Praise for the writ

Master of the Abyss

"A fantastic addition to the phenomenal Mountain Masters series, *Master of the Abyss* is not to be missed!"

– Shayna, *Joyfully Reviewed*

"This story is definitely a page-turner that I could not put down."

– *Whipped Cream Reviews*

Master of the Mountain

Five Stars! "[A] melt your panties right off, intriguing love story that forces you to turn the pages until the wee hours of the night..."

– Brande, *Book Junkie*

The Starlight Rite

"*The Starlite Rite* surpassed each and every hope I ever had about this story."

– Bella, *Fallen Angel Reviews*

The Dom's Dungeon

A Golden Blush Recommended Read! "I recommend, as you read this book, that you keep lots of ice on hand and keep the fans going."

– *Literary Nymphs Reviews*

LooSe Id®

ISBN 13: 978-1-61118-375-7
MASTER OF THE ABYSS

Originally released in e-book format in October 2010

Cover Art by Anne Cain
Cover Layout and Design by April Martinez

DISCLAIMER: Many of the acts described in our BDSM/fetish titles can be dangerous. Please do not try any new sexual practice, whether it be fire, rope, or whip play, without the guidance of an experienced practitioner. Neither Loose Id nor its authors will be responsible for any loss, harm, injury or death resulting from use of the information contained in any of its titles.

This book is an original publication of Loose Id. Each individual story herein was previously published in e-book format only by Loose Id and is a work of fiction. Any similarity to actual persons, events or existing locations is entirely coincidental.

Printed in the U.S.A. by
Lightning Source, Inc.
1246 Heil Quaker Blvd
La Vergne TN 37086
www.lightningsource.com

MASTER OF THE ABYSS

Cherise Sinclair

Author's Note

To my readers,

This book is fiction, not reality and, as in most romantic fiction, the romance is compressed into a very, very short time period.

You, my darlings, live in the real world and I want you to take a little more time than the heroines you read about. Good Doms don't grow on trees and there's some strange people out there. So while you're looking for that special Dom, please, be careful.

When you find him, realize he can't read your mind. Yes, frightening as it might be, you're going to have to open up and talk to him. And you listen to him, in return. Share your hopes and fears, what you want from him, what scares you spitless. Okay, he may try to push your boundaries a little—he's a Dom, after all—but you have your safeword. You *will* have a safeword, am I clear? Use protection. Have a back-up person. Communicate.

Remember: *safe*, *sane* and *consensual*.

Know that I'm hoping you find that special, loving person who will understand your needs and hold you close. Let me know how you're doing. I worry, you know.

Meantime, come and hang out with the Masters of the Shadowlands.

—*Cherise,* cherisesinclair@sbcglobal.net

Chapter One

The sound of melodic laughter added a sweet note to the country-western music drumming through the ClaimJumper tavern. With a slight smile, Jake Hunt tipped his chair back against the rough log wall and took in the view of the women at a corner table. Gina, Andrea, Serena—all of them tall, curvy, feminine. Beautiful women. Over the last two years, he'd dated all three. Perhaps when he'd been only twenty, he might have prided himself on that—but now? No girlfriend, no wife, no children. No plans for any. *That's pitiful, Hunt.*

A fourth woman sat at the table, Kallie Masterson, and he gave her a speculative look. He'd seen her around over the last couple of years but never paid much attention to the grown-up tomboy. However, if Serenity Lodge teamed up with the Masterson Wilderness Guides like he and Logan were considering, she'd be one of the people they'd deal with.

In marked contrast with the other women, Kallie had short black hair that appeared as if she cut it herself—with a knife—and no makeup. Rather than a pretty top like the others, she wore a red flannel shirt that completely hid her small frame. Baggy jeans and scarred boots. He shook his head. Women were definitely equal to men and should be treated that way, but why the hell would a woman try to look like a man?

Or act like one. Serena had once mentioned that Kallie had tried to outmacho the boys all through high school. He sized her up. Maybe twenty-five or twenty-six, she appeared to have turned into a pint-size Chuck Norris.

As he watched, she bounced up, hands waving, relating a story that sent the others into hysterics. Jake grinned. Most women's high-pitched giggles reminded him of champagne bubbles, but Kallie's husky chuckle? *Coke.* Yep, a Coke would bubble pleasantly at rest, but shake it up and it'd froth all over you—and eat the corrosion off your battery too.

"Jake!" Serena abandoned the table of women and glided across the room.

He rose to his feet. "Serena, what can I do for you?"

"I'm twenty-five today, and I want a birthday kiss." She tossed her blonde, wavy hair back over her shoulder and flirted up at him through long lashes.

"I might be able to handle that." He pulled her into his arms, all fragrant woman, and kissed her thoroughly enough to have the mostly male bar cheering. As she plastered herself against him, his cock gave only a few jerks in token interest.

Nothing new and not her fault. She was exactly the type of woman he enjoyed: soft, sweet, and lush. But these days, a good book held more attraction than a good lay. As he pulled back, she clung, so he gently eased her arms from around his neck, then squeezed her shoulder. "Happy birthday, sugar."

She hesitated, obviously hoping for more, but he resumed his seat.

Her face fell. “Fine,” she muttered and returned to her table, hips swaying, every man in the place watching.

Jake tipped his chair back against the wall and drank some more beer. The clock above the bar read nine. Almost time to go meet his brother down the street. Meantime he’d enjoy the entertainment. Pretty women, good music, and…ah, perhaps a little action. In the center of the room, some idiot tourist was taunting Barney, a logger built a whole lot like the purple dinosaur that bore the same name. Did the tourist have a death wish?

And there went the domino effect: Barney rose to his feet and delivered a solid right cross. The tourist crashed into a table filled with loggers. Two pitchers of beer unloaded their contents over the burly men. One soaked man threw his chair at Barney. The chair bounced off and hit a biker. The biker jumped to his feet.

And then the whole bar erupted.

Jake laughed and dropped his chair legs back on the floor. He hadn’t been in a brawl in a year or two—Logan said he’d turned into an old man.

As he headed for the free-for-all, high-pitched shrieks drew his attention to the women’s corner. Blocked from escaping through the entrance, Andrea, Gina, and Serena had barricaded themselves behind the table. Kallie stood in front, one scruffy sprite, boots planted, guarding the territory. Looked rather like Toto trying to defend Dorothy from all comers.

The woman was dumber than—Jake blinked in stupefaction when little Toto sidestepped a drunk, then shoved him hard enough that his trajectory altered to miss the women's table. The man hit the wall with a nice *crunch.* Kallie laughed and bounced on her toes. She slugged another guy in the breadbasket and dodged as he landed on hands and knees. Jake grinned. *Not bad. Not bad at all.* Nonetheless, a barroom brawl was no place for a woman.

He glanced toward the main knot of fighting, where the bikers surrounded Barney. Too close to the front door. Even as Jake looked, Barney threw a man across the room—straight for the women's area. Having turned to check her friends, Kallie didn't have a chance. The biker slammed into her ass, flattening her like a pancake onto the sawdust floor.

Oh hell. Jaw tensed, Jake shoved his way past two brawlers and kicked another out of his way to get to her. He lifted the biker off and flung him at Barney before dropping to one knee. So small. Limp. Not moving.

The gut-twisting memory of a different body—*of Mimi's body*—slid into his brain like an icy knife, and cold sweat slicked his palms. "Kallie?" He touched her cheek. *Don't be dead. Dammit.*

When she inhaled with a harsh sound, relief made his head spin. *Get a grip, Hunt.*

She was already moving—just had the wind knocked out of her. In fact, she was very much alive and using words that would make his mother blanch.

"Fucking son of a bitch," Kallie snarled. What had hit her? She was lying on her stomach on the damned tavern floor. Rising slightly, she wiped sawdust off her face and gagged at the stench of stale beer. *Whoever hit me is going to die.*

With a grunt, she pushed herself up to a sitting position, and for a second, she would have sworn angels were singing. And then, to her regret, the music descended into the noise of men yelling and Swedish curses as the owner tried to move the fighting outside. She took a breath and waited for the world to stop swirling. She'd still kill whoever had hit her—but maybe later.

"Let's see the damage, sugar," said a deep, rumbling voice. Hard hands closed around her arms, steadying her.

She looked up at a darkly tanned, lean face. Strong jaw with a faint cleft in the chin. Thick brown hair. Cobalt blue eyes. *Jake Hunt.* Oh wonderful—of all the people to see her like this. Kallie tried to pull away.

His grip tightened. "Hold still."

"Let go of me."

Ignoring her, he ran his hands down her shoulders and arms, his eyes intent on her face, his touch gentling when she winced. "Banged your shoulder up some."

"I'm fine." The knowledge that she had Jake Hunt checking her over made her want to sink back to the floor in embarrassment. She tried to shove his hands away with as much success as moving a granite boulder. "I don't need any help, got it?"

"Anything else hurt?"

His gaze ran over her body, and she flushed, acutely conscious of her less-than-hourglass shape—more like a two-legged pear. Scarred face or not, the man could have had any woman in Bear Flat and had dated most of the good-looking ones. She wasn't one of them.

"No, nothing hurts," she muttered.

"Your jaw is bruised." He cupped her cheek with a big hand and tilted her face toward the light. "Did you bang your head? Let's see your eyes."

"I said I'm fine." Averting her eyes from his intense gaze, she tried to push his hand away again. Unsuccessfully.

His voice roughened. "Look at me, Kallie."

The low, commanding tone shook her bones, and she shivered. Her gaze flashed up involuntarily.

His eyes narrowed, becoming more intent until she felt like a deer trapped by a cougar. She swallowed hard.

A smile flickered over his angular face. "Well now," he murmured. "Appearances can be deceiving, can't they? Aren't you supposed to be tougher than any man around?" His hand still gentle on her cheek, he ran a thumb over her lips, sending a tremor through her, followed by a wave of heat.

Wimp. Wuss. Her muscles had turned to water, but she managed to grasp his wrist, trying not to notice the thick bones, the steely tendons. She firmed her voice, and it still came out sounding all girlie and weak. "Don't."

"Don't what?" he asked softly. And he regarded her…differently…in a way that sizzled straight to the center of her body.

"Don't look at me like that," she muttered and pushed his hand away.

Amusement lit his eyes, and a corner of his mouth turned up, creasing his cheek. "Oddly enough, I think I like looking at you."

"Oh sure you do. So are you the one who hit me?"

"I don't hit women," he growled...and then his lips quirked up. "There are much better ways to punish sassy wenches."

At the assessing look he gave her, she could feel her face flame red.

"That's a fine color on you, sugar," he murmured and grasped her upper arms, lifting her to her feet as if she weighed no more than a doll. As the room did a fast merry-go-round, Kallie sagged.

He put an iron-hard arm around her waist to keep her upright. She'd had dreams of having his arm around her, but somehow they'd never included being knocked sprawling in a bar first.

"Hey, Kallie." Barney poked his head in the entrance, eliciting a stream of curses from the grizzled Swede who owned the tavern. "I'm sorry. I threw him at the door, not at you."

"You hit me with a person?" When they'd played baseball in high school, Barney's aim had been notoriously bad; it obviously hadn't improved any. After a second, she laughed and shook her head—*whoa, not a good move*. "It's okay. I'm fine."

Giving his gap-toothed smile, Barney disappeared back out the door, and his roar of battle glee drifted in with the night air.

"Nice of you to forgive him," Jake said as he guided her to a chair. When he stepped away, the warmth of his hands still lingered on her waist.

"He's too big to kill easily."

Jake's laugh sent chills across her skin. When her friends surrounded her and their perfume smothered his clean, masculine scent, Kallie felt relieved. Mostly.

"Girl, I can't believe you're all right. You landed really bad." Gina swooped her hands to demonstrate Kallie's dive and face-plant.

Great. Bet he found that just hilarious.

His grin confirmed her opinion, and then he slid a finger down her cheek. "You know, little sprites shouldn't be fighting."

From anyone else in the world, she might have found the remark amusing. From him, after wanting him for so long, it simply hurt. Trying to ignore the way her skin tingled in the wake of his touch, she gave him a cold look. "I'm not little, and I'm not a sprite. Thanks for the help—now go away."

"You're welcome. *Sprite.*" He glanced at his watch, winced, and shot a stern look at her friends. "Someone take her home." Before anyone could respond, he walked away.

As he left the bar, Gina sniffed. "Such a shame that bossy looks so good on him." She patted Kallie's shoulder. "Let me get my purse, and I'll drive you home. You really—"

"I really need a beer," Kallie interrupted. "No, two beers. And a burger and fries. I just got back from a week in the backcountry, and I'm not running home because some pushy"— *gorgeous*—"person"— *bastard*—"thinks I should."

She'd watched her friends turn all syrupy whenever Jake Hunt touched them. Now she'd done the same thing—and she didn't like it one bit.

He watched from the shadows, unwilling to join in the fighting. His battle wasn't against his fellow men—his brothers—but against evil.

The small woman who had fought, who actually struck a male, had caught his eye. Dark hair and dark eyes were often markings of the devil.

He would watch. He would see.

* * *

His coffee sent a thin line of steam up into the chill morning air. With a sigh of enjoyment, Jake set one foot on the porch rail and settled comfortably in his chair as the sun edged up from behind the white-capped eastern mountains. At his feet, Thor snoozed, his black-furred muzzle resting on Jake's boot. The dog had chased a bear away from the cabins last night and apparently felt he'd earned his rest.

Jake frowned. He and Thor needed to have a chat. They had named the place Serenity Lodge, not Barking Dog Cabins. Then again, could anything be more serene than a summer morning in the Sierra Nevada?

Logan's rough voice from inside the lodge indicated his brother was awake, and when Rebecca's laugh floated out, Jake knew breakfast wouldn't be too long in coming. And a damn good breakfast since Rebecca cooked like a dream. Logan had lucked out to find himself such a soft, sweet woman—well, she did have a temper, but that simply added some spice to a relationship. Very feminine, though; in fact, she'd worn tailored shirts and designer jeans on her first visit to the lodge.

Jake grinned and shook his head, thinking of Kallie Masterson, the direct opposite of feminine for whatever reason. He'd known women who worked in male-dominated fields. Some downplayed their charms when on the job, but not all the time. He might have thought she preferred women, but the notion had bit the dust last night when she'd warmed so sweetly under his hands and eyes.

He took a sip of coffee. A man had to wonder how she'd react to a more...personal...touch. And what she was concealing underneath those flannel shirts and baggy jeans. His hands had curved around a nice waist, one that flared out to what was probably a lushly rounded ass. When the thought of peeling her jeans off to see that ass made him harden, he huffed a laugh and shook his head. *Not going there.*

The way her beautiful eyes—so dark a brown they were almost black—had widened at his command told him she wasn't experienced in the games he enjoyed playing. And he sure as hell didn't want another vulnerable woman. The thought of Mimi's face as she had knelt before him and pleaded with him to keep her stabbed his heart. He wasn't cut out for a serious relationship—didn't need one, didn't want one.

Especially a submissive who didn't even realize her nature, let alone one living in Bear Flat. He'd dated quite a few women from town but kept the dates strictly vanilla. When he required a submissive for some BDSM play, he went farther afield. Considering how badly he'd screwed up with a sub once, he never sought anything more than light play.

He watched as the sun warmed the mountain slopes and patches of white fog drifted upward. No. He wouldn't pursue anything with Kallie. Besides, he and Logan were discussing a business agreement with the Mastersons and their guide service.

Yet she appealed to him so much that he couldn't stop thinking about her. Which was rather odd. Since she'd returned to Bear Flat a couple of years ago, he'd never said more to her than good morning, had only been aware enough of her to be irritated by her manner and clothing.

Perhaps he should have been impressed instead. She was a good guide, he knew. And apparently a good friend. He grinned, remembering her defense of the women last night. All that courage in such a small bundle. She'd gotten knocked ass over teakettle and hadn't whined, hadn't cried—just cursed like a lumberjack. When he'd helped her up, she'd fairly vibrated with energy.

And heat.

She wanted him. Jake took a sip of coffee, remembering the feel of her, the sexual sizzle between them. She wanted him and didn't like the fact. He didn't either.

And it didn't seem to matter, especially against the memory of her melting under his command. *A submissive.*

Jake tipped his head back as an eagle soared high, becoming a black speck in the pale gray sky. As he lifted his coffee, his hand stilled. *Submissive. Business.* Hell. He tossed the remainder of his drink into a nearby bush and headed into the lodge.

As he entered the kitchen, he saw Rebecca smack Logan's knuckles with a wooden spatula.

"Keep those fingers away from the bacon," she snapped.

Logan shook his hand, then grabbed her arms and lifted her onto tiptoes. "Little rebel, you're going to pay for that."

The sub's body went limp. She smiled at Logan and said in a throaty voice, "Okay."

Jake snorted a laugh.

Frowning, Logan set her down and glanced at Jake. "Can't even scare her these days. What am I going to do?"

"You're too easy on her, and she gets off on being spanked." Jake leaned a shoulder against the door frame. "Try a whip."

Logan crossed his arms and studied her. "Possible…possible…"

Rebecca's eyes widened, and she sidled away from him, abandoning her bacon.

"Speaking of whips," Jake said. "If I could have your attention before you start stripping her down, there's something we should discuss with the Mastersons."

"That would be?"

"What happens on a guide trip when one of our guests pulls out handcuffs? Or a flogger."

* * *

A few days later, Kallie took her time picking stones and crud out of Midnight's hoof and ignored the sound of Wyatt and Morgan fidgeting behind her. Thank God Virgil had chosen to be a cop, or she'd have all three of her cousins behind her.

The normally comforting scent of straw and horses clogged her throat as she carefully examined the horse's frog and checked the horseshoe. Pity that this was the last hoof to clean. Couldn't stall anymore, despite the bomb her cousins had dropped on her. At least she'd managed to get her face smoothed out to unreadable, although her stomach churned as if she'd chugged a pitcher of beer.

The late afternoon sun streaming into the barn made the dust in the air glow as she turned to face her cousins. "Now what do you mean, we're going to be seeing a lot of the Hunt brothers?"

With her cat sitting at his feet, Wyatt leaned against the opposite stall, a pleased smile on his face. Morgan had the same smug expression. Good-looking guys. Sure they loomed over her like every other person in the world, but she figured they'd be a lot shorter after she killed them dead.

She crossed her arms over her chest. "Well?"

"We talked about this before, cuz," Wyatt said, taking point as he always did on the trails, leaving Morgan to bring up the rear. "You said they wouldn't be interested, but we ran into them at the feed store last week, and they thought it was a great idea. We've had a couple of discussions, and it'll work out well."

Oh wonderful. "So Logan and Jake will pimp our guide services, and in return, we'll book our incoming clients at their lodge instead of in Yosemite Village."

"Yep." Morgan grinned. "Means more business for all of us. Jake will still handle the day trips for their guests, but we'll get any overnights or longer. If our clients spend the night locally, we'll be able to hit the trails earlier."

Fine, it was a practical idea, but it meant she'd be running into Jake Hunt all the time, and that wasn't a comfortable thought. Either the man ignored her or wore a faintly disapproving expression—both were damned annoying. Then again, the way he'd looked at her last weekend…might be worse. She hadn't been able to stop thinking about it.

But to say *I don't like the way Jake Hunt looks at me* to her cousins? No way. So she'd deal with it. It's not like Jake would come on any guided trips, and she could probably avoid him when picking up the clients at the lodge. *Trouble is, will I want to*? "I suppose that makes sense."

"The only drawback we've found is that the lodge has a rep for accommodating kinky groups." Wyatt's brows drew together. "We'd heard rumors about the place; Logan confirmed they're true."

"Kinky like what?" *Jake and kink.* The thought took her breath away.

"Like bondage and BSMD"—Morgan frowned—"or BMDS."

"BDSM, doofus, and swingers and gay clubs. Whatever." Wyatt scratched the three-day-old stubble on his cheek. He never shaved when he was on the trail with a group. "If they have a…specialty…weekend, they'll black out the days, so we don't book clients then."

When Mufasa glided over, Kallie leaned down and stroked the cat's soft fur. "I guess that sounds all right." Surely the clients wouldn't do weird stuff in front of her.

"The thing is their…people…are going to want to…you know," Wyatt said.

She gave him an exasperated look. "I don't know what 'you know' means." Then again, she might. Serena's romance books were pretty…interesting. And Kallie had actually tried a few things when she was in college. Handcuffs. Spanking. In the books, BDSM had sounded thrilling; in real life, it had been a dud. Wouldn't her cousins hit the roof if she mentioned that?

"Yeah. We told Logan you wouldn't."

She snorted. "Like you have more experience?"

Wyatt's dark tan acquired a red hue. "Morgan and I have seen some, and we told Logan that we're okay with it."

"You have?" *Whoa, new information here.* "You are?" *Who are you guys, and what did you do with my cousins?*

"It's not our thing, but we got around when we were younger." Morgan waggled his thick brows. "San Francisco has everything."

Wyatt glared at him. "Watch your mouth."

Kallie sighed. Her cousins usually treated her as one of the guys. With Uncle Harvey's "*Everyone is equal in this house*" rules, they'd been fine with her being a guide, but perversely, equality didn't include anything having to do with sex. If they could dress her like a nun, they would, and Wyatt, with his love of the Old West, was the worst of them all.

"Don't worry about it, Kallie," he said. "You're not going to guide any of the lodge's…special…guests."

The sense of insult was instant. "That's pretty sexist of

the Hunts. I'm as good as you guys, probably better."

Morgan grinned at the long-standing competition of "who's best," then sobered. "It wasn't the Hunt's decision, cuz; it was ours."

"But...why?" Her chest constricted painfully. Were they trying to ease her out of the business? Hadn't everything been going well?

"Kallie, these people are doing..." Wyatt's color grew close to that of a beet. "Those people might have sex—in the open. In front of you."

"Oh, honestly." She shook her head. "Listen. If they do weird things in the forest, I'll just close my eyes."

"Even if we agreed, Logan insists the guides need to be comfortable with guests, uh, *playing* during a hiking trip. And you've never even seen anything..."

She should take the out. She wouldn't have to go to the lodge and would be able to avoid Jake. But she'd worked too hard to fit in and be part of the business...and to live here with them. They were the only relatives who had let her stay, and she wasn't going to risk their love for something as stupid as discomfort. Besides... "It sounds like the lodge will bring in a fair amount of business. We can't afford to have one of us three not handling some of it—it'd screw up the scheduling big-time."

From the unhappy expression on her cousins' faces, they'd realized that too.

She sighed. "So how does Logan suggest we solve the dilemma of me not being adequately informed about 'you know'?"

"A BDSM club will be at the lodge this Friday," Morgan said. "He offered to show you around and explain things."

Wyatt folded his arms over his chest, looking stubborn. "We told him you wouldn't be involved."

"Guess you'll have to tell him different." Kallie crossed her arms too and gave him the same look back. "'Everyone is equal in this house,' remember?" She could see they were torn in two directions—wanting to keep her safe and acknowledging the business concerns. But they couldn't win against Uncle Harvey's maxim.

Wyatt raked a hand through his hair. "Kallie. Even if we let you—"

"You can't stop me, dude."

He leaned over and squeezed her arm, his brown eyes concerned. "Morgan's got a fishing group booked, and I'm going to be guiding that mountaineering bunch. You can't go to that place by yourself. We need to wait for another party, when we're available to go with you. "

"And that will be how long?"

"Another six weeks," Morgan said.

She rolled her eyes. "If you think about it, you might realize that I'll be by myself if I'm guiding them. I might as well go by myself now. Besides, won't Logan watch out for me?"

They still looked unhappy.

"Tell you what—I'll close my eyes whenever something looks interesting."

* * *

Morgan and Wyatt had felt guilty, and Kallie had taken full advantage of them. They ended up taking her turns at shopping and kitchen duty for a week, and she wouldn't have to guide that ego-ridden group of yuppies on Monday.

It helped just a little when contemplating what was to come.

On Friday night, she pulled her Jeep into Serenity's small parking area and turned off the ignition. After a glance at the lodge, she laid her head on the steering wheel in pure misery.

Jake would probably be in there, damn the man. She'd fallen for his looks on first sight—what woman with a hormone in her body wouldn't? But it was the little glimpses she'd caught of him that had done her in: plucking old Mrs. Peterson's grocery sack from her arms and carrying it to the car, kneeling to admire five-year-old Olivia's new kitten, helping push Dan's car out of a mud hole in the pouring rain. He simply assumed it was his job to help the weaker ones—he reminded her of Uncle Harvey. Yeah, she'd fallen for more than his body.

After climbing out of the Jeep, she scowled at the number of cars in the lot and her doubts rose. There must be a lot of kinky people at the party. But still, that didn't bother her as much as the Jake Hunt dilemma. Maybe she should have tried to explain her discomfort to Wyatt and Morgan…

Guys, it's like this: First, if Jake frowns at me like he usually does—as if I'm dog meat—my feelings will be hurt. I'm liable to kick him, and that's considered bad for business relations.

Second, if I have to watch him…doing…some woman, well, that will hurt too. It was bad enough getting secondhand reports from her friends. How wonderful Jake was in bed, how thorough, how caring. She frowned. Wasn't it odd they'd never done anything kinky with him? Maybe only the lodge guests were into the BDSM stuff, and he wasn't. Not that it mattered to her what he did in his bed. Nope.

Third, if he looks at me like he did last time—just the thought made her heart race—*then I'll go belly-up like a whipped dog, beg him to take me, and never be able to look him in the face afterward. Once again, poor business relations.*

Oh, wouldn't those confessions go over well with Wyatt and Morgan. She snickered. Although they knew she dated, they never allowed themselves to think about what that might mean.

She kicked the Jeep door shut and walked into the wide clearing. The cool night air, scented with pine, ruffled her hair. Lights glimmered from the small cabins in the trees, knee-high solar lanterns delineated the pathways, and one larger light beamed from the two-story log building. As she strolled across the open space to the lodge, an owl glided low, wings lit by the bright porch light. Like a tank dropping out of the sky, it landed on a tiny rodent. The poor mouse squeaked helplessly.

She knew just how it felt.

Okay, let's get this over with. Kallie crossed the wide porch and almost stumbled over a massive dog sprawled in front of the door. It stood, some sort of German shepherd mix, and stared at her. She took a step in retreat, then saw his full tail wave back and forth. A nice dog. She wouldn't be getting her throat ripped out tonight, and wasn't that a shame. She petted him and laughed when he leaned his weight against her legs and almost bowled her over. "I'd rather hang out with you, dog. But guess I'm stuck."

As the dog flopped back down, Kallie pulled open the heavy front door. After stepping inside, she waited for her eyes to adjust to the dim light. The room smelled like leather and wood smoke, perfume and sex. It even sounded like sex. Over the music of a Gregorian chant, a man groaned, long and low. Slapping sounds were accompanied by a woman's whimpering.

Kallie swallowed hard as the room came into focus. To the left, leather couches sat around a stone fireplace with a crackling fire, and past that, a naked man bent over, facing the wall. In the firelight, his pale buttocks displayed red welts in even rows.

Kallie's eyes widened. Is this what Wyatt had meant by "you know"?

On the log walls, lanterns with amber-tinted glass cast circles of golden light, leaving other areas in shadow. She saw more seating arrangements here and there, defined by colorful rag rugs and dark red chairs. Farther down the room, people engaged in activities she couldn't quite make out. Wasn't sure she wanted to. The cracking sound—was the man at the end using a whip? Her hands closed into fists.

To her right, a blonde in a shiny latex catsuit held a lit candle over a woman tied to a desk. Wax dripped onto bare breasts. A *splat.* A gasp.

That looked…really painful. What would it feel like? To be unable to move. Naked. Waiting for something hot to land on your nipples. Painful or…erotic?

Her body said *erotic*. Her bra felt…tight, and even her baggy jeans managed to press on disconcertingly sensitive places. Okay, Wyatt had been right; she really wasn't prepared for this.

The blonde caught her staring and gave Kallie an assessing look before smiling. Kallie sucked in a breath and nodded back. *I'm cool. Experienced woman, seen it all in my time. Really*. What the *hell* was she doing here? Morgan and Wyatt should have explained a lot more about the "you know" stuff. Oh, they were going to suffer—painfully—before she killed them. Maybe she could borrow that guy's whip.

Then again, her cousins might not have realized… Maybe the places they'd visited in San Francisco weren't as…much. Whatever. Well, now that she'd done as Logan had required and taken a look, maybe she could just sneak out and—

"You joining us tonight, baby?" A tall, skinny guy in a black biker jacket grinned at her.

Caught. "No, I'm not. Is Logan around?"

"That's a shame. I'll get him."

As Kallie's gaze followed the man heading for the back of the room, she spotted a woman chained, facing the far wall, dressed in only a thong. The guy in front of her held an English riding crop, and when he whopped her on the thigh, she yelped.

Kallie winced and somehow, weirdly, felt excitement trickle down her spine. *Okay, I really, really need a beer.*

"You made it." Logan strolled up, gripping a lushly built woman by the scruff of her neck.

Kallie shifted her weight uncomfortably. Was that his fiancée, Rebecca? Kallie had met her in town only once. Aside from Jake, Serenity Lodge didn't socialize much. A scream came from across the room, and Kallie amended that assumption. They didn't socialize *in Bear Flat* much. "Yeah, I'm here."

Ill at ease under Logan's observant eyes, Kallie glanced at Rebecca and felt even more out of place. The redhead's emerald green corset emphasized every full curve she had, and gave Kallie a moment of envy. *Must be nice to have breasts.* Her garter belt and garters held up black fishnet stockings, and a thin leather collar was around her neck. No other clothes, though—not even a thong.

Rebecca stared at the floor, hands clasped in front of her... Or no, padded leather cuffs fastened her wrists together. This was so not the polished woman whom Kallie had met, and worry gnawed at her stomach. Rebecca looked so subservient; surely Logan didn't beat her. The number of scars on his knuckles suddenly seemed menacing.

"I'm glad you came," Logan said.

She yanked her gaze from his hands. "Ah. I'm pleased to be here." She shrugged, not wanting to say, *You didn't leave me much choice.*

The wicked grin indicated he knew it anyway. "Let's start with—"

"Logan!" A man called from the other end of the room. "Need you and Becca here."

"Never fails." Logan checked over his shoulder and frowned. "Hang loose, Kallie, and I'll be back to show you what's up."

As Logan wrapped an arm around Rebecca, she raised her head and winked at Kallie. A wink full of humor and not frightened at all.

Relieved, Kallie relaxed a trifle. She realized she was wringing her hands and shoved them in the front pockets of her jeans. There. *Look casual.* She swallowed hard. *Hey, I see people manacled to log walls all the time. You bet. It's a popular sport in Bear Flat. Gonna replace fishing soon.*

The Gregorian chants blended with other worrisome noises. Like the hissing of a man cuffed to a big X-shaped frame against the wall. His testicles dangled between his spread legs, and a woman was winding leather around them. Kallie winced. She might not have that kind of equipment, but three cousins and a couple of boyfriends had taught her a little about their painful vulnerability.

"Kallie?"

She jumped at the sound of a smooth, deep voice. A truly gorgeous man stood in front of her, slightly shorter than the Hunt brothers—maybe six feet—and older, with silver flecks in his black hair. He wore a white, long-sleeved shirt and tailored black slacks, a very civilized look for the rustic lodge and a marked contrast to her battered field clothes.

"Yes, I'm Kallie."

He held his hand out. "My name is Simon. Logan

requested that I stay with you until he could return."

Rescued! She shook his warm hand, uncomfortably aware how cold and damp her own must be. "Thanks. I appreciate it."

"Come, we'll sit down by the fireplace. You can observe, and I'll answer any questions you have." He guided her to a massive leather couch and settled himself on the other end, relaxing with his arms stretched out along the back. Polite, friendly, not making any moves. She liked him already.

"I thought there would be more people," Kallie offered after a minute. "My cousins said this was a club weekend."

"In a way. We all belong to a San Francisco BDSM club, but we're mainly friends who enjoy partying together and getting out of the city."

So if Jake and Logan knew all these people, no weirdo would come at her with a whip and chains. *Right?* Just then a man walked past with a coiled whip attached to his belt. She eyed him, remembering the stuff from Serena's romance novels. She would never have dreamed people did this in real life. Her discomfort increased.

Simon smiled. "Relax, pet. We all have our own submissives—well, except for Jake. You won't be harassed, and no one here minds observers or we wouldn't play in public."

"Oh. Good." She frowned. "But I'm not a pet."

"No?" He studied her for a minute and then nodded toward a man in black jeans and a T-shirt tying a woman facedown on a coffee table. "You don't find watching a dom with his submissive to be exciting?"

The woman wore only a bustier and thong. The dom secured her legs open, then touched her intimately. Slowly. The woman wiggled and a minute later was moaning, raising her hips toward him. Smiling, the man stood up. When he patted her bottom affectionately, his fingers glistened.

Kallie released the breath she'd been holding. The room seemed overly hot. "It's like watching a porn flick," she muttered, tearing her gaze away. "Anyone would get interested."

"Somewhat true," Simon agreed. "However that was only the prelude. What do you think of the main act?"

"Excuse me?"

He tilted his head toward the dom and sub. Kallie turned in time to see the man bring his hand down onto the woman's bare bottom with a resounding slap.

Kallie jerked as if he'd hit her instead. She couldn't tear her gaze away as the man thoroughly spanked the woman...the submissive. Dear God. By the time he finished, Kallie was as damp as if she'd sat in a puddle. That was nothing—nothing!—like what she'd tried.

When she finally turned away, the gleam of amusement in Simon's eyes told her exactly how readable her face must have been. "So, pet," he said, not adding any emphasis to the word but making his point nonetheless. "Would you be interested in playing this evening?"

"I—" The thought of being the one tied to a table, having someone—*Jake*—slapping her bottom, touching her... "No. Of course not."

He raised an eyebrow.

She flushed. "Besides, you told me everyone here is…attached."

He looked over her head as if thinking, and his lips curved. "I believe I said Jake doesn't have a sub here tonight."

She snorted. "He doesn't like me. He dates Marilyn Monroe types." *Not breastless, fat-assed women with no sex appeal.*

"Oh? That seems odd. You have rather the appearance of his old girlfriend—same coloring and height."

Jake had had a girlfriend? It must have been before Kallie returned to Bear Flat. And they resembled each other? *Simon must be kidding.*

"I really look like her?" When he chuckled, Kallie grimaced. *How about I just stand up and announce that I have the hots for Jake Hunt?* She stared at her feet. Maybe she'd just watch the hardwood floor until she could escape—*don't want the flooring to turn soft, right?*—and not be looking at any more of this sex stuff.

But a pair of battered brown boots moved to interfere with her view of the hardwood floor. The hems of the jeans were worn to pure white in places. She lifted her gaze. A black T-shirt clung to six-pack abs and a heavily muscled chest. A corded neck. A lean, hard face with icy blue eyes.

Jake.

Chapter Two

"Uh." Kallie's face heated. Why couldn't those floorboards crack open and let her disappear? Where was a good earthquake when you needed one? How much had he heard?

"Yes, Kallie, you do resemble her," he said in an even tone. He'd definitely caught Simon's comment. Her face was probably red enough to light the room.

"Oh. Well." *I look like an old girlfriend.* Reassuring at first, then rather uncomfortable.

He set his foot on the couch beside her hip and leaned forward, his forearms braced on his knee, studying her until she had to force herself not to squirm. His masculine scent had the tang of a high mountain forest, clean and compelling, but he was intimidatingly close. She edged back against the couch cushions, realizing that after flinging her to the wolves, to Jake, Simon had abandoned her without a word. Her heart thudded inside her chest, more loudly than any spanking or whipping going on.

"I had planned to leave you alone," he said, half under his breath.

Well, that hurt. "Then go." She made a shooing motion with her fingers.

"But then you planted yourself in here. Asked questions."

"I won't ask any more." If her heart would only slow down, she'd be able to think. "I don't want to know anything at all about you or your girlfriend, okay?"

"She was also my submissive," he said, his voice deep. Rough as a talus slope and as dangerous. "I was her master. Do you know what that means, sprite?"

Mouth too dry to answer, Kallie shook her head. *Master?*

He stroked one finger along her jaw, slowly enough that she could feel the warmth, the uneven skin of a man who worked with his hands. The strength. "I like the way you heat under my touch," he murmured, then looked Kallie right in the eyes. "It means she did what I ordered her to do. Always. If I told her to strip and bend over the bed so I could take her from behind, that's what she did."

She could feel how his hands would hold her in place, his cock hard between her legs, demanding entry and… The air had completely disappeared from the room.

He gripped her chin, keeping her head tilted up, revealing her face. "I could tell her to lie on the bed with her legs spread, and no matter what I did, no matter how long, she wasn't allowed to come."

Kallie felt a burn start in her nether regions. And couldn't help wondering what he had done. How had he touched her?

His eyes crinkled, and he rubbed his knuckles over her cheek. "You're flushed, little Kallie."

"I…" She put up a hand to push his away.

"Don't. Move." The command swept over her like a strong gale bending the trees in its path, pinning her into stillness. Her body froze...and yet grew even more sensitive. Awake. In fact, she'd never felt like this before...and he'd not even done anything.

He chuckled. "Little submissive." With both hands, he grasped the front of her shirt and pulled her to her feet. "Simon was right. You do want to play." It wasn't a question.

Her heart pounding, her eyes captured by his, she tried to back away, shaking her head. "No. No, really."

"Don't lie to me, Kallie," he said ever so softly, yet all the spit in her mouth dried up.

She averted her gaze and tried to think. She'd wanted him since the first time she saw him. Now she might have him. But here? How brave was she?

She'd never deliberately done anything really outrageous in her whole life, always tried to fit in and not rock the boat. But right now she wanted to swamp the boat completely. If she did some "you know" with Jake this one time, her cousins would never find out. Her lips curved up. *And my dreams will be very interesting. God, yes, I want to try it.* But when she looked back at him, at his level gaze, the words stuck in her throat, and she managed only a firm nod.

"Good enough." His sky blue eyes darkened as if storm clouds had rolled in. "We're playing together only this one time. Only tonight."

"I know." Jake Hunt's infamous "one night only" rule. With the women he dated, months would go by before he'd call again, and everyone knew he wanted physical intimacy without emotional commitment. But at least he didn't try to lie about it like some guys. She could handle it. "Not a problem."

He studied her for a long moment, as if to judge her sincerity. "All right then." One corner of his mouth turned up, his dark five-o'clock shadow making the half smile look dangerous. "Let's start with this." He grasped her country-western shirt, and the snaps spatted like gunfire as he yanked it open.

"Hey!" The air brushed against her hot skin, and she grabbed at the shirtfront.

"Leave it open, sprite. Happens that I like skin." His devastating grin flashed, halting every single protest. Why did he have to be so gorgeous? "Now let's find out what *you* like." He turned, pulling her in front of him so that her back rested against his chest.

Kallie gulped when she realized he'd turned her to face the woman on the coffee table.

The redhead was still restrained, stomach down. One of the dom's hands was between her legs, his fingers obviously inside her, thrusting in and out. With his other hand, he alternated swats on her butt cheeks. Hips bucking, she pulled against the restraints.

Kallie's heart started to pound. She could almost feel the fingers pressing inside her, the stinging of the spanking, and she shook her head. This was way too…too…something. She tried to turn away.

Jake clamped his arm around her waist, an iron bar holding her pinned against him. "Watch, Kallie." His warm breath brushed her ear.

The woman's voice kept getting higher—"Oh, Sir. Oh, oh, oh."—until she climaxed with a scream, her head back and spine arching.

Kallie realized she was panting, and heat pulsed through her with every inhalation. "Let me go." Her voice came out husky.

"Nope." He closed his teeth on the muscle between her shoulder and neck, and she gasped as electricity streaked to her groin.

"You're just full of surprises," Jake murmured.

No, he was the surprising one. Despite her hot, erotic dreams of him, she'd figured he'd never see her as a woman. He didn't like her—he hadn't liked her—so why had he changed his mind? Worry niggled in her stomach like hungry lake trout. "I'm not your old girlfriend."

"Uh-huh," he said, his voice a deep, warm rumble in her ear. He splayed his hand, hot and hard, against her bare stomach.

Every bone in her body dissolved.

But did he understand what she was saying? She tried again. "I'm not her." *And I don't want to be a substitute for some old girlfriend.*

He huffed a laugh. "You sure don't have her personality."

That didn't sound like a compliment.

"Don't worry. I know you're Kallie 'Macho' Masterson."

Despite the insulting term, warmth bloomed in her. He had actually, finally, seen *her.*

He slid his hand beneath her jeans waistband until his

fingers rested at the top of her mound, and as with a match held to dry grass, flames erupted inside her. He pressed her back against him, and she could feel the bulge of his erection. Hard. He wanted her. Pleasure warmed her heart. He really did.

Her breath caught as his other hand slid under her bra, settling right over her breast. Her very small breast. She stiffened and tried to pull away, expecting the usual stupid guy's comment: "*Why do you bother with a bra*?"

Instead he tightened his arms. "Don't move, sub."

The firm command sent heat streaking across her skin. She tried to move—couldn't—and with the feeling of being immobilized came the realization that he could do…anything. Her insides melted into warm liquid.

He chuckled and bit her earlobe. The sharp, unexpected pain sheared straight to her pussy, and a moan escaped her.

"I think I'll enjoy tonight after all," he murmured. "So, short stuff, have you tried anything like this before?"

She barely kept from rubbing against him like a cat. *Touch me.* Why did he keep talking? Asking a question she didn't want to answer. But his expectant silence forced a reply. "A few times. But I never liked it." She'd known this was too good to be true. *Be fair to him, Kallie.* She added reluctantly, "I'm not submissive or anything, so it's okay if you find someone else."

"Sure you're not." He slid his hand another inch, one finger on each side of her labia. So close to her clit that she had trouble paying attention to anything but the throbbing bundle of nerves.

"Tell me about those times. What did you do?"

Her brain didn't want to work. "I… One wanted to handcuff me to the bed, and I wouldn't let him…although it had sounded exciting at first. Another tried to spank me, and I couldn't stop giggling." What else? "Um, pretty much that kind of stuff."

"Uh-huh. Sounds like no trust and no true submission." He turned her around.

The removal of his warm hands left behind cold places on her skin, and she ached down below like she'd wrenched something in a place where things didn't get sprained. *He'll tell me to go home now; I should have lied.*

He closed his hands on her shoulders. "How much do you trust me, Kallie?"

The question was unexpected, and she had to shift directions. *Want, yes. But trust?* "I—"

"Let me rephrase that. Can you trust me in here, surrounded by other people, to restrain you, spank you, and give you pleasure?"

Her mouth went dry. The thought of him—*Jake*—his hands on her, tying her, touching her… She frowned. But spanking?

His eyes crinkled. "You wear your emotions right out there on your face, don't you, sugar?"

She thought of the dom and his sub, how he'd brought her to climax with his fingers. "Does pleasure mean us both or just me?"

"Well, now"—he slowly stroked his finger down her cheek, his gaze intent on her face—"I figured on just you, using my hands."

The words welled up like a balloon expanding in her chest. "I want more; I want you in—" Couldn't say it; just couldn't… "Um."

"You want my cock inside you. Is that what you mean?"

Heat rolled up into her face until she felt as if she'd poked her head in a sauna. "Yes," she whispered, swallowed, and gave him a firm, "Yes."

He cupped her cheek in his calloused hand. "All right, sugar." He smiled. "But that's the last request you're allowed tonight. Now, did any of those boyfriends give you a safe word when you played?"

"Yes." She couldn't remember a one of them.

"Must have been real memorable. How about 'Barney,' since I doubt you'll forget his aim." With a thumb under her chin, he tilted her head up, and the laughter faded from his face. "Kallie, listen closely here. If anything I do bothers you too much or hurts too much, use 'Barney,' and everything will stop, right then and there. And just to make sure you feel safe, 'red' is a popular safe word, so if you shouted it out, people—including Simon—would come over to check on what was wrong. Around here, any dom who doesn't honor a safe word gets flattened."

"Barney. Or red. Okay." Good. Fine. She could stop everything if she wanted. As she stared into his intense eyes and felt the sheer power radiating from him, somehow that little safe word didn't decrease her anxiety. Or her arousal.

"Now the rules." He moved closer, so big that he loomed over her, like her Maine coon cat with its six-toed paw on a mouse. Even the marrow of her bones seemed to quiver.

A flicker of a smile touched his lips, creased his left cheek, and faded. "You have only one thing you may control tonight—whether to use your safe word or not. Otherwise, all the decisions, all the choices, are mine. Everything is in my hands."

She nodded. Why did that sound so wrong and yet feel oddly like freedom?

"You will do what I say. Immediately. No backtalk, no questions, no argument. I want to hear only, 'Yes, Jake,' or 'Yes, Sir.' from you. Am I clear?"

When she nodded silently, his eyes hardened. She hurriedly said, "Uh, right. Yes, Jake." *Maybe add a salute?*

"Much better." He released her. Stepped back. "Strip."

"Excuse me?"

He didn't answer, but when he raised his chin an infinitesimal amount, heat curled through her and melted her insides into compliance. Her shirt dropped onto the floor.

He nodded, and she could breathe again. She unlaced her boots and toed them off, added her socks, sheathed knife, and jeans to the pile. Hesitating, she stood in her cheap white bra and cotton panties, knowing there were others around, but unable to look away from his face. Almost naked, her body there for him to see—or reject. Anxiety made her fingers curl.

"You are consistent in your choice of attire, at least," he murmured. "Come here."

She took two steps forward. He ran his hand over her

underwear, and the noise he made sounded very much like disgust. And then he pulled her panties down.

Oh Lord. Trying to keep the unease off her face, she stepped out of them. He reached around her, undid her bra, and slid it off her arms.

She was naked. In a roomful of people. This was absolutely insane—and she wanted him to touch her so badly she almost screamed.

When his big hands engulfed her breasts, fire liquefied her lower half. "Under all those clothes, you're definitely a girl. And these feel as pretty as they look," he commented. He rubbed his thumbs over her nipples, and her knees almost buckled with the searing need.

"I'm little," she whispered. He dated C-cups, not—

He pinched one peak, a startling bite of pain, and a cry escaped her. Her clit throbbed as if he'd pinched her down there too.

"You have gorgeous breasts, sprite, and I'll take responsiveness over size any day."

Really? A weight lifted from her shoulders, knowing that he'd seen all of her and had liked what he saw. There could be no compliment more potent than that huge erection in his jeans. All for her. Her lips curved up.

He walked over to the couch and, from a big leather bag on the floor, pulled out a set of wrist cuffs. "Turn around, little sub."

Her heart started pounding again. Surely all these changes in speed weren't good for it. Very unhealthy. She stared at the restraints. "But…"

"Your answer to me is what?" He didn't wait for her response but turned her so her back was to him, and fastened a cuff snugly around her left wrist. He ran a finger under it. "Kallie?"

"Yes, Sir." It came out sounding as if she were a strangled cat, and he chuckled.

"Relax, sweetheart."

The second cuff went on. Then she heard a *snick*. She tried to move, but he'd fastened the cuffs to each other, keeping her hands behind her back. Very fancy handcuffs. Virgil, her cop cousin, would be so impressed.

I'm not feeling real relaxed here.

Jake walked in front of her and looked down at her naked body. The knowledge that she couldn't protect herself, that he—anyone—could touch her, could handle her bare breasts, sent a quiver through her. And yet her nipples bunched into aching nubs.

With a faint smile, he did exactly what she'd been worrying about. Watching her face, he ran his hand over her breasts, one then the other, the slight scrape of his calloused hands intensely erotic. When his finger circled one nipple, she jumped and her arms jerked…and got nowhere. The floor seemed to roll under her, and she swayed. Even as her breathing sped up, she tugged harder, each tug emphasizing her helplessness. And how totally arousing it was.

How could that be? And why in the world had she agreed to this: handcuffs, naked, sex. *This isn't who I am.*

He ruffled her short hair, then grasped it and pulled her head back to kiss her. Teasingly, brushing his lips across hers until her mouth opened, and then sweeping inside. She wanted to hold him, to run her fingers through his thick brown hair, to… She couldn't raise her hands. That rolling floor dropped right out from under her, and then he took possession of her mouth, deep and thorough, permitting no withdrawal.

With one hand on Kallie's shoulder, Jake felt her try to move and her quivering, excited response when she couldn't. The instinctive submission from her ripped right through his long-held detachment and brought a strong dominant's needs roaring to the surface.

He'd enjoyed submissive women in the two years since Mimi's death but had kept the interactions to light play, not trying to breach a sub's deeper defenses or reach any emotional core. Serious play—mental play—exposed a dom's soul as fully as his submissive's and created a tie between them.

He didn't want a bond with anyone. Considering how badly he'd misread Mimi, he didn't deserve or trust himself with more.

Yet Kallie pulled at him. Vulnerable. Challenging. *Joyously alive.*

And very, very female without those ugly clothes serving as a barrier. Just as well this was for only one night. He pulled back to tease her soft lips and moved his thumb to cover the racing pulse in her neck. She was definitely aroused and excited and probably expecting him to start beating on her pretty ass. He hardened at the thought of those round cheeks under his hand. The slap and quivering response...

But a submissive's expectations were met at a dom's inclination. He was inclined to take her for a walk. At the moment, she saw only him. What would happen when she remembered everyone else in the room?

He smiled at the thought. Although watching a submissive's face turn pink with embarrassment was one of a dom's small pleasures, he also must determine how public he should make the upcoming scene.

"Come, pet; let's take a tour." She'd learn about the types of play, and he'd observe her reactions. In his first few years as a sexual dominant, he'd learned that many subs hid fears, old land mines buried until something triggered them. Sometimes the sub didn't even realize they were there. Honest communication and their body language revealed most of them.

Not all. Mimi had taught him that. With an effort, he pushed aside his guilt. He grasped Kallie's upper arm, enjoying her toned muscles underneath the soft female padding. Tough little sub.

About five feet out of the small sitting area, she halted as if running into a wall. Jake smothered a laugh as he noted what had stopped her.

Rebecca and Rona had been manacled side by side to the log wall, both clad in corsets and garter belts. Both with their legs held open by spreader bars. Standing in front of them, their doms, Logan and Simon, turned to smile at Kallie.

And Kallie obviously remembered she was naked in a room filled with people. She tried to retreat.

Jake tightened his grasp and deliberately ran his hand up her torso to caress a firm breast. "This is my body for tonight, little sub," he said for her ears only. "Mine to display as I wish."

He answered the fear budding in her eyes before it could bloom. "Display only, sugar. Tonight I will be the only one to touch you." As often happened, the knowledge that more might be asked somehow diminished a sub's fear of what he required right now.

She stopped trying to pull away.

"Very pretty sub, Jake," Logan said as if he hadn't talked to Kallie earlier. He glanced at Jake, speculation obvious in his eyes. Jake remembered telling Logan that he'd drag his toy bag down and help out with the party, but he wasn't bringing a sub and didn't intend to play.

Simon studied Kallie for a moment and smiled in satisfaction. Yep, he'd deliberately steered his conversation with Kallie, hoping to pique Jake's interest. Jake had known it at the time and still could not resist. Manipulative bastard.

Eyes closed, Rona gave a low moan of frustration, and Simon and Logan both turned as if waiting for something. A few seconds later, a chime sounded from Logan's watch. He nodded at Simon, who thumbed a remote device in his hand until the buzzing became audible.

Jake glanced at Simon's sub and the vibrator harnessed between her legs. Tremors rocked the woman, and her full breasts quivered. She was on the verge of coming.

"Time," Logan murmured, and Simon flipped the remote off. The hum stopped. Rona whimpered and squirmed as if she could turn it back on.

"You're an evil bastard, Simon. How long have you been torturing them?" Jake asked and glanced down at his little sub, who was staring at the women, at the breast clamps and harnessed vibrators. Simon's Rona had a rabbit strapped to her, giving vaginal and clitoral stimulation; Logan's sub appeared to have a double dildo, penetrating the vagina and the anus.

"Oh, a bit. Your turn," he told Logan. Logan turned the remote in his hand, and Rebecca's back arched as her vibrator hummed to life. Now Simon was timing while Logan enjoyed watching his sub.

"Time," Simon said, and Logan flipped the remote off. Rebecca whined, sweat trickling between her lush breasts. Her hips tilted out. "Oh, please, pleeeease, Sir..."

"Hell." Logan pulled a five dollar bill from his pocket and handed it to Simon. "You win."

Simon laughed and slapped Logan's back. "She didn't have a chance. My Rona is incredibly stubborn. After years of hospital administration and dealing with doctors, she can hold her tongue under any torment we can devise."

"A sucker bet, huh?" Logan studied the two subs and smiled. "So how about another bet. Whichever sub comes last on a—let's see—a mid setting."

"You're on." Simon turned. "Rona, you may not come without my permission. Do you understand?"

The woman opened her eyes, glazed with need. "Yes, Master."

Logan gave the same instruction to Rebecca.

Jake shook his head and moved Kallie away. Rona was

going to lose this one, no matter how much discipline she had. With the rabbit's tiny ears flickering right on her clit, she didn't have a chance.

He glanced down. From the way Kallie had stared at the toys, she hadn't experimented much on her own. Yes, she seemed like a no-frills vibrator type, if she owned one at all. He smiled. A beginner's introduction to toys was definitely in order. And maybe something else… He ran his hand over her ass, pleasantly round and soft. "By the way, sprite…"

She looked up at him, sexual energy virtually streaming from her. Damned if he didn't want to bend her over a bench and… He took a slow breath and ran a thumb along her soft lower lip. There would be time.

First he'd teach her a little more of the joys of submission. And that brought him back to another thought. "Later tonight, I will require you to not come until I give you permission. Is that going to be difficult for you?"

After she shook her head, a frown crossed her face, and she bit her lip.

He smothered a grin. Probably didn't usually come without a lot of work, but in a steamy atmosphere like this party and with the sexual dynamic between them off the charts, she obviously realized holding off an orgasm wouldn't be easy. Excellent. One more thing for a little submissive to worry about.

It was a fine balance with new submissives—they needed to feel comfortable enough to give themselves, but they also wanted to know they really didn't have any control. Halfway domination just didn't cut it.

Close to the front door, he halted. Angela had covered

her girlfriend's breasts with wax and, from the drops of water here and there, had varied it with ice play. Now she held the candle, working her way, drop by drop, down the sub's stomach toward her pussy. With each tiny, hot impact, the sub's stomach quivered and her hips tilted away, then up. Pain and arousal, intimately mingled.

Jake studied Kallie's face and kept his arm around her waist. Every time Angela tipped the candle to let the wax fall, Kallie flinched. Nope, this wouldn't be her play, at least not tonight.

As he started to turn toward the other side of the room, Angela dropped wax right onto the woman's clit. The sub let out a high-pitched "ahhh" of pain, and then escalating shrieks as she came hard and long. Jake smothered a grin at the horrified...fascinated...look in Kallie's wide eyes.

"Come along, sub," he said, guiding her toward the other end of the room where Caron was using a single-tail on a new male sub.

A few minutes later, he could tell from Kallie's reaction to the long streaks crisscrossing the man's back, she wasn't into serious pain. Then again, tastes changed. For now, toys and spanking, exhibitionism, dominance. It added up to a nice beginning. For tonight only—and the regret he felt at that limitation increased his resolve.

Speaking of toys... He led Kallie over to his bag and pulled out one of his favorites.

Still trying to process the different things people had been doing, Kallie took a minute to react to the object Jake had picked up. Only about two inches around, it appeared to be an amber butterfly tethered by four black straps. It even had tiny antennae. Oh God. Nerves ran up her spine like spider feet. "What's that?"

Her question earned her a frown that silenced her again. He went down on one knee in front of her. With firm hands, he set the squishy-soft butterfly part directly over her clit.

A sex toy. He was putting a sex toy on her. In public. Her face scorched from embarrassment, and so did her whole body. As he secured the straps around her thighs and hips, her clit was so sensitive that each heartbeat made it pulse against the light pressure. *I want sex now.*

"Patience, pet," he murmured, obviously catching her thought. He taped a small controller to her outer thigh. Hellfire, this was as bad as what Logan and Simon had been doing. She wanted Jake, not weird games. If he tried to tie her to a wall, she'd belt him…only her wrists were still cuffed behind her.

And then he flicked the switch. The thing started vibrating, right over her clit. She froze as she was swamped by the surging need, the contracting of her muscles, the—

Jake gave a low laugh, and the vibrations stopped. "Well, I can see the challenge won't be in getting you off, but in keeping you from it." He still knelt, and his breath brushed her thigh. So very close to her sex. *Oh, God. More.* But all she could do was stand and wait. Let him play with her. Touch her when and how he wanted. She closed her eyes at the erotic thought—he could do anything to her that he chose.

"Spread your legs," he murmured, and she did. He touched her then—oh, finally—stroking her calves. She jumped and tried to move closer, but a stern "Be still" stopped her. When his calloused hands skated across the soft inner flesh of her thighs, her toes curled. *Higher, touch me higher.*

She bit back a whimper. If he didn't do something, she'd end up begging just like Rebecca had. *No, I won't. Absolutely not.* But her pussy felt swollen, and her clit throbbed painfully. Everything she'd seen tonight, every time Jake had touched her, had increased her need. And then he'd teased her with that too-short vibration.

"Poor sprite," he murmured. He slid his hands up farther and traced the crease between her hip and pussy. She stilled, barely breathing, legs apart, her pussy open in front of him. His finger glided around the edges of the little butterfly, over her mound, and down to stroke through her swollen folds. She was very wet, and she wanted more so badly that she shook. And that stupid thing covering her clit blocked him from touching her there.

When she opened her eyes, she realized he was watching her, his blue gaze intent. Suddenly he pushed a finger up into her, a thick, shocking intrusion.

"Ah!" She shuddered as the pleasure ballooned so hard and fast that her knees wobbled. Biting her lip, she steadied her legs. Movement caught her gaze and she realized Logan and Simon were watching. Hell. She was naked, her legs spread, a man's finger up inside her. Heat rushed into her face. Oh, no, she really couldn't do this. "Jake, I don't—"

The butterfly thing turned on, vibrating right against her swollen clit, and everything inside her clamped down. Pressure built within her, coiling tighter with every second that passed. She panted, needing…needing…

When the vibrator stopped, she stood, paralyzed for a moment, totally unable to breathe. He slid his finger out and closed his hands on her hips, holding her as her legs buckled. His chuckle seemed to shake her bones.

As her heart raced, everything down there hurt, burned, throbbed with need. She barely kept from yelling at him, managed to hiss only a simple: "You bastard!"—and even then her words came out too loud, too angry.

His laugh was deep. Strong. Melting her bones like chocolate in the sun. "Such language. Now you've earned that spanking I've been wanting to give you." He rose to his feet, his eyes crinkling with amusement. "Of course, if you hadn't earned one, I've have given you one anyway. Just because I feel like it."

Her mouth opened.

"Yes, and you would have taken it." He gripped her arm as she tried to catch her breath. A spanking. Yes, he'd mentioned that before. But…but what about sex? When he'd stood up, she'd thought…

A tremor shook her as his intent registered. A spanking, here, in public, not in his room. And not a boyfriend she didn't take seriously, but Jake. How hard was he going to hit her? Her stomach sank as her anxiety ratcheted up. This was Jake, who she already knew wouldn't just slap her butt a couple of times, wouldn't stop if she was uncomfortable, wouldn't stop if she yelled. Only if she used the 'Barney' word. Her breathing increased to that of a terrified Pomeranian.

Ignoring the way she dragged her feet, he tugged her to

a leather couch in front of the fireplace and stopped behind the back. After removing her cuffs, he spun her to face the couch. “Bend over it, sub.”

She eyed it. Her bottom would be toward the room…the people. She tried to turn, to check who was watching.

“They’re not your problem. I am.” He set his hand between her shoulder blades and steered her firmly into position. “Don’t worry. Everyone will admire your pretty ass, especially when it’s glowing pink from my hand.”

Oh dear God. Embarrassment surged through her and, disconcertingly, a little thrill at being so exposed, especially in front of men she now knew. Logan and Simon—what would they see? What would they think?

Not waiting for her compliance, he pushed her shoulders down. The top of the couch hit her right at her stomach, cool and smooth, and she inhaled the scent of leather. As she bent farther, he ruthlessly pulled her hips upward until she was bowed in a V, with her bottom high in the air and her legs dangling. Her mound lay against the couch, pressing the butterfly into her clit.

She braced her hands on the seat cushions to keep from sliding right off. “Jake!”

He casually slapped her butt. “Silence, sub.” Just the mild sting and the feel of his hand sent more anticipation curling inside her. She closed her eyes and rested her forearms on the cushions as need swamped her embarrassment. From farther back in the room came the sounds of a whip, each crack accompanied by a man’s groan. A woman begged in a high voice near the front. The low hum of conversation rose above the moody music.

Something closed around her left ankle—a cuff—and he drew her leg toward the end of the couch. A metallic clatter and a click. When her leg wouldn't move, she realized he'd restrained it—with a chain? He cuffed her other ankle and pulled outward, tethering it to the opposite end of the couch. Her butt in the air and now her pussy wide open.

She wiggled, trying to move her legs. No give. Fear tensed her muscles.

He stood, and his jeans brushed against the back of her thigh. "Very pretty, sugar," he said, his voice a dark caress that slid her fear into heat. "I like seeing your ass high and open. I can play just how I want...as long as I want."

Her breath shuddered out.

He kneaded her bottom with strong hands, then teased the crease at the top of her thighs. The butterfly pressed on her clit, and she wanted it back on, dammit.

His finger brushed between her legs, sliding through her folds—oh so wet—around and around her entrance until her entire pussy swelled with need. Each time he nudged the butterfly, a jolt of exquisite pleasure pierced her clit. She wiggled helplessly, trying to get more.

"A squirming little sub, nicely positioned for my enjoyment." His rumbling voice seemed to fill the air around her. "Ten strokes, I think, for mouthing off to your dom."

"What?" she gasped.

"Eleven." He swatted her bottom like she'd bat at a mosquito, a mild slap. It didn't hurt but sent her nerves to zinging. Suddenly he pushed a finger into her, a fast, merciless intrusion, and his other hand slapped her lightly again. Her attention, every nerve inside her focused on how his finger slid in and out of her swollen tissues, ever so slowly. Oh, she needed more.

She pushed up with her arms, trying to raise her butt, and received a stronger slap, a bite of pain. “Be still or I’ll tie your hands too, Kallie.”

She stopped, afraid to move. His finger thrust in, out, never stopping. Her breathing turned to shallow panting. And then the butterfly thing turned on.

“Aaah!” She quivered as it drove her higher, until all she could feel were the vibrations.

His hand came down on her bottom, hard this time, the stinging overwhelming the sensations on her clit. Amplifying them. He pushed another finger inside her, stretching her, pumping in and out. And then the vibrations increased.

Her back tried to arch; her hands closed into fists. She was going to come, needed to come, just a little more…

He spanked her harder, and each blow alternated with the forceful thrusts of his fingers. Burning pain on her skin, followed each time by sizzling pleasure from inside. The vibrations seemed to grip her clit, and she tightened around his fingers, the pressure inside her growing to an explosive point, waiting for one little…

He stopped the spanking and slowed the vibrations—*damn him*. The sensation of his fingers inside her became everything, and each slow slide flooded her senses with exquisite, overwhelming pleasure, keeping her right on the precipice. Her legs strained against the cuffs as every muscle in her body grew taut with the wait.

Slap. Her bottom burned from the severe blow, and even as the harsh bite of pain ripped into her and tears filled her eyes, his fingers plunged deeper and she plummeted off the precipice as sheer pleasure blew outward—fierce, bright waves of sensation exploding through her until the world itself seemed to move. And move. And move.

Eventually, her brain turned back on, although her heart still tried to pound out of her chest.

The vibrations had stopped.

He stood between her gaping legs and massaged her burning bottom until her pain tangled itself with pleasure. She heard herself moan and choked at the powerless sound. *This is not me.* The spasms still reverberated far inside her. *I don't want this to be me.*

"Let me go," she demanded. Her attempt to make her voice strong failed utterly.

"Oh, I don't think so, pet," he said, and she heard something. A *zip.* A crinkling of a wrapper.

"Jake?" Her pulse that had finally slowed picked up the pace, and her muscles tensed.

He gripped her hip with his hard hand, and then she felt him, huge, pressing into her at a snail's pace, stretching her painfully despite how wet she was. He eased deeply into her. Her breathing had barely slowed, and now she gasped for air. She felt overfilled.

She squirmed against the sensation, and his strong hands flexed on her hips, keeping her immobile. "Hold up, sprite."

As the feeling of being overpowered swept through her like an avalanche, she tensed, then relaxed. He was in charge. She wanted him in charge.

"That's right, sweetheart." His low, rumbling voice stroked her like a warm, comforting hand. "That's a good girl."

Her insides throbbed, and then, as if a switch had been flipped, he felt shockingly good, as if every nerve inside her blazed awake—even before he started to move. *Oh dear God.*

Slow. Faster. Each slide of his cock was thrilling; each new thrust stretched her again, and spasms of pleasure rocked her. As her need built higher and higher, the sensations began to overwhelm her. She clutched the edge of the couch cushion, the only thing she could control in this universe. The restraints kept her open for him, with her bottom placed just right for his penetration, and his powerful grip immobilized her. The feeling of helplessness rocked her, returning like the tide with even more arousal.

Each thrust shoved her mound against the soft little butterfly. And suddenly it came to life, vibrating against her still-engorged clit.

"Oh, fuck..."

Jake grinned when the little sub muttered the curse, and her hips started wiggling uncontrollably. He anchored her well and drove in hard and deep. Damn, she felt good: hot and tight around him. And despite being new to submission and being embarrassed, she responded honestly.

Joyously. The wonder wrenched at his heart. And then she came, her voice raised in husky cries.

He flicked the remote off and bent to cup her breasts as

he took his own pleasure. Like a hot fist, the powerful contractions of her vagina milked his cock, and soon all the willpower in the world couldn't stave off his own climax. The bulldozer rolled over him, starting at his feet, squeezing all the blood into his balls until they drew up to his body. He groaned as his cock jerked, as the white lightning of incredible pleasure ripped through him with each one. He sagged against her back for a second and realized her hand was rubbing his wrist.

Damn, she was sweet. Tough little Kallie. According to her family and friends, she'd been the terror of the high school, trying to outmacho her big cousins and every other male also. But here? She was all woman. He kneaded her breast gently and felt the quiver shoot through her body and her cunt spasm around him. Smiling, he nuzzled her neck, stroking her gently, not ready to break the connection yet.

What connection? He closed his eyes and sucked in a breath. *There is no connection.*

And yet energy flowed between them. As her surrender and response heightened his own pleasure and increased his ability to read her, he could play her better, which increased her response, and on and on, spiraling upward into the instinctive dance linking a dominant and submissive.

"Stay put for a minute, sugar," he murmured and pulled out. After disposing of the condom, he untied her, removed the butterfly, and stood her on her feet. Her eyes looked dazed, her mouth soft and swollen. Come to think of it, he hadn't sampled her pretty breasts yet.

Those ugly clothes she always wore had definitely concealed her body and the very responsive female inside them. He might have felt foolish for not looking closer, except that she'd had the attitude to go with it. Why the attitude and the unfitted clothes?

"Come here, Kallie. Let's sit a bit." He scooped her up, the size of her giving him a pang of memory—*Mimi*—that disappeared at the wholehearted way Kallie snuggled against him. Mimi had always held something back, her reserve rarely broached except during a scene. From what he saw, Kallie's nature was *hold nothing back, full speed ahead.*

As he took a seat on the couch they'd fucked on, he noticed Simon. Leaning against a table and talking with his sub, the dom had obviously been watching.

Jake freed one hand and pantomimed drinking. Simon nodded, and a minute later, Rona carried over two bottled waters. Her heavy-lidded eyes spoke of recent satisfaction, and he grinned. "Thank you, blondie. By the way, can I assume you lost the second battle against Becca?"

She flushed.

"Is Simon going to make you suffer for your lack of control?" Jake raised an eyebrow. "Maybe I should offer him a few suggestions. Perhaps a good flogging?"

The crackling sound from one bottle indicated she was tempted to dump the water on him even though she knew he was teasing. A glance at her master—yes, Simon was still watching—evidently changed her mind. She glared at him for a second before giving up and laughing. "You're such a jerk."

When he chuckled, Kallie stirred. "Here, little one." He curled her fingers around the bottle and spotted an annoyed look on her face. *Two glares in two minutes. Doing well,*

Hunt.

"I am not little," she muttered and sipped the water, then drank thirstily.

"I'm sorry to tell you this, sprite, but you are definitely little."

The bum. Kallie sighed. So far the evening had been…magnificent. Why did he have to ruin it by calling her little?

His eyes gleamed with amusement. When one half of his mouth turned up in a smile, a crease appeared in one cheek. Unable to help herself, she reached up and ran her finger down the line, and it deepened. Because she'd touched him.

Her gaze lingered on his lips. He'd possessed her mouth and taken her, spanked her. Her butt burned, and her insides still shook.

And God, she wanted him to do it all over again.

He raised an eyebrow, making a line through the long, white scar on his forehead. After setting his drink down, he ran his fingers along her jawline. His thumb rubbed her lips. "That looked like an interesting thought," he murmured. Without asking, he leaned her back on one arm. She expected a kiss. Instead he dipped his head lower to brush his lips over one breast. She stiffened as a whole new set of nerves leaped into the action.

He closed his mouth around her nipple, and his tongue, so incredibly hot and wet, played over the peak. Her back arched, pushing her breast against him. Men had fondled her breasts before, but never when she'd been so sensitive already. This was…almost too much. Almost.

He sucked hard.

She inhaled sharply as each unrelenting suck shot electricity straight to her clit. Hellfire, if he kept this up, she'd be as aroused as if she hadn't come at all. He tongued the peak against the roof of his mouth and bit down gently, not releasing, and the edgy pain only made her soar higher.

She whimpered and couldn't believe the sound had come from her. She tried to pull away, and the arm behind her back was unyielding, holding her still for his mouth.

He switched to the other breast, and suddenly his hand touched her mound. God, she wanted that, and yet…

"Open your legs, little sub." He tapped his fingers against her thighs. "Now."

When she parted her knees, he slid his hand down into her wetness, stroking her folds and then moving to her clit. He firmly rubbed just one side of it, over and over, until she could actually feel it swell and the coiling of approaching climax, and then the bastard moved his finger to the other half of the nub, toying with the hood, occasionally grazing across the top. Lightning shot through her body as her whole clit swelled and pulsed with need.

Oh, God. Her hips lifted.

He chuckled, his breath warm on her breast, and then switched breasts again and sucked that nipple fiercely. A finger slid into her—two fingers—and his thumb pressed down right on her clit. Pain, pressure, penetration—everything in her spasmed uncontrollably. A blast of white filled her vision, turning to a roaring in her ears. Waves of pleasure broke over her again and again as her hips bucked against his hand.

When it all stopped—and somehow he'd kept her going longer than she'd ever thought possible—she lay like wilted grass in his arms, staring at his lean, hard face. How did he make her feel so safe with him that she'd just let him do…anything?

He nuzzled his cheek over hers, and she felt…cherished. She set her hand on his face and lost herself in the blue, blue eyes. After a minute, he sighed. "Little sub, you could worry a man." His kiss was gentle. Sweet.

When he sat up, she realized his hand was still between her legs. He moved his fingers, and her insides spasmed around him, sending more pleasure fizzing through her veins.

He chuckled and withdrew. Keeping his gaze on hers, he licked her wetness from his fingers. His cheek creased again, and he said softly, "Next time I'll taste you there." He tilted his head. "Tie you open…maybe even gag you so only I will hear your whimpers."

A sound escaped her, and the sun lines at the corners of his eyes deepened with his smile. "Yes. Like that."

God, he made her feel helpless. And yet, his control filled a…a need inside her that she hadn't realized was there, a longing to be treated like this.

He stroked her, petting her like a cat; then turned his hand over and rubbed his knuckles over her pebbling nipples. "Did being restrained bother you?"

He waited for his answer, and she realized his patience

was something else she wasn't used to, his total focus on her. He watched her so closely, her eyes, her face, noticing every time she tensed or took a breath. It made her feel...special...and somehow exposed also.

"Kallie. I asked you a question."

He wouldn't permit secrets, she realized uneasily. But she didn't have secrets, really, so... "Bother me? No." She hesitated, searching for the right words. "I liked...knowing I didn't have the reins. Sometimes during sex, I feel like I have to decide what happens, how far to go, all that. You didn't give me any control at all."

He nodded, unsurprised by her answer.

"Did you enjoy your spanking?" He slid his hand under her bottom, and the unexpected pain from her tender skin made her squeak and try to lift her hips away. He grinned. "A little sore, pet?"

She glared at him. The skin there still felt hot and swollen, and his abrasive fingers didn't help any. "No, of course not."

He squeezed and made her yelp. "Now try again, and be honest."

"Damn you."

His second squeeze was just plain mean. "Ow!" And she could feel herself getting wetter, not just from the pain, but from the way he made her bend to his will. The world shifted around her like she'd strayed off the trail into an unfamiliar forest.

"Kallie?"

"The spanking hurt...and it made...made me come

harder." And part of that had been because he'd controlled her, that he could make her take the pain.

"Better." He brushed a kiss over her lips, whispered low, "Next time I'll use a paddle."

The flush of heat that went through her worried the hell out of her. She tilted her head. "Next time? I thought..."

"One night only. But the night's not over yet."

Chapter Three

Jake hadn't called.

Kallie slid out of her Jeep and slammed the heavy door shut, letting the loud *bang* express her feelings on the subject. *That asshole bastard rat fink.* She'd been so sure that he would call her—that there had been something between them.

So little she knew. Obviously. No word from him in the last five days. She shoved her sweat-dampened hair off her forehead. Wonderful damned day, wasn't it? *It's dry air*, people would say, like dry helped when the temperature soared over ninety degrees. The heat wasn't helping her simmering mood. Or her desire to wallop someone named Jake. He was such a… *Okay, be fair.* He'd told her "*one night only.*" Repeated it, even.

But still…

Morgan had visited Serenity Lodge yesterday, and Jake hadn't asked about her. Now Morgan wondered why Kallie had asked if he had. *Gah! I might as well be back in high school.* As Kallie stalked into the small grocery store, she barely kept from slamming that door too.

At least Logan hadn't discussed any details about Friday night with Morgan or Wyatt. He'd simply said she seemed comfortable enough with his guests' activities. Since she'd reported the same, her cousins had accepted the matter. After all, they sure wouldn't ask her for descriptions of anything related to sex.

She stopped inside the door and picked up a basket. Behind the counter, the owner, David Whipple, was going over paperwork with a redheaded delivery guy, who smiled at her.

David asked, "How are you, Kallie?"

"Just dandy." Wyatt had stocked the kitchen as per the bargain, and for, oh, at least the first two days, she'd thought she had the better of that deal. No shopping or cleaning for a week, and she'd enjoyed the best, most exciting sexual adventure of her very limited life. With Jake, of all people. As her breasts tingled, she mentally shoved that memory into the toilet…and flushed.

Turning her attention to her errand, she studied the shelves of crackers and cookies and chips. A sack of potato chips went into her basket. Sour cream dip from the refrigerated section.

She said hi to Mrs. Jenkins and smiled at the small dog perched in the child seat. Looking like a furball that had encountered a light socket, the Pomeranian gave a series of shrill yaps, then panted with exhaustion. Yeah, she remembered panting just like that at the lodge.

After consideration, Kallie added two bottles of Sierra Nevada Stout from the beer fridge. Only two, just for her. All three of her best friends had dated Jake, and although they tended to share almost everything, she'd never confessed to having the hots for the man since she'd first seen him in town. All long legs and broad shoulders, that hard, rough-cut face, the cleft in his chin, and eyes the color of a mountain lake. And don't forget his large, competent hands. Oh, she remembered how those hands had slapped her bottom, stroked her pussy, pushed her down onto her hands and knees and... *Well.* She let out a slow breath. She sure wouldn't be sharing details with Serena or Gina. Nope.

So with no friends to line up on her side and call him the appropriate names, she had to hold a pity party all by herself. She studied the contents of her basket. Almost all the essential food groups: salt, alcohol, grease. Missing sugar and chocolate.

Obviously she needed Ben and Jerry's contribution to the ice cream world: chocolate fudge brownie. She dropped in the small container, hesitated, and added another. The chances that she'd feel better by tomorrow were slim. Real slim. Holy crapola, but she'd been stupid.

Setting the basket on the counter, she managed a smile for David.

He beamed at her. A bit short of six feet and stocky, he'd filled out a lot since high school, probably from hefting groceries around. She hadn't really known him then; he'd been in the geeky crowd, and she'd hung out with the jocks, playing soccer and baseball.

Not basketball, unfortunately. When all the other kids passed her in height, she'd discovered that, no matter how fast she was, genetics ruled on the basketball court. Life really sucked sometimes.

"That'll do it, Andrew." David signed the electronic device for the delivery guy. "You joining us next week for poker?"

"I'll be there."

As the man walked away, David glanced into Kallie's basket and gave her an odd look. *What, people didn't normally fill a basket with junk food?* He took the beer out and rang it up. "I enjoyed our date last month."

"Yeah, I did too," she said. They'd gone out for dinner and a movie. He was a nice man. Certainly a lot nicer than Jake. But not—

"Are you available this week?"

She hesitated, thinking over her schedule. The weekend was out, since she'd invited Rebecca to join her friends at the ClaimJumper on Saturday. On Sunday, she had a women's group booked for an overnight on Little Bear Mountain.

Earlier in the week was possible, but going out didn't sound particularly appealing. *I want Jake.*

As if she'd called him, she glimpsed him crossing the street, shoulder to shoulder with Logan. Big guys. She'd heard they were ex-military, and despite their casual stride, the two men gave as deadly an impression as the Earps heading for the OK Corral.

And oh, could this day get any better? They came into the grocery.

Jake saw her. His gait hitched, and the laughter faded from his face. He said, "Morning, Kallie," his voice as polite as if she were…a tourist. As if he'd never kissed her or been inside her or sucked on her breasts. Obviously he'd meant that "*one night only.*" The bastard.

After a quick frown at Jake, Logan smiled at her. "Good

morning, sugar."

The annoying lump inside Kallie's chest made it hard to speak, but damned if she'd show how much Jake's attitude hurt. "Hey, guys."

When the men had entered the store, David's face had gone expressionless, almost a match for Jake's. The grocer greeted Logan and continued ringing up her snacks. "So what about Thursday night?" he asked her. "Mike's having a barbecue that night."

Kallie's attention, despite her efforts, drifted back to the Hunts. While Logan checked over a list on notepaper, Jake was studying her pile of groceries on the counter. A frown creased his brow and lined his scar. His intense blue gaze moved to her.

Surely he didn't know what chocolate ice cream meant. As her face heated, she turned her back. *You are nothing to me.* "I'd love to go out, David. What time?"

* * *

In a filthy mood, Jake carried two grocery sacks through the lodge's back door into the kitchen and thumped them down on the counter.

"Just in time for supper." Rebecca opened the refrigerator and started unloading a bag. "I'm going to make chocolate cake tomorrow. Did you remember to get ice cream?"

"I think so." Hopefully. He didn't remember picking up a carton.

"*I'd love to go out, David.*" He scowled at the memory of

Kallie's low voice, of the victorious smirk that Whipple had given him. *Bastard.* Jake headed back out, passing Logan on the way in.

Get over it. She not only had a right to date, but he wanted her to. He had welcomed the fact that she hadn't gotten hung up on him and hadn't expected anything after their night together. As he stepped off the porch, the heat sent a trickle of sweat down his back. Kallie had been sweating by the second time he'd taken her. He'd licked between her tiny breasts, tasting the salt on her skin, and then pushed her knees up. She'd been so wet by then that he'd entered her snug little pussy with one thrust.

A hard shove made Jake stumble. "We've got more groceries," Logan said. "You planning to stand there all day?"

"Right." Jake moved forward, shaking his head, as if that would dislodge the memories. Hadn't yet. And now he had a serving of guilt to join them, because he couldn't lie to himself. Maybe she would date that asshole Whipple, but Jake had seen what was in her grocery basket: chocolate ice cream. Chips and dip. *Hell.*

When Mimi had been sad, she'd cried. A simple solution. But he'd lived with enough women to learn the other remedies females used to feel better. Whereas an unhappy man might get roaring drunk, a woman would curl up with a bowl of ice cream. Or chips.

Kallie's basket had contained both. It didn't take a leap of logic to figure he was the cause. The look she'd given him as he entered the store had held pain, then anger. The stiffness of her shoulders when she'd turned her back said he'd hurt her pride as well. But although she'd been hurting, she hadn't yelled, been rude, or cried. He admired that—she was a strong woman. No surprise there.

He sighed and hefted the forty pound sack of dog food onto his shoulder.

What he hadn't known was how Little Miss Macho could turn so fucking *female*. He shouldn't ever have played with her...because it had become more than play. The way she'd submitted, warily at first, and then, as her defenses lowered and her trust grew, with a stunned wonder that had left him humbled. And the way she'd welcomed him into her body—with such joy—had played hell with his control.

"Jake. Bro. Take the dog food in the house."

Jake focused, saw Logan's exasperated face. "Right. Doing just that."

It was good that she'd moved on.

Jake entered the kitchen, opened the plastic bin where Thor's kibble was stored. Good that she was going out with Whipple. He was relieved—happy—to know she wasn't pining over him.

Logan punched his shoulder. Hard. "Jake. Pour the damned food into the bin."

* * *

Kallie pulled the scrub pad out of the mouth of the oversize wooden frog and patted its green nose. After returning from Alaska two years ago, she'd whittled the figure out of basswood and carved its bushy eyebrows and beard to match Uncle Harvey's. When he'd seen it, his roaring laugh had shaken the windows. *I miss you, Uncle.*

As she soaped up the pad, she wrinkled her nose at the mess in front of her. Seems like no matter how many bargains a girl made, she still ended up doing the dishes. Her "I'm so macho" cousins only washed dishes on their kitchen-duty day and could be oblivious to any putrid stench between times. Did testosterone kill the sense of smell?

After stepping around Mufasa—like any self-respecting cat, he'd commandeered the center of the tile floor—she unloaded the dishwasher and filled it again with food-encrusted bowls and plates.

Maybe she should dump the plates in her cousins' beds. Would they take a hint?

She grinned. But when she imagined the guys' reactions, her amusement disappeared, and the icy spot lurking in a corner of her heart pulsed painfully as if in warning. These weren't her dishes, after all; this wasn't her house. Not really.

She was just the poor relation Uncle Harvey had taken in after Aunt Teresa had dumped her. After everyone had dumped her. She never forgot her place. Ever.

She swiped at a dried spot of tomato sauce. Maybe she went a little overboard in being careful—okay, maybe she'd gotten a bit hung up on the idea—but she knew how quickly someone could turn off the love faucet. Her mom had loved her, but she'd died when Kallie was eight. Not fair, so totally not fair to lose your mommy, Kallie thought, scrubbing the counter until the pad started to fray.

Two years later, her stepfather had shoved her off on Aunt Penny. At least he'd told her why: "*I'm getting married, and Annabelle already has two children.*"

She was twelve when Aunt Penny shipped her off to

Teresa. That time, she received no explanation other than, "*I'm sorry, Kallie, but we can't keep you here any longer.*"

She'd cried herself to sleep for a month after leaving Penny, but eventually the fun and bustling activity in Aunt Teresa's home had drawn her in. And then a couple of years later, Uncle Pete and Teresa gave her a little *vacation* to visit Uncle Harvey, and put her on a plane to the West Coast. They hadn't taken her back.

It still hurt, dammit. Kallie drizzled soap into a frying pan. And she'd suffered through the transition. From a city home filled with younger cousins and an affectionate, bubbling aunt to a wilderness cabin with three older cousins and her giant-sized uncle. They'd terrified her.

This place had been her last hope. If the Mastersons didn't like her, she'd have had nowhere else to go. Maybe if she'd known what she had done to get kicked out of the other homes…

Poor Uncle Harvey and poor Morgan and Wyatt and Virgil, having a teenage girl dropped into their lives. She'd spared them her tears; she'd already learned that crying didn't help. But she was the quietest, sweetest mouse they'd ever seen, at least until she'd figured out what they wanted. Her cousins didn't know what to do with a girl cousin, so she'd turned herself into one of the boys. Kallie smiled at the memories. They'd treated her like a little brother, coaching her on how to backpack, fight, shoot.

Being tough suited her.

If only she could break them of the overprotective crap. Sometimes they acted as if she were a fragile little girl or something. It was a wonder she hadn't developed a split personality.

Losing Uncle Harvey last year had been…bad. He'd loved her; she was sure that he'd loved her. When she had returned to Bear Flat after working in Alaska, he'd cheered so loudly the town must have heard him.

She'd missed him too, missed them all, but she'd forced herself to get a college degree and some experience before joining the Masterson guide business. Moving away had been incredibly difficult. At least she'd gone to a college close enough to drive back frequently. But Alaska… She'd deliberately accepted the distant job so she couldn't run home, but damn, she'd felt so empty without her cousins and uncle. She'd missed the noisy meals, the arguing and teasing, the bossing her around and laughing when she tried to reciprocate.

So although sometimes she thought about moving out again—she wrinkled her nose at the dirty dishes—the independence she'd gain wouldn't be worth what she'd lose. The others must feel the same, since they'd also returned. Or maybe they were just lazy. With the livestock and erratic schedules, it was easier for everyone to live here.

Good thing her uncle had built a huge house. Whenever one of them had turned eighteen, Harvey added on to the cabin, and eventually each bedroom had transformed into a mini-apartment. It had been the sneaky old man's way of keeping his children around.

She stared at the brick-colored wall. What would she do when the guys started getting married?

The ringing of the phone saved her from the dismal thought, and she hurried into the dining room to answer it.

The noise stopped, so Wyatt must have picked it up. As she stacked the dishes left on the table, she heard him say, "I don't know, Logan. Morgan and I are booked on Tuesday. Kallie is too." She stepped into the office.

Wyatt looked up, his hair shoved into angry spikes. He hated doing the accounting.

Serenity Lodge must have some clients for them. She ignored the little voice going, *don't, don't, don't.* Her desire to avoid Jake didn't matter. This was business.

She ignored Wyatt's motion for her not to talk and said loudly, "The women's group I'm guiding will return Monday, so I'm free on Tuesday."

"I'll get back to you, Hunt." He punched the Off button hard. "You just had to keep talking, didn't you? I don't want to book you with anyone from the lodge."

"That's what I thought. We've been over this, remember?" She glared at him. "Honestly, Wyatt, they can't be worse than some of the yuppies I've taken out—the ones who think a female guide provides sleeping bag services."

His face went dark, and he shoved to his feet. "Who? Who the hell… Did they touch you?"

Not a good argument to use, stupid girl. "Not for more than a second. Understanding was achieved quickly." She rolled her eyes. "Cuz, I sleep lightly, I carry a knife, and you guys are the ones who taught me to fight. It's not a problem. *Sit.*"

With a grunt, he sank back into his chair. "Okay. But those people from the lodge—that's something else. Virgil reamed me and Morgan a new one about letting you anywhere near them." He gingerly fingered a dark purple bruise on his jaw. "He said the Hunts are actually involved in that stuff."

"Oh?" *Involved? If he only knew*... God, they'd haul her to a convent. "Who cares? If the guests start swinging from trapezes while they"— *screw*—"mess around, I'll just step off the trail and wait until they finish."

Wyatt scowled.

"They're probably safer to be around than the clients who think camping means you don't need deodorant."

He barked a laugh. "You might have a point."

"I have several. I'm part of the business. 'Everyone is equal in this house,' remember?"

"Pa might have gone overboard with that rule," Wyatt muttered. When she crossed her arms, he held up his hands. "Fine. You win. We'll outfit a party of four—two couples—for an overnight next Tuesday."

For her own comfort, she asked, "Just the four people? Not either of the Hunts?"

"Doubt it. Why would they go?"

Good. That's good. "Have Logan fax the details." She shook her head. The Hunts and the Mastersons were doing business together, so she might as well resign herself to it and shut down the part of her that felt hurt. Yeah, when she ran into bastard Hunt, she would act just as "ice cube up the butt" as he had.

"Will do." Wyatt picked up the phone. "By the way, I invited the Hunts to our party on the Fourth. Logan said they'd come."

"Oh." She swallowed her frustrated scream. "How nice." She made it back into the kitchen before losing it, and then she slammed the counter with a fist, growling like Mufasa if someone tried to steal a newly killed mouse.

Growling. Hitting. Very antisocial. She'd better visit her sanctuary and de-stress or she'd rip Wyatt's head right off his shoulders. Not that it would affect anything—his brain must be located elsewhere.

* * *

Jake and Logan walked into the ClaimJumper. The country-western music hit Jake first—"Good Hearted Woman" with Waylon and Willie. Not bad. At least the owner, Gustaf, hadn't put on his beloved Johnny Cash. Yet.

The scent of beer, burgers, and french fries overwhelmed the traces of maybe-I'll-get-laid aftershave and perfumes. At first glimpse, he thought the entire thousand-plus population of Bear Flat had jammed into the tiny tavern, but no—just another Saturday night. Tourists from the handful of bed-and-breakfasts and the local motel mingled with loggers and locals and a few fishermen from the river lodge. And delivery men. Sitting at a table near the door, the redheaded, muscular guy who delivered sodas to the lodge nodded. "Fellas."

"Evening, Secrist," Jake said. He noticed most of the preponderantly male population watched the eye candy in the far corner where Serena and Gina sat with Logan's fiancée.

On the way out the door, Rebecca had announced she

planned to indulge herself during the girls' night out—which was why Logan had talked Jake into driving him into town. He would take no chances of his pretty sub splattering herself all over the zigzagging highway.

Avoiding the antlers festooned with baseball and cowboy hats, Jake leaned a shoulder against the rough log wall and studied Becca. The curvy redhead looked happy—she usually did—but right now, she appeared both tipsy and giggly. He glanced at Logan. "She looks like a girl hanging out with girls."

Logan set a foot on a chair, his hands braced on his leg as he studied his submissive. "She's been missing this, hasn't she?"

"Seems so. Sociable as she is, she probably had a bunch of girlfriends in San Francisco."

"And none here. Fuck me for being so blind. I'll make sure she takes more time off and gets into town, even if I have to drag her."

Jake winced. "No dragging, please. My stomach isn't up to another of your wars." The last time business called them to San Francisco, Rebecca had insisted she'd stay at the lodge. Unwilling to risk his city girl alone in the woods, Logan had swatted her on the ass and stuffed her into the car. Bad mistake. The redhead was a magnificent cook, but the following week, nothing he or Logan ate had been edible. Damned if he knew how she'd ruined their food and still fed the guests well. And he was still pissed off that she'd included him in the battle.

Logan grinned. "Wimp. But I'll let her decide. Bless Kallie for inviting her tonight."

"Kallie invited her? Kallie will be here?" Jake's gut twisted like a worm impaled on a hook. Hell, he wouldn't have come if he'd known.

"Yeah." Logan watched Rebecca for a minute, smiling each time she laughed. "God, she's beautiful."

"She is that." And she'd turned his brother's world around. *Thank you, Becca.*

"Looks like we might as well get a beer." Logan jerked his chin toward a burly man across the room. "Bart's here, so I'm going to check on our hardware order. Grab me a beer."

"You bet." As Logan headed for the lumberyard owner, Jake scoped out the rest of the room, nodding to the people he knew. Was the sprite here?

She was—at the bar beside David Whipple, and as Jake watched, the grocer wrapped his arm around her. Possessively.

A growl escaped, startling Jake as much as a flabby tourist nearby, who edged farther away. *Hell, put a lock on it, Hunt. She's not yours.*

Is too.

In her own unique scruffy pixie way, Kallie was even more beautiful than Rebecca. Her short hair was tousled, like she'd just got out of bed. *It had looked like that after I spanked her.* She'd taken her flannel shirt off and tied it around her waist, and her tank top showed off her tanned arms. Her skin had been so smooth…

I should leave her be.

Her head tilted back, and he could tell she was laughing. Damn, he liked her laugh. Her dark eyes would be dancing and…

Don't do this, Hunt. Even as he reached the end of the bar, she slipped away from Whipple and headed to her table, carrying two of the four drinks lined up on the bar. Well then, he'd just wait right here until she returned. His displeasure at seeing Whipple touch her had wrecked his judgment—and he didn't give a damn.

Whipple glanced over, then scowled and averted his eyes. The animosity was mutual. Mimi had broken up with the grocer just before meeting Jake, and after seeing her black eye and swollen lip, Jake had paid the bastard a visit. So no hugs and kisses from Whipple, and wasn't that just a crying shame?

"Hunt." The old Swede serving drinks looked as battered as his tavern. "Gutt evening, youngling. What can I get you?"

Jake grinned. The old man was the only person who'd called him young in two decades. "A couple of drafts."

Gustaf filled two glasses and set them on the bar top after swiping up a few miscreant drops with a grimy towel.

After paying, Jake picked up his beer. Unfortunately the icy cold liquid didn't divert his mind—or body—from Kallie. He was already half-erect from one look. Had he actually worried about his dick's lack of interest?

He leaned an elbow on the bar and watched as Kallie handed off the beers to the table of women. She said something to Rebecca, laughed at the retort, and headed back to get the two drinks she'd left on the bar.

Jake moved a few steps out to intercept her.

Why'd they decide to sit so far from the bar? Kallie wondered as she headed back to fetch the rest of the drinks. She dodged a staggering tourist, veered too close to Ben's table, and had to slap the damned lecher's hand away from her butt. A few steps later, she pulled old Verne to his feet and two-stepped down the middle of the room with him. She'd never seen him sober, but he was a happy drunk. Ten years ago, he'd given her country dance lessons in the parking lot after some jerk whose name she couldn't remember had made fun of her. By the time Verne had been satisfied with her progress, she could outdance most of the town.

He cackled and patted her shoulder. "Still got the moves, girl."

"So do you, Verne." Her kiss on his leathery cheek made him grin so wide that his silver fillings gleamed at her. Laughing, she turned away and ran into a wall. A wall of very hard man.

She heard a low chuckle, and firm hands gripped her arms to steady her. "Careful there, sprite."

Like snow in the hot sun, every cell in her body turned to slush. Knowing he'd undoubtedly notice his effect on her, she muttered, "Hi, Jake," to his chest without looking up.

"Kallie." His voice rumbled across her like a mountain avalanche and had the same effect, knocking down every one of her resolutions. Her heart picked up speed, and even worse, she could feel her breasts contracting, her skin absorbing the heat of his hands. She might tell her mind to forget, but her body well remembered the feel of him against her. Thick inside her. His powerful hands—

She tried to step around him.

He put a finger under her chin and tilted her head up. "Are you not talking to me, Kallie?"

His eyes were too blue in the tavern light, and the warm look in them made her long to burrow closer. But he didn't want that. She didn't want that. *Okay, don't lie.* She *shouldn't* want that. And she really, really didn't know how to handle this. She forced a smile. "We're having a girls' night out, dude, and you don't have the proper equipment."

She yanked away and continued to the bar. If he touched her again, she'd plant a fist in his gut. Maybe that was excessive, but, hey, he was into BDSM, right? What was a little pain between friends?

Next round, she'd send Serena to fetch the drinks.

When she reached the bar, David had an odd expression on his face. "Is he bothering you, Kallie?" He put his arm around her again.

Is this what a chicken between two hungry dogs feels like? She stepped out of reach. "Nothing I can't handle." She lifted the two last drinks so quickly that beer sloshed over the sides. "Well—"

"I had fun at the barbecue," he interrupted. "How about tomorrow night? There's a—"

"No." The word was out before she thought, the bluntness rude enough to make his mouth thin. But she meant it. "I like you, David, but not—Dating isn't—" Hell, could she be any more tongue-tied?

He scowled. "It's him, isn't it? Jake Hunt."

Kallie glanced over her shoulder and sucked in a breath.

Jake stood beside Verne—undoubtedly listening to one of the old guy's interminable jokes—but his eyes were focused on her. No chill there tonight; his stare was like molten silver, hot enough to burn. She turned to the bar and could still feel his intense gaze on her back.

David caught her arm. "Don't be with him, Kallie. You're better with me. We're good together."

"Ah…thank you, David." She pulled away, unsettled at his show of emotion. He had always been reserved. Polite. No fire like Jake—who didn't want her. The thought sat in her stomach bitterly. "I don't think I'm right for anyone."

She headed back to the table, giving Jake a wide berth, and thumped one of the two beers down. "Here you go, Rebecca."

After dropping ungracefully into her chair, she lifted the last beer and drained half of it in one long pull. A covert glance showed Jake still talking with Verne. Kallie shook her head, remembering Verne's story of how Jake had jumped into a flooding river to rescue him. Dammit—like she needed to hear glowing tales of the jerk's bravery?

When David walked past the two men on the way to the restroom, the glare he directed at Jake's back should have put a smoldering hole in Hunt's black T-shirt. Well, she felt the same way.

Serena and Gina were chattering about the gorgeous star of a new TV show and—thank you, God—hadn't noticed the interlude with Jake. Rebecca, however…

"Very interesting." Rebecca sipped her beer, her gaze on Jake. "You know, I've never seen him watch anyone like he does you. He's always so easygoing; very little upsets him.

When he does a scene with a woman, it's like his emotions are switched off. But not last week at the party, or tonight." She raised her eyebrows at Kallie.

Kallie kept her back turned to the asshole and her voice low. "Don't look at me like that. There's nothing going on." She drank the rest of her beer and scowled. "We played one night, and he gave me the 'this is only tonight' lecture. Repeated it, even."

"A one-nighter lecture?" Rebecca snorted a laugh. "He's so honest I can just see him doing that. And it's true; I've never seen him with any woman more than once in a row." Rebecca tilted her head and regarded Jake. "He isn't acting like a one-nighter right now. I don't think he's taken his eyes off you."

"I don't give a damn how he acts." Dipwad. If he'd wanted to see her, he knew where the phone was. He'd barely said hello in the grocery store. But tonight, yeah, he'd probably had a beer or three and now wanted a quickie as a chaser. And then he'd go back to ignoring her again.

Rebecca tapped a finger on her lips. "Maybe if you flirted a little? Wore something sexy?"

"I don't know how to flirt or be sexy."

"No way. How can you grow up without learning the essentials?" The horrified expression on the redhead's face made Kallie snicker.

"Three older cousins and a conservative uncle. I wanted to fit in, so I dressed like them… And they got so used to that, they'd harass me if I wore something provocative. Or looked at a guy." Kallie smiled ruefully. "I didn't even date until I got to college, and then it was too late to change."

"Girl, it's never too late to change." Rebecca tilted her head and assessed Kallie. "I can guess your size. And then maybe a little—"

God help me. "So how did you meet Logan?"

The diversion worked. Rebecca flushed a light red and leaned closer so only Kallie could hear. "You know how wide-eyed you were last weekend? Well, you should have seen me the night I met Logan. See, my boyfriend had talked me into a holiday at Serenity." She hesitated and glanced at Serena and Gina, who were now debating whether a man's size could best be determined by the length of his thumbs or his feet.

Interesting. Kallie's gaze slid to Jake and his—*oh, yeah*—big, big boots.

Rebecca's eyes followed, and she burst out laughing, drawing the attention of every guy in the place, including Logan. The look he gave his fiancée was hot enough to spark a forest fire, and it sent a spike of envy right through Kallie's heart. No man had *ever* looked at her like that. She took a slow breath and tried to remember what they'd been discussing. "Okay, you went to the lodge with your boyfriend. Go on."

After checking again that the other two weren't listening, Rebecca said, "With my boyfriend and his swinger's club."

"Swingers…that's when everybody kinda sorta does everyone else, right?"

"Oh yeah. All out in public." Rebecca rolled her eyes. "Major mistake on my part. So when my boyfriend brought someone back to our cabin to…enjoy, I couldn't say anything since—hey, swinger's club, right? Anyway, I stomped out. Logan found me freezing to death on the front porch…and took me upstairs to his rooms."

Kallie snorted, remembering the commanding way he'd wrapped his hand around the back of Rebecca's neck. "I just bet he did."

"Shy, he's not." Rebecca gave Kallie a mischievous look. "He discovered I was submissive, and sucked me right into a whole new kink. I would never have thought I'd do anything out in public, but being watched adds a certain…something."

Kallie averted her gaze, the words bringing back more than she wanted to remember. Light glinting off muscled arms, calloused hands holding her legs apart, her whimpering, even knowing others could hear the sounds she made… Warmth seared her cheeks. Then she remembered she'd never do that again with Jake. She drained her beer.

He stared at the bitch from across the room. So rude. A ballbuster who would humiliate a man in front of his friends. There she sat, satisfied with herself, probably even gloating. The darkness of her hair and eyes echoed the blackness in her soul.

Laughter spilled across the tavern, ugly, vicious noise, ripping holes in his mind, letting memories ooze into him. The first demon had challenged his manhood. "*Can't even get it up. Loser. I've had it with you.*" Had tossed her dark hair over her shoulder and turned her back.

His fingers clenched, squashing the burger in his hand into nothingness. Catsup dripped onto the table in bloodred splatters.

A woman could get under a man's skin, stealing his thoughts, his very essence until she owned him. And then he'd return to her over and over, letting her tear pieces of him away until clawing darkness streamed through him. Until he felt that life wasn't worth living.

He dropped the remains of his food and stared at the redness covering his hand. Drops of red had spattered the long white scar on his wrist where he had sliced so cleanly and watched the blood of his body pour out and soak into the carpet.

He'd been wrong to do that and wrong to blame himself instead of her. The knowledge had come to him as he'd recovered. The doctor who saw him had a voice of an angel as he kept repeating that the failure of the relationship hadn't been his fault. Not his fault at all.

And then he knew—it must have been hers. Some women were evil.

She'd been evil. He'd hit her, then hit her again and again. He saw that by his actions, he'd destroyed the evil and removed it from the world. The shrieking of the demon inside her had confirmed it, hurting his ears until his head pounded with pain. When the noise stopped, he'd known the foulness had gone, for once again, his manhood had responded to his command.

Dark hair and dark eyes. Marks of the devil. Some

females fought successfully against the encroaching malevolence; some were overcome by the demon. The fallen ones taunted the men—his brothers—ruining their lives and shredding their souls.

Carefully he wiped the redness from his hand. Now he would risk his own life and soul to destroy this demon.

Chapter Four

An hour or so later, Kallie shoved her chair away from the table. Time to go. By now most of the alcohol had to be out of her system.

Logan had bribed Gustaf to give Johnny Cash a rest—thank God—and play a waltz. He'd snatched Rebecca right out of her chair to dance. In one corner, Serena and Gina flirted with the loggers, but none of the men looked interesting. Not with Jake still sitting at the bar.

Jerk.

Aside from talking with Rebecca, the evening had been a crappy one—because of Jake's presence and the effort it took to ignore him.

Kallie pulled on her flannel shirt and slipped out. The parking lot was wonderfully cool after the stuffiness of the bar and silent after the loud music. Shaking her head, she slid behind the wheel of her Jeep and turned the key. *Rrr-rrr-rrr.*

Excuse me? She tried again. *Rrr-rrr-rrr.* With an exasperated sigh, she thunked her head on the steering wheel a few times, then got out and scanned the area. Nobody in the parking lot to jump-start the car. Didn't that just figure? She eyed the door of the tavern. Did she want to ask for help…in front of Jake…looking like a wussy girl who couldn't even get her car to start?

He'd undoubtedly offer her a ride, thinking she'd changed her mind and wanted him, after all.

Nope. It'd be a hot day on the glacier before she accepted help from him. She glanced at the sky. A few clouds. The fat curve of the silvery moon didn't provide the greatest light, but it would do. She rummaged in the glove compartment for a flashlight. Only half-dead, so it might last long enough.

Oh well. A few miles in the cold air wouldn't hurt her any. Walking didn't take that much longer than driving the twisty gravel road. She headed across the parking lot, glancing back as a young man staggered out the back door and bent over in the unmistakable way of someone being sick.

She shook her head. Poor guy. Then again, this wasn't the way she'd planned to end the evening either. Maybe she should have gone home with David and made new memories to replace the ones of Jake. Like that song, "I'm Gonna Wash That Man Right Outta My Hair," she might have screwed that man right out of her thoughts.

She huffed a laugh. Interesting as it sounded, it wouldn't happen. The thought of having sex right now with anyone—*except Jake*—felt wrong. With *anyone*, dammit, she told herself firmly. She stuffed her hands in her pockets and strolled down Main Street. Past David's grocery store across from the police station, past the two antique stores, the tiny museum. Clouds floating in front of the moon sent shadows wavering along the clapboard buildings.

Damn her for being an idiot, anyway. Ever since seeing Hunt for the first time, she'd wanted him. Everything about him appealed to her, from his low voice and quick smile to his broad shoulders—even the way a day's growth of beard shadowed his square jaw. And nothing had changed since then.

Her boots thudded on the boardwalk, and then she crossed the street, leaving the downtown section. One night of having sex with him—she couldn't call it making love—had only added more to dream about. How she'd felt with his cock inside her while he'd held her in his arms so tightly that there didn't seem to be any part of her he hadn't touched. How his fingers had dug into her hips when he'd come. How he'd watched her when he'd pinned her down, not letting her move at all as he'd...

Great. Now she ached in all the wrong spots. *Dummy.*

About a mile up the gravel road, houses sat acres apart, and the trees thickened into forest, blocking some of the moonlight. A car approached, its lights shining between the trunks, and disappeared down a side road. Pity. She could have asked for a ride. Occasionally using the flashlight for the darker sections, she forged onward against the ever-steepening rise of the road. Her footsteps crunched on the loose gravel. A slight breeze rustled the trees, bringing the crisp scent of snow from the surrounding mountains.

She'd walked over two miles when a shiver ran up her spine, and she slowed. Stopped. Something—or someone—was watching her, the feeling identical to when she'd spot a cougar or coyote watching nearby. Turning in a slow circle, she studied the area. No eyes flashed in the moonlight. Lights from the distant houses were barely visible through the heavy forest. No self-respecting cougar or coyote would try to worm through the thick undergrowth beside the road.

A human? Whatever it was, right now she felt way too much like prey.

Her shoulders tensed. Whatever it was didn't make a sound. Great. Where was her rifle when she needed it? Hellfire, she hadn't even strapped on her knife. Should she head back to town? She caught a movement out of the corner of her eye and spun. A small shape sprang across the road and disappeared into the blackness of the ditch. *Someone's cat.* The antsy feeling didn't leave.

Suck it up and keep going. Faster. Her skin crept as if the tiny nerve endings could detect whatever was watching her. Muscles tensed, she started walking again. A rustle sounded behind her, and she turned. On the other side of the road, the bushes swayed. Something big was over there. A bear? Bears hung around campgrounds, true, but they didn't stalk humans.

Her hands clenched into fists. More likely a human animal—some bastard was following her. The dying flashlight was too weak to reach the other side—and would simply pinpoint her location. Well, thanks to her cousins' lessons, the cowardly lurker wouldn't find her easy prey.

The rumble of a vehicle sounded, and a truck came slowly around the curve. The headlights blinded her as she moved closer to the shoulder. It stopped.

"Get in." Jake's voice.

She blinked, trying to restore her night vision, started to say no, and stopped. *Don't be dumber than you have been already.* As she neared the passenger side, he leaned over and pushed the door open.

She stepped up and slid onto the seat. The sweeping feeling of relief made her voice shake. "Thanks."

Despite the dash lights, his expression was unreadable. He regarded her for a long moment, then turned the heat to high. As the blast of hot air hit her, her tense muscles started to unravel. *Warm.* She sagged against the seat, inhaling the fragrance of leather and Jake's musky forest scent. *Safe.*

His prey had been removed from his grasp. When her car wouldn't start, he'd thought it was a true intervention, but he might have been wrong. Perhaps darkness had not yet totally consumed her soul. He watched the truck, the red taillights glowing at him like demon eyes as it accelerated up the road.

With both relief and disappointment, he tossed the heavy branch into the underbrush and turned back to town. He must not act without certainty, although he'd hardened like a true man at the thought of vanquishing another.

But he'd watch.

Jake shoved his anger down…again…and kept silent as he drove up the road. The winding curves required concentration, although he'd stopped drinking a while back. The tension eased out of him slowly, but he was still damned pissed off. He'd seen her depart—alone—which had pleased him more than he found comfortable. He'd left later, only to spot her Jeep parked next to Rebecca's car in the parking lot. A green-faced young man slumped against the tavern wall told him a short woman had left the Jeep and taken off. Walking.

Walking. If she'd been his sub, he might well have pulled down her pants and spanked the hell out of her for her foolhardiness.

Might anyway.

They'd both enjoy it.

At the sign MASTERSON WILDERNESS GUIDE SERVICE, Jake turned off onto the tiny gravel road and drove downhill almost a quarter mile into a tiny valley. The forest continued on the left but opened to fenced pastures on the right and a clearing in front. As he pulled the truck to a stop, the moonlight showed a massive barn near the pastures and a two-story log cabin nestled up against the trees. No lights on.

"Nobody home?" Jake asked.

She shook her head. "Virgil has night shift this week. Morgan and Wyatt are out on Gray Mountain with a big group. They'll be back tomorrow afternoon."

As if doing the calculations—empty house all night—Jake's cock hardened. Bad idea, he told it, but when had a man's dick ever listened to the voice of reason?

He swung out of the truck and walked around. As he'd expected, she didn't wait for the common courtesy of having her door opened, but hopped out on her own. Steady on her feet too. "For someone who drank as much as you did, you're pretty sober."

"I stopped early," she said. "Besides: cold air, nice hike. A little scare."

She was on the wide front porch by the time her last three words registered with him. She didn't mean him, dammit. He took her elbow and spun her around. "What scare?"

"Nothing important."

Her nonchalant manner was starting to annoy him.

"Thanks for the ride, Jake."

He took the keys from her, ignored her futile snatch to get them back, and opened the door. Setting his hand on her lower back, he nudged her inside…and followed. Definitely a home, not a fancy house. The small entry to dump gear and outer clothing and boots led into a huge living room. The log walls had been polished to a muted sheen. Some shelves held books; some held the clutter of DVDs and change. One displayed intricately carved Old West figures. He walked over. A corral, a barn, tiny men with weapons drawn. He could almost see the shots being exchanged, and he chuckled as he figured it out—a depiction of the fight at the OK Corral. Old Harvey Masterson's passion. "These are remarkable. Where'd you find them?"

"I whittle."

"You? Well, damn. I might try to talk you into doing some for the lodge." He glanced around at the rest of the room. Comfortable, oversize furniture, coffee tables that you could put your feet on, heavy-duty woodstove. "Nice place."

"Yeah, it is, isn't it?" She took her keys back and tried to shake his hand, as gracious and distant as a queen. "I appreciate the lift."

Here's your hat and what's your hurry, eh? He took her hand and pulled her closer. "We'll discuss the need for that lift later," he said, unable to keep the roughness out of his voice. “Meantime—hell!”

He shoved her behind him as a massive cat stalked across the room and sprang onto the back of the couch. Black ear tufts stuck up like a bobcat’s, and a tail puffed out as big as a raccoon’s. “That can’t be a cat. What the hell is it?”

Her husky chuckle was as effective as fingers stroking his cock.

The beast stared at them with golden green, unblinking eyes.

“He’s a Maine coon cat, and his name’s Mufasa.”

“Mufasa in *The Lion King*? Simba’s kick-ass father?”

Her eyebrows rose. “Very good. I’m surprised.”

“I’ve got a hoard of nieces and nephews.” From the size of those front paws, the cat could probably disembowel a person with one swipe. He kept an eye on it as he pulled Kallie to face him. Cupping his hands under her pretty, round ass, he slid her up his body to take her mouth.

Seductive lips—and damn him for thinking about how they’d feel around his cock. Her sigh whispered into him, and her muscles started to yield, turning soft and supple. Then she slapped a hand against his chest. “Stop.”

With a disappointed grumble, he released her and stepped back.

She blinked in surprise. “You know, it’s nice not to have to struggle when I object.”

“A dom should be able to hear when a woman is or isn’t playing.” The dom in him also noted the arousal heating her cheeks, the redness of her lips from more than his kiss. But her brain had overruled her desires. And unfortunately that brain was still working. Her mouth firmed into a stubborn line that made him want to kiss it back to softness.

"You told me 'one night,' Jake. You made that quite clear, and I appreciated your honesty. Obviously you meant what you said—you haven't called me since." She crossed her arms over her chest, high enough to conceal the peaked nipples apparent through her tank top.

He had to bite the inside of his lip to keep from smiling. "This is true."

"So you have a couple of beers, and suddenly you want to screw around. No."

Her eyes held anger…and hurt. His amusement disappeared.

She saw the laughter fade from his eyes and his jaw turn to stone, and somehow it only made her want him the more.

"First, alcohol isn't a factor. Second…" He stroked a finger down her cheek, and she felt as if she could fall into his eyes, as clear as a high mountain stream.

"Kallie, I refuse to get involved. With anyone. Ever." He paused and added, "And yet, I want to make love to you. I want you on your knees in front of me, those soft lips around my cock. I want you bound and helpless on my bed. I want to spank you and take you so long and hard you'll walk bowlegged for a week."

Oh. God. Her breathing turned ragged. She cleared her throat. Why had she said she appreciated his honesty? "Well." She swallowed and tried again. "You want to…to play…without any involvement, is that right?"

"Is that possible?" He caught her chin, keeping her from looking away.

I want him. But could she take the inevitable end? Her feelings had already taken a blow from only one night. How many could she survive before she fell? "I need to think about it."

"Fair enough." He brushed a kiss over her lips. "Come and lock the door behind me."

She flipped the lock and listened to the sound of the truck fade into the night. As she stepped away from the door, she remembered…something…had lurked in the darkness by the road. Maybe she'd latch the windows too.

Tomorrow she'd take a group up the mountain and be able to relax. No place was as safe as the wilderness.

* * *

Early the next week, Jake loafed on the ground with his back against a log and contentedly sipped a cup of coffee. The day was just starting to chill off now that night had fallen. They'd hiked an easy three hours, enough to give his muscles a nice workout, and stopped early to make a leisurely camp. On the other side of the crackling fire, the older couple, Steve and Evelyn, sat side by side, watching the campfire and talking quietly. With more energy, Heather and Andrew had walked down to the nearby stream for a quick washup. Across the clearing, Kallie did supper cleanup, having refused any help. "My job," she'd said, and insisted he and the clients should simply enjoy the evening.

And they would, he thought with a smile.

Originally Logan had planned to accompany these two couples and continue their instruction in BDSM, but when Rebecca had picked up a nasty flu, he hadn't wanted to leave her. Jake shook his head. His bro gave new meaning to the word *doting*. So Jake had taken his place.

With Kallie as the guide… Well, he'd planned to allow the sprite more time before calling her, but he had to admit her presence added to his enjoyment of the day. The woman was a cheerful bundle of energy, and she'd delighted the two couples. She was everything a person might want in a trail guide: she managed to spot any wildlife in the area, from mule deer to porcupines, could identify all the plants and trees, and knew both the geology and the history of Yosemite. Rather than lecturing, she'd drop tidbits of interesting facts and elaborate if anyone expressed interest.

He considered himself a damn good guide. With growing pride, he'd come to realize she was better. His tough little sprite.

No. Not mine.

Heather and Andrew appeared, and Jake motioned both couples over. "All right, are you ready to get started?"

Nods all around. Good enough. He smiled at the two women, then glanced at the men. "Your submissives, gentlemen. Here to do anything you want them to." Within reason, he didn't add, but to remind everyone that there were limits, he asked, "Heather, what is your safe word?"

A pale blonde with the coloring to match, she flushed beautifully. "Diamond."

"Evelyn?" Jake nodded to the round brunette in her early forties. Although she gave a motherly impression—someone who would make cookies and snuggle children against her small, cuddly body—she was a renowned orthopedic surgeon.

"Darth Vader," she said.

"Interesting choice."

Steve stroked his goatee. "I believe she accompanied it with a nasty threat: 'Don't make me destroy you,'" he added in a raspy voice.

Jake stifled a laugh. "Well, if she uses it, you'd best pay attention." He studied the group for a minute. Anticipation and a few nerves. Good enough. "Gentlemen, please direct your submissives to remain here, and then join me over there." He pointed to the other side of the campsite.

The professor gave him a blank look, but Andrew caught the clue. "Heather, kneel. Hands behind your back." He waited to be sure she'd done as directed before strolling across the clearing with Jake.

Jake saw the unspoken *got it* from Steve. "Evelyn, the slave position. Now."

Ah, someone had been doing his homework and learning the positions. Jake watched as Evelyn knelt, spread her knees open, and placed her hands on her thighs. *Very nice.*

Steve joined them, and Jake nodded approval. He added for the men's ears only, "Subs in the kneeling position should keep their eyes down."

Both men snapped orders, and the women complied.

Jake leaned against a tree and smiled at the pretty sight. "Look at them," he murmured to the men. "All worried about what you have in mind. Anticipating pleasure but possibly pain. Knowing you might push them past what they're used to. Quivering inside."

"God, you're right. I've never seen her like this," Steve said.

"With her eyes on the ground, a sub can't read your face, can't see what's coming," Jake said. "It increases their sense of helplessness and worry. This is the space you want them in. Excited and eager to please."

Nods.

"What else could you do to make them feel more vulnerable?" He smiled as the men considered. A lawyer and a professor, both with professional wives. Used to equality in their marriages, they needed some mental adjustment to take on the dominant role.

"Naked," Andrew said. "Being without clothes would..." He gestured, a lawyer at loss for words.

"Good choice. Go for it." When the men started to speak, Jake held up a hand. "A command can certainly be given at a distance, but in this case, with new submissives, you want to be hands-on. Enjoy your submissive's body as she strips. Make her stop at your command. Savor the fact that you can touch as you please. Tease her. Let her know how much the sight of her and the softness of her skin pleases you."

Two nods and the men strolled back to their wives. Walking taller. Yes, they were already beginning to own the power. Any idiot could use handcuffs. Dominance required more.

He checked the area. Kallie had finished stowing dishes

away and was sitting near her pack, pretending to whittle. He'd expected her to turn her back or retreat into her tent when he started the lessons. But she watched instead.

When she glanced his way with a wistful look, his blood surged through his veins like a flash flood. Damn, he wanted her. Had she had enough time to think? How badly did she want to play? "Kallie. Come here."

She opened her mouth to reply.

He lowered his voice. "Now."

After setting her knife and wood on top of her pack, she came to him. Slowly. He could almost hear her arguing with herself. *Submit. No, don't.* With eyes so dark they appeared black in the dim light, she stood in front of him and rubbed her hands on her jeans. He almost smiled. Sweating already.

"Did you finish thinking, sprite?"

"Yes." She licked her lip and said resolutely, "I want to play."

So do I. In fact, he'd never met anyone he'd wanted so badly. Getting control of himself, he set a finger under her chin and lifted her face. "The commitment between us is only for one more night. Tonight. Can you live with that?"

"Yes." Her acceptance showed in her eyes.

"Yes, what?"

A tremor ran through her. "Yes, Sir."

"Very nice." He stroked her hair, then ran a finger around the delicate curve of her ear and down the line of her jaw to that stubborn chin. Obstinate enough to be a challenge and vulnerable enough to pull at his heart…dammit. "I will enjoy having my hands on you again."

The way her breathing deepened pleased him. He firmly grasped her upper arm to increase her feeling of being controlled. "There are many things I want to do to you, Kallie."

Chapter Five

Kallie swallowed hard as her imagination went wild. What did he mean…"*do to her*"?

Hell, what was she thinking, agreeing to this? But she wanted tonight—wanted more than one, but oh, well. Over the past few days, she'd had time to think and had decided that she could handle the limits he'd put on their relationship. The other times she'd been tossed aside had come as a total shock. Knowing up front that he didn't plan to stay with her, she wouldn't be surprised when he moved on. That had to be better.

He undid the top buttons of her flannel shirt and slid his hand inside. The touch of his fingers on her breast and the slight abrasion from his roughened skin made her toes curl. She saw his lips curve up as he teased her nipple. God, her knees were liable to give out.

"What is your real name?" he asked, switching to the other breast.

"What?"

His eyes darkened.

Oops. A sub didn't ask questions. "Ka-LEEN-da, spelled K-A-L-I-N-D-A. My mother said my father was born in India."

"Ah. That's where your gorgeous eyes come from."

Gorgeous? She had gorgeous eyes? She looked down to hide how much pleasure his compliment gave her.

"Considering the size of the Masterson men, you must have inherited your height from your father's side."

He was calling her a scrawny midget, wasn't he? She scowled at him.

After threading his fingers in her short hair, he pulled her head back, and his voice turned rough enough to match the skin on his hands. "I don't like being glared at by submissives."

She tried to move and discovered his grip had her completely in his power. Helpless. Her whole lower half seemed to melt.

"I'll accept an apology this once. The next time, you'll be punished."

Punished? The thought sent warring sensations through her: heat at the memory of being spanked and the shattering orgasm afterward—and then anger at his threat.

"Kalinda. I'm waiting."

She stared up at him. Firelight flickered over his stern face, heightened his cheekbones, and shadowed his eyes—and she wanted him so badly she shook with it. "I'm sorry, Jake," she whispered.

"Very well done, sprite." Still holding her head back, he brushed his mouth across hers and bit her jaw. The small pain jolted through her and sizzled her insides. His lips were gentle, warm, and he took his time, nuzzling under her ear, nibbling on the curve between her shoulder and neck. Never letting her move as he pleased himself. As he set her every nerve to quivering with need.

She wanted to touch him, to grab his shoulders, lace her hands behind his head, but somehow, barely, she kept her hands at her sides. The effort of obeying his unspoken wishes—of pleasing him—sent sparkles of excitement shooting into every nerve.

He straightened and studied her. One corner of his mouth turned up. "Good little sprite," he murmured. "Working so nicely to stay still."

She had only a second to enjoy the pleasure of his words before he took her mouth hard. Possessively. The way he kissed was more devastating than she remembered. When he lifted his head and pulled her into his arms, she laid her cheek on his broad chest. His erection pressed against her lower abdomen, and satisfaction filled her. He wanted her too.

A laugh rumbled under her ear, and she realized he was watching the others. She tried to turn to see. His grip only tightened. Not a chance. "Gentlemen, when you are finished, join me and my sub, please."

His sub. The sound of that was…much too nice. She shouldn't like it, but she did. She put her arms around his waist and sighed when he didn't stop her. He had the fragrance of soap—he must have washed by the creek—and a head-spinning, masculine scent. Pushing her face against him, she sniffed. Why did he have to smell so good?

He chuckled. "I enjoy the way you smell too, sugar. Like vanilla ice cream."

She heard footsteps as the other two men arrived.

"Very good. Now look at your sub. Study her. Has her breathing increased? Is she flushed? Did your actions arouse her—and how can you tell? Each woman is different. Pay attention, and don't assume anything."

He paused. After putting his arm around Kallie, he moved her to stand beside him, facing the men.

Her cheeks heated. This was a mistake; these were her clients. She tried to pull away, but he had her trapped.

"Gentlemen, like your wives, Kallie is a career woman and the best guide in the area, as you've seen. For this evening, for the enjoyment of us both, she chooses to give up control to me." He glanced down at her, and a corner of his mouth turned up. "However, if I tried this without her acceptance, she'd probably cripple me for life. As you work out the parameters of your play with your partner, remember that a woman can delight in submission with the right man and in the right place, and yet rip the guts out of someone in the boardroom the next day."

Kallie met his gaze, warmed at the understanding. Her breath sighed out; she hadn't realized she'd been holding it. All right then. It helped to remember the two women here also had careers.

Jake ruffled her hair, then closed his fist around the short strands, pulling her head back as he'd done earlier. His other hand cupped her cheek. She felt the warmth of his body as he pulled her closer. "Steve, Andrew, you've started seeing how verbal control works. Physical control is very similar—exerting your will and keeping your submissive feeling helpless. She must know she has no choice except to do what you want and take what you give.

"Holding a submissive by the hair succeeds on a couple of levels. Immobilizing her so you can enjoy." Jake kissed her. "Baring her neck to you—the animal in us interprets that as the ultimate submission. There is nothing more vulnerable than a throat." His free hand curved around her neck to press very, very lightly, and a flash of instinctive fear shook her.

Jake turned her and pulled her back until her bottom rested against his thighs. After trapping her with an arm around her waist, he started flipping open the snaps on her shirt.

"Hey!"

"Be still."

She bit her tongue to silence a protest. Her heart pounded. Hellfire, this *would* be the time she went without a bra or tank top.

"Good girl," he said, the roughness in his voice gone. He nuzzled her cheek in approval, and warmth filled her.

When he stopped, her shirt hung open. "Part of the exchange of power is that your submissive agrees that her body belongs to you: to use, to show, to share at your will. However, each sub has her limits, and you must discover those. Some won't want any play except in private and in the bedroom, some desire a little public exhibition, some won't mind if you let others touch her, and some will be thrilled if you give her to others to enjoy."

Horror went through Kallie at his last words. Share her with these men? She shoved at the immovable arm around his waist.

"As a dominant, you'll have your own limits also. For example, I enjoy sharing the beauty of my submissive, but I'm too possessive to let anyone touch."

Oh. She relaxed slowly, curling her fingers around his muscular forearm and leaning back against him.

When he closed his hand over her breast, she inhaled sharply. No questions, no hesitation; he just took what he wanted. Like he'd been saying. His warm palm covered her.

"Your heart is pounding, little sub," he whispered in her ear.

Fear, trust, worry. Arousal. She felt as if she'd climbed on a rollercoaster of emotions, and it was a good thing he was holding her up.

"Gentlemen, you'll find blindfolds in my pack. If you are uncertain at some point or feel that you're taking too long to figure out a piece of equipment or bondage technique, simply blindfold your sub. Not only does it remove the pressure of someone watching, but it also increases the sensual enjoyment and anticipation for your woman. Touch her as you're restraining her. Watch how she strains upward toward your hand."

His fingers closed on Kallie's nipple, squeezing the sensitive peak, and the pleasure was so acute she arched her back.

Jake chuckled and continued, "I've set up equipment around the campsite and flagged the spots. Show each one to your sub. Keep your hands on her, listen closely to her, and discover which type of bondage sets her heart to pounding. If it also appeals to you, then use it. Call me if you have questions or problems."

From the flushed faces and obvious erections, the two men were definitely ready. Of course, watching Jake playing with her breasts probably hadn't cooled them off any. Sure hadn't cooled her off.

While the men headed back to their wives, Jake guided Kallie over to the fire and took a seat on a log. He made Kallie straddle his legs, facing him. "Last time, we didn't discuss all the various types of play. Bearing in mind what you've read or seen, is there anything that you hate the idea of doing?"

He slid his hands under her open shirt and settled around her waist. Not only steadying her on his knees, but the unwavering grip let her know he intended to keep control. *My body is his.* She shivered at the appalling...erotic...thought.

"Kallie, answer me."

Oops. What did she hate in the reading she'd done, or at the party? "I don't want holes poked in me or scars or anything to make me bleed."

He nodded, his gaze on her eyes, her mouth, her hands, her body. Reading her like he'd told the other men. "Go on."

Why did he have such a rumbling, deep voice? As his thumbs stroked over her lower ribs, everything on her body seemed to scream *more*! Her breasts had swollen and were now so sensitive she could feel the cool air alternating with his warmer breath. Between her legs felt so puffy that her jeans were uncomfortable. What would he do if she yanked her clothes off and just climbed on him?

Probably spank her.

She shivered.

His lips curved. "I think your mind went off task, little sub." He brushed his knuckles over her bunched nipples. "You're supposed to be thinking of what turns you off, not the reverse."

She leaned into his hand.

"Not yet, sugar." He moved his hand. "Continue. Are there activities you're not sure about?"

She snorted. "Everything?"

"Not exactly. We both know you enjoy being restrained. Using toys. Being spanked. Being exhibited as you just were." Amusement danced in his eyes. "You watched the flogging last weekend. What about that?"

"Well." All those strands of a whip hitting her bare skin. *Fear. Heat.* She licked her lips. "I-I don't know. I didn't know I'd like being spanked until…"

He palmed her breast again, caressing her gently. A reward, she realized, when he said, "I appreciate your honesty. Anal sex?"

"I've never done it." She flushed at the thought of him touching…taking her there.

"But not a no." He lifted her off his legs. "Good enough for tonight. What's your safe word?"

"Barney."

"Perfect."

She glanced around. The others had selected their spots. Heather stood by a tree. The chains hanging from a branch connected to her wrist cuffs and kept her arms over her head. Evelyn was restrained across a log.

"Time for a student break." Jake rose. "Kneel here with your eyes down."

She started to kneel, halted at his frown.

"What do you say?"

Oops. "Yes, Sir."

He nodded, then strode across the clearing, stopping to pick up a blanket from beside the fire. He showed Steve how to check Heather's circulation. He stopped a short distance from Andrew, waited until the man noticed, and handed him the blanket to put between the rough bark and Evelyn. That was nice. Jake glanced toward Kallie, and his brows drew together.

Oh hell, caught. She winced and dropped her eyes.

His footsteps crunched back to her, and boots entered her field of vision. "Stand up and strip." His voice was soft. *Cold.* Her stomach clutched at the wash of fear.

She pulled off her shirt. She'd heard him tell the other men to have their wives undress and savor them. Touch them. Jake wasn't doing any touching *or* savoring. She risked a glance up under her eyelashes. His eyes matched his voice, and his jaw was like stone. After a moment's hesitation—being totally naked was so much worse than being topless—she unlaced her boots and pushed them off. She removed her belt and knife, then her jeans and panties.

"Bend over and grab your legs."

No way. Not going to do that. She stared at him.

His face didn't change. As she stared up at him, the confident power in his eyes made her resolve evaporate like water under a hot sun. She closed her eyes to block him out, then leaned down, curling her fingers around her ankles. *See, nice and flexible, does that count?*

He moved closer until his thighs rubbed against her hip. He set a hand in the middle of her back. And then he slapped her bare bottom. *Whap!*

"Ow!" The abrupt pain, even though she'd kind of known what he intended, was too much, and she started to stand.

"Don't move, sub." He pushed her back down. "I expect obedience." *Whap.*

She gritted her teeth. Mouthing off or giving insults right now would be suicidally stupid. What happened to a warm-up? This hurt!

"If I don't get obedience, I'll be disappointed"— *whap*— "and you'll be sore." *Whap.*

He wasn't pulling his blows much, and her bottom burned like he'd dumped acid over her skin. *Fucking A*. Her hands tightened on her ankles as she prepared for the next blow. He'd not get any whimpering or crying from her.

He stepped away. "Kneel."

Her body had been so tense in preparation for pain that it took a second to move. She slowly lowered herself to her knees. The dirt and pine needles prickled her bare legs. As she sat back and her bottom met her heels, she winced at the bite of pain.

"Apologize."

"I'm sorry, Jake." Actually she did feel sorry. She'd gone into this with open eyes and didn't mean to cheat by disobeying. But the fact that he hadn't let her and wouldn't let her satisfied something inside her…as if a hunger had niggled at her without her realizing it. "Really, I am."

"That will do." His voice had returned to a rough croon that sent shivers down her spine. Grasping her by the upper arms, he raised her to her feet and pulled her to him.

It felt…strange…to be naked and held by a fully clothed man. Disconcerting. Vulnerable. His big hand pressed her face against his chest, and he rubbed his chin on the top of her head. "You're forgiven, sugar. I know you'll do better next time."

If a man had said that to her somewhere else, she'd have shoved his words back in his face. But here, being naked…aroused…in Jake's arms, she only wanted, really wanted, to please him, to hear the approval in his voice and see it in his eyes.

"Jake?"

"What's on your mind?"

"It drives me crazy when my cousins boss me around. Why—how can I like it when you do?"

"Ah. It's normal to want to make your own decisions in life most of the time. But a submissive finds handing those choices to a dominant—one she trusts—to be freeing, especially in a sexual context. There's no thinking, no trying to figure out what I want, no ability to hold back or fake your response, or to choose words that are tactful." She could actually feel the power radiating from him, hear it in his uncompromising voice. "Because I will tell you exactly what I want, and you will have no choice except to respond, and no choice except to give me the utter truth."

She shivered, and a corner of his firm mouth tipped up.

He stood for a minute, holding her and watching his students. "They're doing well." He smiled at her. "Let's go play." After picking up his bag, he wrapped an arm around her waist, keeping her close as they walked across the clearing toward his tent. The fabric of his flannel sleeve felt soft against her skin, belying the iron-hard arm beneath.

"Don't I get to choose?" she asked, eyeing an odd arrangement of straps crisscrossing a log.

"Nope."

Well, that wasn't fair. She frowned at him and caught the flash of his grin.

"This place is more private. You'll like it."

Private sounded good. Anticipation rippled across her skin as he grabbed a blanket out of his tent and led her to the far side of the clearing, where the trees partially enclosed a small area. The glow from the firelight diminished, but the quarter moon floated high in the western sky, the light angling above the treetops.

He snapped the blanket open and onto the ground, then pointed. "You belong there, little sub."

Her heart gave a thud. A cool breeze from off the still white-clad mountains brought the scent of pine and wood smoke, and Jake's wonderful fragrance of soap and man. She dropped to her knees. Was she supposed to kneel or lie down? She worried, then remembered it didn't matter. Jake would tell her; she didn't have to think about what to do...at all. The decisions weren't hers to make. She hadn't noticed the knot in her stomach until it disappeared.

He stripped off his shirt and knelt beside her on the blanket. In a smooth move, he wrapped his arms around her and tipped them both over, putting himself on top. She grazed her fingertips across the contoured muscles of his shoulders as he leaned down for a long, hungry kiss.

He tasted of the hot chocolate they'd been drinking, and took his time, teasing her lips, plunging deeply inside.

When he pulled back, she sighed. *Chocolate. Camping. Sex.* What more did a girl need? And it definitely looked like the sex would be great.

Setting his hands on each side of her face, he asked, "What put that smile on your face?"

"Uh." What the hell. "I was thinking that you taste like chocolate, and there can't be anything better than sex and chocolate."

His rumbling laugh made her grin. He brushed his thumb against her lips. "Under all that bluster and men's clothing, you are such a girl."

If one of her cousins had said that, she'd have punched him. But from Jake… A warm glow lit inside her.

"But considering the way you dress, I should probably check and make sure." He nuzzled her temple, her cheek. When he kissed the sensitive area under her ear, she got goose bumps.

Jake grazed his tongue over the hollow of the sprite's collarbone, tasting her skin, putting a firm hold on his need to taste her more deeply, to move straight to the most delicate, fragrant places. But leisurely exploration had other rewards. A kiss between her breasts, and she arched a little. Sensitive breasts—the memory of her response to his touch had given him several sleepless nights. This night would be sleepless also. He smiled—he would take his time tormenting them both. He brushed his jaw against the gentle curve of her right breast. The day's growth of his heavy beard scraped, and she inhaled sharply. Slowly he drew his chin across her breast, up and over the puckered peak. Her fingers dug into his arms.

He did the other breast, back and forth, until her fingernails embedded in his skin. Then he closed his lips around one swollen peak.

She gasped.

Damn but she was sweet. Her nipple had a velvety texture, the tiny tip just a little rough when he stroked his tongue over it. He licked the other nipple, then left it wet, chilling in the evening breeze. He sucked the other, hard and strong. Her back arched, and she cried out, a beautiful sound in the quiet night.

He lifted his head to gaze down at her, and her eyes had that dazed look he loved. *More.* He did the same to her other breast and felt her tremble under him. She could offer him still more. He cupped her small breasts, pressing them upward, then carefully closed his teeth on one tip and heard her suck in a breath and give a husky moan.

He licked the burn from the pink crest. Bit the other gently. Another moan. *Welcome to another type of carnal pain, sprite.* He grinned as she tried to push him away with one hand, to pull him closer with the other.

Her attempts to move him reminded him of their

location. He took her wrists in one hand, raised them above her head, and found the Velcro cuffs that he'd tied to a tree with a few feet of rope. Quick and simple bondage. He had her wrists secured before she caught on and tried to pull her arms down. Her eyes widened, and he could feel her arousal increase.

Sitting back, he slid her down on the blanket until the ropes turned taut, pulling her arms almost straight. He ran his finger under the cuffs to check the fit, and then straddled her curvy thighs and enjoyed the sight before him.

Her skin gleamed white in the moonlight, her jutting nipples still wet from his mouth. Her lips were swollen, and he pleased himself with another kiss.

He knew she'd liked the sensation of being restrained at the lodge, but outdoors bondage added another layer of helplessness. Especially the way he intended to do it. He located the thigh cuff lying in the pine needles and wrapped it snugly above her left knee. He did the same on the right. When he finished, her legs were still straight, only slightly bent, and she looked at him in puzzlement as if to say, *What's the point?*

He started to adjust the ropes.

He watched her body tense as the shortened rope pulled her left leg upward and outward. When he started on her other leg, her thigh muscles flexed, subconsciously resisting as she registered how exposed a position he intended.

He finished, and she lay open to him with the moonlight shining straight down on her glistening pussy.

"Now that's pretty," he murmured, smiling at the excited, vulnerable look in her eyes. Sex in the lodge, with the music and noise and people, tended to be intense and fast, whereas out in the forest, surrounded by trees growing at their own pace, the soft sounds of the pines sloughing in the breeze, distant coyotes barking along a moonlit trail, a groan from the others by the dying fire… Out here a man was encouraged to take his time. To sample and savor and learn everything about the sweet little sub in front of him.

His finger along the delicate crease between her thigh and pussy made her tremble. He ruffled the soft curls on her mound—maybe he'd shave them off next time—and slid his finger along her folds, spreading them open. Her eyes shut, and her face darkened with a flush. Embarrassed. Adorable.

Not that her modesty would stop him. On the contrary.

Moonlight showed that her clit was slightly swollen but still tucked inside its hood. He smiled and touched a finger to the soft, soft tissue. She moaned, and her hips wiggled.

"Yes, you're definitely a girl." How long would it take before her little nub engorged and pushed out of its cover? It reminded him of trying to tame a feral dog. It took patience. Several approaches might be needed. Push too forcefully and it would retreat back into hiding. Coax gently, reward often, keep the touch light.

Occasionally back off entirely.

He'd stopped. What was he doing? Kallie opened her eyes. He lay down between her legs, resting his weight on his forearms. His head was over… Oh God. The touch of his tongue right on her clit sent a jolt of pure electricity sizzling down her nerves, the sensation too, too much after all the waiting. Her cry broke through the clear air, and humiliated, she tried to muffle the next one.

He chuckled. "I enjoy hearing you, sugar. Please continue." He closed his mouth around her clit and sucked...once, twice...and she moaned as everything inside her clamped down. He drove her straight up toward an orgasm—and stopped.

"You taste like honey," he murmured. "Vanilla-scented honey."

"Please," she whispered, the ache overwhelming her tongue.

"'Please.' Please I want something inside me, please?" he questioned.

Oh, yes. She really did. "Um-hmm. Yes, Sir." She wiggled—tried to wiggle. Difficult when her legs were lashed open.

"All right." He bunched the blanket under her hips, raising her bottom slightly, and ran his hands over the soft skin of her inner thighs. Her breathing increased as she thought of his cock pushing into her.

Only he pulled his bag over instead. Oh, *condom*. How amazing that he could remember these things.

Cold liquid drizzled down between her buttocks. "Wh-what are you doing?"

"You requested something inside, remember?" His deep voice held a note of amusement. That *something* pushed against her anus.

"No!"

"You weren't sure about anal, so I'll let you try this little plug, and you can tell me if you like it."

"I don't like it."

He snorted. "Afterward, sugar. You tell me afterward." The first smooth part pressed her open. But it got bigger, burning as it stretched her opening, and then, thank God, smaller again. His fingers nudged between her cheeks as he moved it around. "All in, sprite."

God, what a feeling. Fullness and a quiet stinging and strange sensations, as if new nerves had been created. Her excitement had cooled with the surprise, but now as he knelt between her legs and watched her reaction, it shimmered through her like a heat wave.

"You are so very beautiful, Kallie." He ran his hands, so hard and confident, up and down her body. "I'm going to have fun playing with you tonight."

More? Weren't they getting close to being done?

He took something else from the bag and held it up. Long and slim with an almost flattened end. He took another kiss and then firmly pressed her labia apart. The thing slid up inside her pussy, which seemed overly occupied considering the toy was so slim…only she had something in her butt, didn't she?

The full feeling was wonderful—and a little disturbing. Two things in her. She couldn't move…couldn't remove them or do…anything. Her breathing increased, and the corners of Jake's eyes crinkled. But he asked, almost politely, "Doing okay, sprite?"

He knew the answer; she could tell from the crease in his cheek and the laughter in his eyes. She wanted to wiggle, to be touched, to moan—not to have a fucking conversation. "You know the damned answer," she forced out, sounding as if she'd just hiked up Half Dome.

He pinched her nipple in reprimand, and her pussy clenched and made the stuffed feeling more…more.

The moan escaped.

"When I ask a question, I require an answer," he said patiently, the steel edge of command only half-hidden. "Yes, I might know already. The point is, you need to be able to tell me." He tilted his head, waiting for his answer.

"I'm fine. Great. Wonderful." She bit her lip, tried to wiggle, and things moved inside her. "Do something, da—" She bit back the curse. "Please, Sir."

"Something like this?" His gaze stayed on her face, studying her as he touched her, as his fingers circled her breasts, then her nipples. The sensations blazed through her like lightning strikes in dry grass.

Answer him. "More? Please. Sir." *And may God strike you dead if you keep this up.*

He snorted a laugh. Then he slid down until his shoulders rubbed the insides of her thighs. His breath wafted over her mound, and she tensed. He stroked up her thighs too, too slowly, and finally reached the apex of her legs. When he traced his clever fingers over her labia, she inhaled sharply. He chuckled. "You're swollen and peeking out. Ready to play." A fingertip brushed her clit, just enough to make her gasp again.

He bent his head and licked over her, and oh, God, her whole body jumped at the feeling. His tongue was warm and soft as it circled her clit. He didn't stop, kept going around and around, never close enough for her to come, and the coiling pressure inside her grew as if her insides were being squeezed. Each repetition increased her sensitivity until the whole area felt swollen and tight.

"You know," he murmured, stopping for a second. She whimpered. How could he want to talk now?

"You might have wondered why I put something so thin into your pussy. Although I'm sure you enjoy having it in there, it's actually designed to vibrate. But only on one small place—right on the G-spot." She felt him move the vibrator inside her and turn it on. It didn't feel all that special, nothing compared to his mouth on her. He moved it again.

She tried to lift her hips, to suggest he go back to—

He moved it again. And her breath caught, stalled dead, as the vibrator hit something inside her. Hit and sent waves rippling outward, forcing her toward a climax as if someone were rubbing her clit from the inside. "Oh, oh, oh."

She hung there, on the pinnacle, as the world narrowed to just that, his intent gaze holding her as it pushed her higher and higher. Her muscles strained for release.

"That'll do," he murmured. He leaned down and licked right on top of her clit once, twice, and then sucked it into his mouth.

The pressure inside her burst into billions of sparking nerves, expanding out from her clit, from inside, merging and exploding through her body. Wave after wave of heat, pleasure, everything. The stars above her turned into white novas. And she screamed…

His tongue slid over her in slow, gentle strokes like a rodeo rider staying on until the last second, until her whole body pulsed with sensation. She heard herself "oh, oh, oh" over and over and couldn't stop. Her body wasn't hers; he'd disconnected her brain.

One final lick and then he moved up to lie on top of her. His belt pressed cold against her stomach. Still half-dressed, damn him.

"You come so beautifully," he said, the approval in his voice and eyes easing the shakiness trickling in. His body was warm; the hair on his chest tickled her breasts. His heavy weight was comforting, anchoring her back to the earth.

He chuckled. "Although the coyotes probably fled the area."

"I—"

"Shhh." He kissed her so gently that—oh, she wanted to touch him. To hold him.

"You didn't get off."

His lips curved, his eyes hot and yet the fire inside him controlled. "I will, sugar. Don't worry. I'm looking forward to the extra snugness from that anal plug."

She swallowed. He'd been almost too big for her before. "You're going to leave it in?"

The sun lines beside his eyes crinkled. "Oh, yes."

Slowly he worked his way down her body, inch by inch, kissing her shoulder, her collarbone, her breasts, one and the other. Kissing the undersides, which she discovered—and obviously so did he—were almost as reactive as her nipples. He stopped right there to nibble and tease until her hands fisted.

Down her stomach and farther until his tongue touched

her clit.

"Oh!"

A low laugh. "A little sensitive, sugar?"

He had no idea. The whole area had become so sensitive that the lightest touch almost hurt, but not quite. And it was the *not quite* and his clever tongue that had her head spinning.

He slid the vibrator out, making her arch up at the slick sensation. He played with the anal plug and put one hand on her hip to still her squirming as he tormented her. Wiggling the plug, moving in and out slightly, stimulating all those nerves. He watched her, his gaze roving from her face to her breasts to her hands.

When he slid his fingers into her wetness and over her clit, she bit her lip as her body started to really awaken again. "Jake, not again. I can't so soon," she whispered.

"Sprite, you can." He rubbed his big finger along one side of her clit, not close enough to cause pain, but firmly…so firmly that she seemed to have no choice. She felt the nub tightening, the feeling of drawing in preparatory to an explosion.

As always, damn him, he stopped right when it was getting good. At the sound of a zipper and the rustle of a condom wrapper, her eyes popped open. He captured her gaze as he pressed his hard cock against her opening and entered her with one powerful thrust. Her back arched as her insides clenched, sending a wave of pleasure through her. The plug inside her suddenly felt huge—or he felt huge, something…

The wait had been well worth it, Jake thought as he gave her a second to adjust. She'd come so beautifully that he'd had a difficult time not grabbing her ass and taking her right then. Damn she was lovely when she climaxed. Her eyes would go blind as her cheeks and nipples flushed a dark red. When he'd felt her pussy convulse around the vibrator, he'd hungered to replace it with his cock.

And now he had. His entry alone had set her pussy to spasming around his cock. And the plug made her vagina even snugger. With his first movement, she gasped, and her hands closed into fists. After seeing her fight the restraints, he unsnapped the Velcro cuffs from the rope.

She wrapped her strong arms around his shoulders, and it was a sweet feeling—one he could get used to far too easily. As she ran her hands over his biceps, she grinned, openly pleased to touch him, and asked, "What about my legs?"

Her gaze still didn't appear quite focused, as if half her concentration remained elsewhere. He shoved in forcefully and withdrew, saw her eyes blur, and chuckled.

"No, little sub," he said and bit her shoulder. Her cunt clenched. "I like your legs stretched open, and your pussy secured so I can play without you doing anything about it."

Submissive that she was, his words alone made her pussy clench again.

He'd had enough of talking. He moved in and out slowly, saw only pleasure in her eyes, and started driving into her, hard and fast, the way he'd wanted to after watching her come. Raw, gut-wrenching sex. Possessive sex.

Her fingers dug holes in his shoulders.

The slick slap of him against her flesh merged with her tiny moans. Almost. He balanced on one arm and reached around to grasp the plug stuck up her ass. Moved it and heard her shocked gasp. Her legs began quivering uncontrollably.

With each driving thrust, he pulled on the anal plug, then shoved it back in when his cock withdrew. Her moans changed into a constant low hum of need. Her thigh muscles strained against the restraints, her whole body tightened, and then he released the plug.

"Come for me, sugar." He ran his fingers directly over her slick, jutting clit.

She came like a shooting rocket, exploding in his arms. Despite the restraints, her hips managed to buck against his. And her pussy—damn, the contractions were like a whirlpool, massaging his shaft in heat and softness until his balls swelled, hardened like boulders, and poured fire up and out his cock in mind-blowing spasms.

Eventually, when his mind seeped back into his skull, he lifted his head and simply stared at his little sub. Flushed and sweaty, swollen lips, closed eyes showing him those long, dark lashes. How could this little sprite get to him like this? He'd had submissive women, responsive women, stubborn women—she was all those and more. Tough. Vulnerable. Joyous.

Her nipples had flushed a dusky red color from his attentions. And he could feel her heart hammering away. He brushed a kiss over her mouth, and her eyes fluttered open. Her lips curved. "I came again. So soon." She sounded as if she didn't know whether to be proud or shocked.

"So you did. And very nicely too." Damn, she was cute. He took her lips, surprising himself with the feelings welling up inside him. Tenderness. Protectiveness.

With an effort, he levered himself up, pulled out, and then removed the anal plug. Apparently she didn't appreciate the removal of either, and her muttered curse made him laugh.

Chapter Six

Kallie felt empty…and alone as he moved away to dispose of the condom. Her body, covered with sweat, began to cool. She sat up and tried to undo the restraints on her thighs. The excitement was gone, the letdown beginning. She'd never liked the awkward after-sex period. At the lodge, there hadn't been any "after sex"—they hadn't stopped until he tucked her into her Jeep just before sunrise.

But this time she'd have to suffer through the postsex stuff. Trying to conduct small talk, realizing you'd bedded someone you didn't know that well.

It had been great sex. Really. Her insides still quivered, but…

"Let's get you loose," he said. He unfastened the leg cuffs, and his powerful hands massaged the muscles around her hips as he straightened her legs. A second later, he straddled her and dug those strong fingers into her aching shoulder joints. She yelped as pain zipped through her, then eased, disappearing entirely.

She stared up at him, watching him concentrate. When he stopped, her shoulders hummed with warmth.

"Better?" His eyes met hers, shadowy in the moonlight yet still a punch to the system.

Odd how she didn't feel nearly as alone, as distant, as she usually did after sex. "Thank you. How did you know…?"

"That you hurt?" He rolled her onto her stomach and dug his thumbs into the tense muscles in her lower back. "The way you moved, experience from years of tying up subs, and a few times being tied myself."

"You?"

"Not long after I started topping, I asked a friend, a domme, to give me a taste of what it feels like to submit."

"Did you like it?"

"Not in the least. But I do know what bondage can do to muscles." He ruffled her hair. "Time to get up, sprite. I need to check on my students."

She wiggled a little, then sighed. "Okay."

"Try again," he said in a cold voice.

What? Still on her stomach, she craned her head far enough to see the expression she'd grown to recognize…his don't-fuck-with-the-dom frown. "Yes, Sir. Right away, Sir. Anything you say, Sir."

She heard the snort of laughter and had a second of pleasure before he slapped right on the already sore area of her bottom. She scowled at him and won herself another slap. Dammit. Maybe she didn't like him after all.

He smiled at her, running his finger down her cheek. "We're new to each other, and testing is inevitable. You might save yourself some pain if you realize that I try to be consistent with my requirements. Respect and obedience, Kalinda."

Her butt hurt enough that her reply was sullen. "Yes,

Sir."

"I'm fairly easygoing, sugar. There are some doms who would expect you to say, 'Whatever Master wishes,' no matter what, whether it was beating the hell out of you or giving you to his friends."

Ugh. Way further than she wanted to go. She rubbed her cheek against his hand and couldn't figure out why being with him could feel so right, so rewarding. He'd just swatted her butt as if she were a kid, for God's sake.

And yet…it did feel right, as if there was a sanctuary for her—just her—when he held her.

He kissed her cheek, then rose. After putting on his shirt, he pulled her up. He handed her the blanket and picked up his bag, then guided her back to the fire. She bit her lip, her feet slowing. Would he want her to sleep in his tent?

She took a step toward her clothing, still in a pile by the tents, and he stopped her. Taking her wrists, he snicked her cuffs together behind her back. She stared up at him, and his eyes crinkled. "The moon will set soon, but it'd be a shame to waste all this nice firelight, don't you think?"

Her body seemed to spring to life, and she blurted, "There's more…? Are…?" She stopped before more than the faintest disapproval crossed his face. "Yes, *Sir*." He'd see just how polite she could be.

"That sounded very nice." He pulled a black piece of material out of his pack. Uneasiness ran through her when he held it up with the ribbons dangling from the sides. A blindfold.

He fitted it over her face, tied it snugly, and sat her on the log. "Enjoy the darkness for a minute until I return."

Another sliver of insecurity slid across her nerves. "You won't leave me?"

"Hey." His hands closed on her face, ever so gently. "I'm not going anywhere, sprite. I'll be right across the clearing talking to Andrew and Steve. I want you to simply sit here and wait. Can you do that for me?"

What a wuss. She made her voice confident. "Of course."

She heard his footsteps walking away. The low buzz of conversation grew fainter. Had he left? No, he wouldn't. She knew that. He... Doubt crept into her, eating away her certainty like ice eroding a mountain, crack by crack.

Apprehension kept tensing the muscles Jake had massaged, until her body ached. She tipped her head to listen, but her pounding pulse drowned out any sounds in the clearing. Maybe they'd gone. All of them.

Her breathing increased. Her brain tried to reason out why she was wrong, but her thoughts had tangled into a knot. All she knew was she'd been left. Again.

The fabric covering her eyes absorbed her tears—but she never cried. That didn't seem to matter in the sadness swamping her mind. She'd known he wouldn't stay with her, and now it hurt... She'd known it would hurt when he left.

She pulled at the cuffs, needing the blindfold off, and couldn't move. How would she ever get out of this stuff? But it didn't seem to matter. He'd left her alone. She'd always be alone.

Suddenly the blindfold was yanked off, and she looked

up through her tears at Jake. His face resembled granite as he reached around her and undid her cuffs. He picked her up effortlessly and carried her across the clearing. With his foot, he shoved one of the fireside logs sideways, perpendicular to the fire, then sat on the ground and leaned on the log. He didn't put her down, merely cradled her like a baby with her back against his right arm, and her bottom on his hips. She'd been a baby.

But he hadn't left her. Relief trickled upward, barely making it through the dam of emotions.

"Are you hurting, Kallie?" he asked. His face was in the darkness, the fire burning brightly behind him.

She shook her head, her throat still constricted.

"Then why the tears?" He rubbed her shoulder, easing the tenseness out of her muscles.

She swallowed and edged away from the blackness inside. "I thought you left," she whispered and realized how pitiful she sounded. She tried to swallow, but her throat was too constricted.

"Shhh." After a second, he asked, "You think I would leave you cuffed and blindfolded?" Anger threaded through his deceptively mild voice.

"I'm sorry." She stared down at her hands, seeing the rich brown leather cuffs still around her wrists. He'd never do such a thing. How could she have thought it?

"When you and your boyfriends played games, did one leave you alone?"

She shook her head and hauled in a shuddering breath.

What the hell had happened with her? Jake wondered. She'd never left his sight. If she hadn't been crying so quietly with the blindfold concealing her tears, he would have caught her distress sooner. But she hadn't moved, hadn't made a sound.

She hadn't expected him to return. He pushed aside his outrage and focused on the problem instead. Something had created such an expectation, but apparently not a past BDSM experience.

Scrubbing away the tears, she said in a stronger voice, "I'm sorry, Jake. I never cry."

And why was that? He'd deliberately turned the log before sitting down so the firelight would light her face. He studied the tight muscles around her eyes, the lips compressed to hide the trembling. "Who left you?"

She tried to turn away, and he gripped her shoulder, keeping her in place. A tremor shook her. Damn. Sometimes sex, especially with an overwhelming orgasm, could expose a woman's emotions as thoroughly as he had exposed her body. Apparently he'd triggered a land mine, all unknowing. Now he needed to dig it up and identify the problem—without blowing them both to pieces. "Look at me."

The vulnerability in her liquid dark eyes made him want to simply hold her and comfort her and tell her it would be all right. In fact, he wanted more than that. He wanted to uncover those walls hiding her inner self, to be more than a top in BDSM play for one night—he wanted to be her dom.

He couldn't. *One night, Hunt. No connections, remember?*

But something had caused her reaction, and he needed

to find out what.

"Now answer me. Who left you, Kallie?" He tried to recall what he'd heard of her past. Lived with her cousins, involved in the guide business her uncle had started. No parents? "Where's your father?"

She shook her head. "I… He stayed long enough to name me and then returned to India."

"Ah." Didn't sound like an emotional tie, not enough for tears from this tough little sub. "How about your mother?" She tried to get up, and he simply set his arm over her legs. "You're not going anywhere, sprite, and neither am I. Your mom; tell me."

"She died. A long time ago, when I was eight." She frowned at him. "I'm sorry I wussed out on you. It won't happen again."

Sure it won't. "That's a rough age to lose a mother. So who did you live with?"

She jerked as if he'd slapped her instead of asking a question, then answered in an unemotional voice, "My stepfather, but he didn't want me. I lived with different relatives." She stared across the clearing, not meeting his eyes.

"But you ended up with Harvey?" Jake remembered the old guy. Tough as granite up to when he had died of a heart attack last year.

A sweet smile appeared. "I was fourteen. *He* kept me." The note of wonder in her voice made Jake's heart constrict. God, how could the assholes have left her so insecure?

He frowned. This was nastier than could be dealt with in

a night, but he could reduce one minor worry. "Kallie."

Her eyes met his.

"I never, ever leave a sub who is restrained. I was just on the other side of the fire. In fact, if you hadn't been blindfolded, I'd have realized you were crying sooner." And damn him for not checking more closely. "I'm sorry you were frightened."

She shrugged, although her lips still quivered slightly. "I'm sorry for being such a wimp. I don't know why…"

Why it hit her so hard. But restraints, pain, even orgasms could dissolve layers of defenses, leaving a sub vulnerable. Old emotions could surface without warning. He'd work on this insecurity of hers more in the future—no, he wouldn't. No ties. What the hell was he thinking? In fact, what was he thinking when he'd blindfolded her, doing something that increased dependence and deepened trust—he never used blindfolds with play subs. He scowled and saw her worry double.

Damn, he sucked as a dom tonight. "Sugar, you haven't done anything wrong. I'm angry with myself, not you."

Her gorgeous, big eyes searched his face, and her muscles slowly relaxed. Good.

"But, Ms. Show No Fear, you need to tell your dom if you're nervous. Not being omnipotent, we don't always catch the signs." He rubbed his knuckles over her cheek, feeling the slight dampness remaining. And damn him for missing the clues. "A dom might still go ahead, but he'll watch more closely if he knows something worries you."

Her brows had drawn together, but she nodded.

"And you have that safe word for a reason, sprite. It's not just for physical overload, but for an emotional one as well." He paused again. If she went further into the lifestyle—and the thought of someone else topping her bothered the hell out of him—she needed to be able to communicate. "I don't want you to forget that again."

"Yes, Sir." Her tense little body had relaxed into the snuggly one he had trouble resisting, so he sealed the discussion with a long, gentle kiss.

When he'd taken his fill and her arms had crept around his neck, he pulled back and glanced around. The others had left to get dressed and returned to talk quietly by the fire. "Heather, could you bring me a cup of hot chocolate?"

"Sure, Jake."

A minute later, she handed him a cup, and he sipped. Just right. "Here you go, pet."

Kallie squirmed to an upright position on his lap and took the cup with steady hands. She took a drink, smiled, and had some more, then tried to hand it to Jake.

"No, I don't want any more tonight. Rebecca insists chocolate is a remedy for all woes, but for me it's just a nice campfire drink."

Her husky chuckle lightened his evening. Then she tilted her head. "But you drank some…"

"Just testing to make sure it wasn't too hot for you."

The look she gave him held outright disbelief.

He laughed, then sobered. The sprite suffered from a serious lack of pampering, dammit. And damn him for wanting to fix that.

* * *

Early Friday evening, Kallie hopped out of her Jeep and trotted into Serenity Lodge. Although the air outside was hot and dry, her hands were cold. Her skin felt itchily sensitive. A little voice inside her chanted *maybe Jake will be here, maybe Jake will be here* until she wanted to thump her head on the door frame.

She wandered across the empty main room and spotted Rebecca setting the table in the dining room. It was almost a relief not to see Jake. Almost.

Rebecca smiled. "Kallie. Are you guiding someone today?"

"Nope. I think Heather left this in the gear." She held up the flat electronic reading device. "Is she here?"

"They decided to run into Yosemite Park for the day." Rebecca waved off Kallie's attempt to hand it to her. "Nah. I don't have time to deal with it right now. Jake's in the rec room. Give it to him."

Kallie opened her mouth to reply and noted the smug expression on Rebecca's face. Nothing like being set up. "Now that's just mean."

"I know." Rebecca pointed to a door at the far end of the main room. "Put on your big-girl panties and go on in."

That did it. "City girl, I'm looking forward to that trip to Little Bear Mountain with you." Not waiting for an answer, she continued. "You'll discover the wilderness is full of life: bears that steal your food, cougars that attack the horses, rattlesnakes looking for a warm sleeping bag to crawl into."

Rebecca's mouth dropped open.

"If the goddess—and that would be me, by the way—is displeased, you'll get bats in your hair and mice in your boots." Kallie gave her a thin smile and then stomped across the room. *She thinks I'm a coward? Just because Jake and I have done...kinky stuff...doesn't mean I worry about facing him. Or how he affects me.*

She stepped into a room that would have her cousins drooling with envy. Dart board, pool table, foosball, and Ping-Pong tables.

Jake leaned against the wall, drinking a beer, while Logan racked the balls and the massive dog sprawled off to one side. When the men smiled at Kallie, her cheeks turned hot. Dammit. "I—"*Not affected, remember*? "Heather left this in the gear. Can you get it back to her?"

When the dog padded over, she bent to pet it for a few seconds, hopefully hiding her blush.

"Not a problem." Logan took the electronic device. "Thanks for bringing it out. How 'bout you stay for supper as a reward? We're eating in half an hour, and Becca's a fantastic cook."

"No, but thanks for the offer." She took a step toward the door. Jake hadn't said a word. Wasn't he even going to greet her? "I need to get back."

Jake tilted his head and studied her. "Do you really have something planned?"

"I—" Hell. "I always have things that have to be done."

As one half of his mouth quirked up, that tantalizing crease appeared in his left cheek. "In other words, no." He set his beer on a card table and glanced at Logan. "Tell Becca one more for supper."

Kallie pulled up straight. "Listen, I—"

He advanced on her, as unstoppable as a forest fire in a strong wind. When she held up her hand in protest, he chuckled and used it to haul her over his shoulder. "We'll be upstairs, bro," he said. "I have a craving to play dress-up."

"Damn you, Hunt. Put me down."

Ignoring her orders and her fists pounding his back, he hummed a tune and blatantly fondled her butt. They crossed the main room, going past Rebecca—not that Kallie saw her, but the snicker was evidence enough. An electronic keypad beeped, a door opened, and Jake started up a flight of stairs.

Kallie gave up. She hadn't expected to be hijacked, but face it: she'd hoped for...something. If Jake Hunt wanted his hands on her, she wasn't about to argue. She laughed and thumped him one more time with her fist...just because.

He wasn't even breathing hard when he entered a door down the hall and dumped her on a couch. "Stay put for a minute, sprite."

As he disappeared into another room, she struggled to a sitting position. How did he do this to her? She'd dated before, made love before. And yet the man made her feel like a teenager out with a guy for the first time.

She rose to her feet. *"Stay put?" Dream on, Hunt.* She strolled around the room, trying to ignore how snug her bra had grown and how each step scraped her jeans over her increasingly sensitive clit.

Nice place, she decided. Cream-colored walls with original paintings of Yosemite...signed by Rebecca. Kallie checked the signature again. Rebecca had mentioned she painted. She was really, really good.

A chess table stood in one corner. The shelves over it held seashells and coral. The next wall displayed framed photographs of family and friends in settings that ranged from a cattle ranch to tropical beaches. Apparently he not only liked to travel, but he also had a lot of friends. Mr. Sociable himself.

A wide-screen TV—of course—on the far wall. Considering the decor downstairs, she'd expected more leather up here, but his oversize furniture was upholstered in a dark blue fabric. Rag rugs in a mingling of blue, green, and white covered the hardwood floor. The room had a homey atmosphere.

Her sense of comfort disappeared when Jake returned, his arms filled with fabric. "Strip."

She narrowed her eyes. "You know, we need to work on your social skills. You can't snap out orders to a guest."

"Oh. Was I too terse?" He cocked his head and gave her a mean smile. "Kalinda, you will remove every item of clothing immediately or suffer the consequences."

She took a step back as the steely glint in his eyes did funny things to her heartbeat.

"Was that better?"

"Uh, not exactly what—"

"Now, Kalinda."

Her mouth went dry. *But there's only half an hour before supper* kept running through her head, as if that made a difference to someone like Jake. She unbuttoned her flannel shirt, shrugged it off, and removed her boots, socks, and jeans.

And then he got that disapproving expression again, as if the sight of her body displeased him. "Would you stop looking at me like that?" she burst out.

He lifted an eyebrow. "What way?"

"If you don't like the way I look, why do I keep ending up—"

His laugh rang out, full and strong, and she balled her hand into a fist. If he tried to touch her, she'd belt him one.

He yanked her against him so quickly she didn't have a chance. His ruthless hands roamed over her back and her butt, and her desire to punch him burned to ashes in the blast of heat.

"I love your body, sprite. So much that what you wear offends my senses." He unfastened her bra and tossed it on the floor, then ripped her panties in two. "You have the ugliest underwear I've ever seen."

"My underwear? You've been frowning at me for two years because of my *underwear*?"

He eyed her face and started laughing so hard that she swung at him. He caught her fist as easily as if it were a buzzing mosquito. "You hit me, sugar, and I'll spank your ass—even if we're late for supper."

She tried to yank her hand out of his grasp and got nowhere, and then he palmed her right breast, teased the nipple, and turned her legs to water.

"And I not only dislike your underwear, but the rest of your wardrobe too. I understand the need for hiking gear when you're hiking, but why don't you wear girl clothes at other times?" He asked the question in an easy voice, but there was nothing casual about the way he scrutinized her.

She started to answer and stopped. "Well." She vaguely remembered the last sexy top she'd bought, back as a teenager, and how her cousins had behaved, like she'd turned into a slut or something. "It's easier"— *to not rock the boat*—"to stay in the same clothes." She shrugged. "I don't even own anything fancy."

"Ah." The sense of satisfaction that the sprite had never dressed provocatively for a man was a little unsettling. As was the impression that laziness had little to do with her choice of attire. "Well, if you like it easier, I'll do all the work this time."

That delightfully suspicious look appeared on her face—the one that said he had all the control and she didn't think she should like it. Even if she trusted him completely, he'd still enjoy provoking her. A dom shouldn't allow a sub to get too comfortable, after all. But in her case, it didn't take much effort.

Right now, he intended not only to please himself by putting her in feminine clothing, but he wanted to see what effect a change of clothing would have on her. Push the boundaries a little. He paused. He shouldn't be doing this.

And then he slid the bra he'd chosen up her arms and fastened it.

"You bought me underwear?" She sounded so appalled that he chuckled.

She stiffened when he reached into the cups to adjust her breasts, so he took his time until her nipples puckered under his palms. He stepped back to survey the results. The push-up bra gave her the prettiest cleavage, and when she looked down, her eyes got big.

Damn, she was cute.

He dropped a deep pink top over her head. The low neckline with an edging of lace framed her breasts nicely, and he nodded approval, then added a long, silky skirt.

"What is it with you guys and pink?" she muttered, staring at the clothes.

"It's feminine," he said, and pulled her to the bathroom mirror. "And a damned good color on you too."

Her mouth formed an O as she took in her appearance. The top hugged her breasts and waist, and the dark pink skirt flowed smoothly over her grabable, full ass.

"What about…briefs?"

"You'll go without tonight," Jake said.

She whipped around. "I can't go without underwear."

He crossed his arms and stared her down, enjoying the way her eyes lowered. The flush of pink in her cheeks now matched her skirt. "You can. You will. Because that's how I want it."

She swallowed.

He stepped back and smiled, showing her the pleasure he found in her appearance. "You look lovely, Kallie. You're a beautiful woman. Now and then you might give us poor men a treat and dress like one."

That she should look so confounded saddened him.

Hadn't anyone ever complimented her beauty?

"Thank you," she said softly. Then her stubborn little chin rose. "But why no panties?"

He stepped closer and cupped her cheek and whispered back, "So that when I decide to take you—downstairs or up here—there's nothing in my way."

Her response was beautiful…and now he'd have to suffer from having a hard-on all through supper. *Hell.*

* * *

On the day before the Fourth, he settled into a chair beside his tent in his favorite Yosemite campground. He'd start a fire, make some supper. Then maybe hike one more time before sundown. The forests comforted him and dimmed the discordant noise in his head. One or two years ago—he lost track of time—he'd realized the clamor and the incoherent voices came from the evil ones. Some people, like him, could sense demonic energy—could actually hear it.

He'd enjoyed the short hike he'd just taken, and the peaceful trail had allowed his tension to ease away.

But now a woman's shrill voice scraped across his nerves. He turned and spotted the young couple at the campsite next to him. The woman wore a purple tank top that displayed her lush breasts, and her hair spilled over her shoulders. Her dark, dark hair. Her voice grew louder as she deliberately yelled at her poor boyfriend in front of their tent, right out where everyone could witness the man's humiliation.

He watched as the demon rose inside her and peeked out

of her brown eyes, so clearly visible he was surprised everyone didn't scream and run. But no one else saw. This was his gift—his curse.

As the demon screamed in a mind-piercing voice, the boyfriend hunched his shoulders, clenching his hands at his side. Short but muscular, the young man could have flattened her with one blow, but no, men didn't hit women. The fool. Couldn't he see that his girlfriend wasn't there anymore, that a demon had shredded her soul into such darkness that it shone through her eyes?

No, instead the man simply took her abuse, feeling like a failure. A loser. Less of a man.

He couldn't let that continue, and it would. Over and over until the man had nothing left, as the demon tore his spirit down with words and screams and insults.

Face set into calm lines, he watched her give one last high shriek and then stalk off on one of the myriad of trails leading away from the campground. Her poor victim walked into the tent. A minute later, a rolled-up sleeping bag hit the ground outside. Then a backpack. The boyfriend obviously planned to leave.

Another brother hurt, perhaps damaged forever.

He leaned forward and laced his hands together. The evil had gone up the trail, and the miasma of her passing floated above the ground, an ugly dark green like a bruise. His duty was clear; the world would be a better place without her.

In his jeans, his manhood hardened. He hated disposing of demons, of the noise, the smells, the darkness—but the heavens had provided compensation, showing him that his way was right. The scream of the demons sent masculine heat through his body, and over the years, he had grown to anticipate the battles. And the time afterward when he would show in an unmistakable way that he had the victory.

Taking his time, he wandered across the clearing and headed up the adjacent trail. Once out of sight, he slipped through the thin forest until he came to the trail the dark-haired woman had used. A heavy branch offered itself for his weapon, and he picked it up. The foul scent beckoned him onward.

Dark would come soon.

* * *

Carrying a platter of raw hamburger patties, Kallie stepped out their back door onto the low cedar deck. The hum of conversation was broken by the occasional clanking of a horseshoe and victorious shout, the screams of the younger children enjoying the waterslide, and yells of disappointment at missing a Frisbee catch or a badminton swing. The scent of barbequing meat filled the evening air, and her stomach growled. Maybe she'd have a moment to eat soon.

She set the platter on the to-be-cooked table to the right of the massive barbecue. Clad in a chef's apron, liberally stained with grease and catsup, Morgan grinned at her and flipped another burger before returning to his conversation with Gina.

Kallie bent to pet Mufasa, who had positioned himself strategically close to the barbecue, where Morgan could toss tidbits, especially when reminded by a paw placed firmly on his sneaker. The cat rubbed her hand and then returned his attention to important matters.

After transferring cooked burgers and hot dogs to the long buffet table, she checked the offerings with the experience of a decade of Fourth of July parties. The ice under the salad section was maintaining well, enough buns were available, condiments not empty. Red, white, and blue paper plates and napkins vied with the sparkling pinwheels lined down the center. Parties went in three stages: first families with small children, secondly the ones with older children, and finally adults without children and older teens to close down the night. The first wave of hungry people had already gone through.

"Hey, Kallie, hold up a second." Gina patted Morgan's butt before trotting over.

"How are you?" Kallie asked.

"Not bad." Gina pursed her lips and gave Kallie a once-over. "And you're looking very, very good."

Kallie flushed. "Thanks. Feels weird though." Just before lunch, Rebecca had arrived like a military godmother with a mission, wielding makeup and clothing like advanced weaponry. Before leaving, she'd mentioned that prior to artist and cook, she'd been a manager. *No kidding.*

"Maybe, but you're getting a lot of interested looks." Hands on her hips, Gina surveyed the pickings of men with an experienced eye. "And there are a lot more single guys this year to be looking. Nice job."

Kallie grinned. Some people were so easy to please. "Virgil has two of his cop friends here—the other two and the chief had to work—and Wyatt invited his buddies from the black-powder rifle club." She nodded to the group of guys around Wyatt, most of them bearded, one with hair braided halfway down his back. "They had a great time this morning shooting and throwing tomahawks and knives." And Wyatt had dragged her down to show off how well he'd taught her to throw a knife.

"Mmmmh, mountain men. The one in the red T-shirt is downright hot. Then again, the two men in buckskins look really…primitive." Gina fanned herself.

"Stop drooling, or I'll get you a bib."

"Hey, a girl's gotta look." Gina licked her lips. "And mmmhmm, there's a gorgeous sight."

Kallie followed her gaze. Logan and Rebecca walked around the side of the house. Then she saw Jake, and her libido gave a massive roar like a Harley that someone's boot had kick-started. She couldn't blame Gina for lusting after him. The summer had darkened his skin and put gold streaks in his collar-length brown hair. He'd dressed fairly casually in jeans and a white polo shirt, where the sleeves stretched around his hard biceps in a way that made her fingers want to touch.

"I've never seen them at any party before," Gina commented. "Only the ClaimJumper now and then."

As Wyatt sauntered over to greet the Hunts, Kallie said, "I got the impression they're more sociable now because of Rebecca." Standing here gawking at the man wouldn't do, especially since she had no idea of her place in his life. Him and his damned "for one night only" rules. Did he want her to ignore him or pretend to be a casual acquaintance?

This was so confusing.

"Well, I'm going to be...sociable...and say hi to Jake," Gina said, her eyes bright. "It's been a couple of months since we went out last; maybe I'm close to the top of the rotation."

Oh. Damn. "Ah, Gina?"

"Yeah?" Gina paused.

"Never mind." What could she say? That the man had taken her so many times that her jeans rubbed uncomfortably over her still-swollen private parts? Yesterday morning, he'd kissed her good-bye, and she hadn't understood the look he'd given her. All the way home, she'd worried over it. Had that been a the-night's-over-and-so-is-our-time-together look or a this-was-wonderful-I'll-be-calling-you look. She'd sure jumped to the wrong conclusion last time.

If she went over there, he'd probably give her another of those chilly greetings. Maybe she should encourage Gina to have at him? *No no no.* Before she could decide, Gina sashayed over to hug Rebecca and say hi to Logan. Then she turned on the flirt switch for Jake.

When Jake greeted Gina, his smile lightened his lean face. Kallie's throat constricted. *Not mine. Never mine.* Maybe she'd go check on the kitchen for a few minutes. To provide an excuse for fleeing the scene, Kallie picked up a dish that had held cherry pie. Stepping back, she bumped into someone. "Oh. Sorry."

The guy in the red T-shirt, one of Wyatt's friends from the mountain-man club, grinned down at her. "Totally my pleasure. You can bump into me anytime you want."

She blinked at his flirtatious expression and smiled. *Thank you, God.* Right now she needed someone to help make her feel attractive. "I saw you shooting a muzzle loader earlier. You're good."

His smile widened. "Yes. I am. Very good." He ran a finger down her arm and glanced at the dish she held. His voice dropped suggestively. "Cherries. I love a good cherry, you know. Maybe you'd like to see?"

Ew. Some men looked interesting until they opened their mouths. This one should have stayed in the gutter where he belonged. She took a step away. "Well, I—"

An arm encircled her waist and yanked her back against a rock-hard body. Jake's baritone sounded rough enough to take someone's hide off. "If you're a black-powder reenactor, you should know how to talk to a lady. Apologize."

The guy's mouth dropped open, and his face turned the color of his shirt. To her surprise, he manned up and said, "You're perfectly correct, sir. My apologies, ma'am, for getting out of line." Not waiting for a response, he gave a short bow and retreated back to his cohorts.

Kallie tried to step away, but the arm around her waist didn't loosen. Instead Jake swiped her fingers in the leftover cherry filling, lifted her hand to his mouth, and licked her fingers.

The blast of heat swirled from her hand straight to her pussy, and her legs wobbled. His embrace tightened, keeping her shoulders against his chest. She could actually feel his cock thicken and press against her butt, and her lower half grew liquid—ready to be taken. *Damn him.*

She pulled in a shaky breath and tried to get her hand back.

"Don't move." His sharp nip on her thumb streaked straight to her groin. Taking his time, he finished cleaning her fingers, sucking on one after the other. And she felt each pull of his mouth as if his lips circled her clit instead.

Finally, when her body was in flames, he let her tug her hand away and turn to face him.

"Mmm. Any more pie left?" he asked, his voice so casual she wanted to belt him one.

She glared, dying to drag him to bed…after she punched him a few times. "I can't believe you gave that man such a rough time, and then you do this."

"Ah, sprite." He glided his knuckles over her cheek. "The difference is that we're not strangers. I know what you taste like…everywhere, what your whimpers sound like. I have your scratch marks on my shoulders, and my sleeping bag carries your scent."

The air felt like the Mohave Desert, hot and thick, scorching her brain cells until she couldn't seem to think. The sun lines around his eyes deepened as he smiled. "You know, sometimes you're drop-dead beautiful…and other times you're just damned cute."

Cute? Chipmunks were cute. Before she really could hit him, he grasped her upper arms, yanked her up on tiptoe, and kissed her so thoroughly every thought in her brain melted into goo.

He tasted like cherries.

He lifted his head slightly and whispered, "By the way, I like the top."

He'd noticed the sleek blue shirt Rebecca had given

her—one formfitting enough to get a frown from Wyatt. Before she could wallow in the compliment, he took her lips again. When he pulled back this time, he had to hold her up or she would have staggered like a drunk. Chuckling, he drew a finger over her wet lips. "So if I promise to help with the cleanup, do you think I can get more of that pie?"

Damn, she really was cute. As Kallie walked toward the house, Jake admired the snug fit of her jeans over her pretty, round ass. He might have thought his efforts had prompted the sexy improvement, but he'd seen Rebecca leave the lodge with a sack full of clothing. He owed her.

He noticed Kallie's stiff-legged walk and tilted his head. Not used to tight pants? Or she might be a tad sore. He'd taken her a lot the night before last. Wanted to again. He moved and adjusted himself surreptitiously.

Why the hell had he kissed her? But he'd forgotten how quickly she turned him hard. And how she brought out every possessive trait in his dom's nature. After seeing that asshole coming on to her—*Face it, Hunt, you staked a claim as blatantly as a bear putting claw marks on a tree.*

Kallie wasn't the only one with uncomfortable jeans. Even thinking of cold showers and mountain glaciers didn't help. Annoyed, he walked across the deck. After grabbing a cold Sierra Nevada Stout from the ice-packed cooler, he leaned on the deck railing festooned with red and white streamers, and hoped his cock would ease eventually.

Nice setup for a gathering. From the wide cedar deck, the lawn sloped down to a tree-lined creek. Picnic tables and patio chairs held various sets of people: a group of local merchants, a few cops flirting with some of Kallie's friends, the buckskin crowd, and a handful of loggers who lived in the area. A batch of older citizens kept grandchildren running to serve their requests. Teens hung out down at the creek or playing board games, toddlers and moms had taken over the wading pool, older kids used the waterslide or kicked a soccer ball. Some climbed on the hay bales stacked two and three high and scattered around the lawn. Looked like two poker games going on in the shade, and dominoes reigned at a picnic table. He'd heard about the Masterson's Fourth of July gathering for years but never realized it drew in the entire population of Bear Flat. And more continued to arrive.

Just as he took a hefty drink of beer, something rubbed against his calf. He jerked his leg away and looked down. Kallie's monster cat sat at his feet.

Jake knelt on one knee and offered a finger. Hopefully the beast wasn't in a bad mood, or he'd be drawing back a stump. "You know, I like cats, but I think you're descended from something a lot bigger." Maybe the tufts on his ears resembled a bobcat's, but the thick fluffy mane looked more like a lion's—if lions came in brown tabby coloring. And those paws were huge.

The dark pink nose touched his finger gently. Jake petted it for a bit and started to stand. The cat deliberately lay down on Jake's boot, all twenty-some pounds of him. "Ah-uh. If I move at this point, I'll have scratches all the way up my leg, right?"

A snort came from the direction of the beer cooler, and Jake glanced up.

Kallie's cousin Virgil, clad in jeans and a short-sleeved shirt, opened a can of Coors. "Takes a lot to make him really mad. He's more mellow than he looks."

Jake stroked Mufasa and grinned. The beast had a purr like an outboard motor. "You're the only people I know who keep a guard cat rather than a dog."

"Yeah, well, Kallie was so upset when my dad's cat got savaged and died, that he picked one not so tempting to the critters outside."

"Good choice." The beast wouldn't survive a cougar, but any fox or coyote would think twice before taking it on. Jake rose to his feet very, very carefully. His rest disturbed, the cat twitched its fluffy, raccoonlike tail and stalked away. Back to the food, Jake noticed. Not a dumb cat at all.

"So, Hunt. Welcome to the party." The flat tone didn't sound welcoming, and Masterson's eyes were as cold as the icy beer. They weren't friends, although they'd exchanged greetings a few times. The man had a rep as being an honest, tough cop.

"Thanks. Appreciate the invite."

"We've always invited you. This is the first year you've shown."

Uh-huh. The man's voice matched his eyes. Protective family. Jake understood perfectly; he was that way himself. "Rebecca wanted to come." He wiggled the bottle. "Good beer."

A corner of Virgil's mouth drew up slightly. "Kallie likes that brand, so we indulge her, even though the rest of us prefer light. We like her to be happy." Virgil gave him an unwavering stare. "And that's why I'm not busting your chops right now. If she kissed you, then that's what she wanted."

Jake leaned a hip against a picnic table and waited. There was obviously more to come.

"I know about you and your brother and the games at the lodge. I'm not going to go into that." Virgil scowled and then drew a figurative line in the sand. "Kallie's got a soft heart, and she's collected some hurts in her life. Don't fuck with her heart, Hunt, or I'll pitch the badge and beat the shit out of you."

"You could try," Jake said mildly. "But I understand your concern. I don't play games—but sometimes people get hurt anyway."

"I hear you. Best it not be Kallie."

"Fair enough."

As two other cops raided the cooler for beer, Virgil turned to greet them and introduced Jake. Warning delivered, the cop had moved on, shedding the animosity.

Excellent control, Jake thought as he shook hands and listened to the cops complain about an incompetent coroner who apparently had just retired, to everyone's relief.

He watched her. She laughed often, almost sparkling with energy. She treated the children sweetly, like a mother, but demons could be devious. Sipping a beer, he stood in a group of townspeople, smiling at the jokes and evaluating the woman.

She was small. Sneaky-sized. Black hair showed the

darkness in her soul. Surely the evil had taken her. Surely he needed to act, to destroy her face, her body until pain forced the demon to sink back into the depths. He could almost hear the sound of the club striking flesh, feel the impact as it shattered bones. He shuddered at the memory of a demon's shrieks as it was torn from the physical world—from a body.

His stomach twisted with nausea. Sweat coated his skin. Forcing his muscles to calm, he carefully swallowed some more beer. His job. To save his brothers, his world. He would do it no matter the cost to himself.

He'd have his reward at the end, when he'd triumphed over the demon. His manhood rose, strong and proud, as he watched her.

Chapter Seven

Kallie smiled at the pies lining the kitchen counter, brought by the townswomen.

On the first Fourth of July party, her uncle had been overwhelmed by offers to bring food. A man who loved rules, he created guidelines for what people should bring. Like the party itself, the guidelines turned into tradition. Women brought desserts, men over forty brought beer, men under forty brought munchies. Teens brought soft drinks. The Mastersons provided hamburgers and hot dogs, baked beans, and an appalling amount of potato salad.

She found a cherry pie and cut a hefty slab for Jake, smiling a little. He'd not greeted her coldly today—he'd kissed her in front of everyone. She pressed a hand to her chest. That had been a great kiss. He'd noticed her shirt too. If he hadn't coaxed—bullied—her into changing how she saw herself, she'd never have considered wearing it. *But I'm really not just one of the guys.*

Jake had cared enough to bully her that way. Did that mean he cared a little bit for her?

Dammit, she wanted him to, because he was sucking her willpower away. He made her feel safe. Wanted. Cherished. And dammit, how would she ever find someone like him?

She didn't need gorgeous—although that was wonderful—but who else would have his strength, his intelligence, his sense of humor and honor?

She glanced out the window to indulge in another look at him, and her breath caught. Virgil stood in front of him in a posture that said her cousin wasn't being polite. He must have seen Jake kiss her, she realized, and her stomach sank.

She'd dated off and on over the years, had a few lovers, but she never, ever brought them back here. It just seemed...safer...to downplay her love life. She didn't want her cousins to be disappointed in her, to think she didn't belong with them. She'd sure never tested them with someone who would blatantly kiss her in front of everyone.

When Virgil's face suddenly turned hard, the air left Kallie's lungs as if she'd slipped off a trail and belly flopped onto a slab of granite. She took two steps toward the door and stopped.

Nothing she could do would keep Virgil from trying to protect her. And Jake would go his own way no matter what Virgil said. Having lived with a bunch of obstinate men, she knew that intervening only made things worse.

Unable to watch, she abandoned the pie. Heading down to the creek, she was intercepted. Gina grabbed one arm, Serena the other, veering her off to one side.

Hands on hips, Serena gave her a spill-it look. "Okay, girlfriend, it's confession time."

Oh, hell. "Well..."

"I've never seen Jake come on to someone so blatantly," Gina said. "Not since his girlfriend died. He'll buy someone a drink at the tavern and take her home, and that's about it. He doesn't attend parties or anything."

"Died? His girlfriend died?"

"Yeah. Don't you remember the big deal...? No, you were still in Alaska," Serena said. "Anyway, when did you start dating Jake?"

"Uh, I'm not sure dating is the right term." Kallie grimaced. "I got the 'one night only' lecture, after all."

Gina tilted her head at the sun, half-hidden by the western mountains. "Seems like daytime to me."

"Let's just say he wants to take it one...um, interaction...at a time."

"Oh. Gotcha." Serena snickered. "That was a really nice interaction you had going on there on the deck."

Kallie tried to glare, but witnessed or not, the memory was sweet. "Yeah, it was."

"Well, be careful, okay?" Gina clasped Kallie's hands. "I don't want you getting hurt."

Kallie glanced up the slope. Jake had joined the older men. As he threw a horseshoe, the muscles under his shirt flexed in a way that made her mouth water. "It'll be worth the pain." Her gaze shifted to the deck. Wyatt stared down at her, then shifted his attention to Jake. "Maybe."

"By the way..." Serena's gaze ran over Kallie. "You look fantastic."

"Way fantastic. If Jake hadn't branded you, the other guys would be following you around, wagging their tails for attention." Gina frowned. "I think Serena and I should have pushed harder to fancy you up. Then again, maybe it took a different kind of incentive to get you in girl clothes."

Kallie laughed, her face heating. "*You have the ugliest underwear I've ever seen.*" Interesting type of incentive. But it felt...nice...to know she looked good.

"Kallie," one of the children yelled from the deck. "The sun's going down. Morgan said to ask you if we could play now."

As the little boy jumped up and down in anticipation, Kallie laughed and did a quick visual of the party. In the dimming light, people started to pack up the board and card games. The air had cooled, and the wading pool had emptied of toddlers—it would now become the loading area for weapons. The war would begin as the twilight deepened.

"Morgan, break out the vests and guns," she yelled. "It's time to win our independence from England!"

All the potential soldiers cheered. A second later, twinkle lights flashed on around the property, designating the boundaries of the battlefield, as well as giving light to the seating areas and the deck.

From the deck, Morgan tossed vests to the combatants: red for the English, blue for the patriots. Cheers and complaints came from the recipients. Meantime, Virgil and Wyatt cleared the battlefield of tables and chairs and other obstacles.

As Kallie reached the deck, Jake appeared, tucking his fingers under her waistband to stop her. "What's going on?"

"Water tag—or should I say, the American Revolution fought on the Masterson battlefield with water for bullets. Want to play?"

Jake stared at the soldiers suiting up—donning vests—and choosing their weapons from a variety of water pistols, and he had to laugh. The Mastersons were definitely insane. He grinned. "Damn right."

Kallie patted his chest and shook her head. "You are such a boy."

"True. Very true." He pulled her forward, keeping his eyes on hers. Seeing the heat spark to life. He leaned down to brush her lips with his. "You'd best be careful, soldier. If I capture you, I'll be forced to conduct an interrogation," he whispered. "There are many, many ways to make an enemy talk, and I know them all."

Even in the dim light, he saw a flush darken her cheeks and the way her nipples peaked inside her tight shirt. Her laugh came out husky and low. "Well. You'll have to capture me first, won't you?" She raised her chin in a definite challenge. "By the way, beware of the artillery and their bombs."

"What?"

She nodded at a group of older guests lined up behind the deck railing. Tubs filled with red and blue water balloons waited at their feet. "Bombs."

"You people are amazing. Bombs, huh?" His laugh broke off as the word registered. *Bombs. War.* Where was Logan? He spotted his brother standing inside the kitchen, oblivious to the game starting up outside. *Hell.*

"Jake, are you all right?"

"Where's Becca?"

Kallie turned and pointed. “Down by the creek with Serena.”

“Thanks.” He jogged across the grass, not slowing when he realized Kallie trotted beside him.

“What’s wrong?” she asked.

Not taking time to answer, he stopped by Logan’s woman. “Becca,” he said sharply enough to have her spinning around. “There’s going to be water tag, and it’s set up to simulate a war. Guns. And bombs.”

Her face paled.

“Dammit, Jake.” Kallie slugged his arm to get his attention.

Bad little sub, he thought, then explained. “When we were overseas, Logan and his team were sliced to bits by an IUD. He’s the only one who survived, and still has nightmares.”

“Hellfire,” Kallie muttered. “Being a macho idiot like you, he won’t leave the party either, right?”

Becca shook her head. “Probably not.”

“*Men*. Okay then, coax him into the living room. Seems like there should be a game on—the World Cup for soccer?”

“That’ll work. Thanks,” Becca said and sprinted up the lawn toward the house.

“Nightmares?” Kallie asked Jake.

“Better now, but they were pretty ugly for years. After counseling, he managed all right during the day, but any noise might set him off at night, and he’s a hell of a fighter, especially when he doesn’t realize he’s not back in battle. That’s why I got him out here, why we started up the lodge—to get away from city noises and sirens." He frowned at the creek, unconsciously rubbing the scar on his forehead.

Her eyes narrowed. "Did he attack *you*?"

His hand dropped, and after a second, he nodded. "On the ranch one night, I heard something getting at the calves, so I yelled at him to get his ass up. He got up...but he wasn't awake." He shrugged. "Scared us both a tad."

That was a damned big scar. A chill ran down her spine as she realized how close Jake had come to dying at his own brother's hands. But Jake still stood loyally at his brother's side. Her heart turned over in her chest. Damn him, why did he have to be so...perfect? "Did you *want* to run a lodge?"

The corner of his mouth turned up in a wry smile. "Hadn't considered it when I went to college. I'd planned to buy a spread next to my parents."

"Ranching?"

He nodded. "Eastern Oregon." Kallie followed his gaze to the glow on top of the mountains, the dark sky, and the stars popping into existence one by one. "But I would have missed this. And it suits me far better than ranching." He added, "I miss the horses sometimes."

A rancher. A soldier. No wonder he had an I-can-do-anything attitude. And even though his brother had attacked him, had left that scar on his face—something far, far worse than anything she'd ever done—Jake hadn't abandoned him. Instead he'd changed his whole life to support Logan. Her heart wrenched, and she couldn't help but wrap her arms around his waist.

"Hey." He stroked her hair, then tilted her head. "You

okay, sprite?"

Her lips trembled. *Logan knifed someone and was still loved—so what horrible thing did I do that no one could love me?* She pressed her mouth into a straight line, ignoring the way he narrowed his eyes. With a small laugh, she said, "I thought I'd cop a feel before I slaughter you in battle."

His gaze stayed intent for a moment. Then he obviously decided to let her evade. He rubbed his knuckles along the line of her jaw. "You're not going to play on my team?"

"Pfft, no way in hell." She grabbed his hand and started toward the house. "I have a memory of someone beating on me very recently." In fact, she could still feel the imprint of his palm on her butt. "You're going to die. Uh…Sir."

"Good luck, imp." He caught her nape and pulled her close enough to murmur, "But you should know, I do take prisoners, and I'm looking forward to having you in my custody."

The sheer carnal tone in his deep voice sent a shiver down her spine, followed by a blast of heat. She could feel the controlled strength of his hand on her neck—just enough to restrain, not enough to hurt. What would he do to a prisoner?

He chuckled, tugged a lock of her hair, and raised his hand to join the fray. Morgan tossed him a red vest. Looked like she'd wear patriot blue tonight.

* * *

Despite the sprite's warning, the first so-called bomb took Jake by surprise. The water splashed across his vest and into the specially designed pockets that held water and determined the score, according to the rules Morgan had explained. If and when his vest pockets completely filled, he'd be considered dead and out of the war. He'd managed to evade most of the water from the pistols—all his military training should count for something—but nobody escaped the water bombs.

He eased around a stacked hay bale—and now he knew the reason for the scattered bales—and dodged back in time to escape a stream of water. Kallie's army had slaughtered—well, drenched—his redcoats until only five or so remained, leaving them seriously outnumbered. And perhaps outplayed, he thought as another of his team fell over with an enthusiastic screech.

Catching a glimpse of Kallie edging around a hay bale, Jake took aim. Before he could fire, a balloon splattered over her, winning a yelp of surprise and then a low scream. "Ice water! Wyatt, you bas—you jerk."

On the deck, Kallie's cousin hooted and grabbed another bomb out of an ice-filled cooler.

Jake took advantage of her distraction and shot at her, catching her square in the back. She yelled and jumped out of sight, and then her infectious laughter mingled with the sounds of battle. Jake grinned. *Damn, she's fun.* Now he'd best keep an eye behind him for a tricky little sub. He checked the remnants of his army: two youngsters and a college boy. Maybe if they split up and tried attacking from the flanks…

Not much later, as the twilight faded to black, the bombers increased their activity to end the war. A barrage of water balloons killed Jake and another two soldiers. The last man standing was an adorable little girl, a patriot about nine years old, and the sneakiest minifighter he'd ever seen. As he ruffled her wet hair and congratulated her, his gaze went to the second sneakiest: his own little sub.

Not mine.

Mine.

As Jake watched Kallie strip off her waterlogged vest, a surge of heat almost scalded him. The sprite was braless, and the ice-water balloons her cousin preferred had made her nipples contract into jutting points.

She didn't notice, and he considered his choices. Let her stay clueless so he could enjoy the sight…but let others also enjoy? *Mine.* He wrapped an arm around her. "Leave your vest on, sprite."

Her puzzled expression made him chuckle despite the burning need to lift her shirt and warm those cold, thrusting peaks with his tongue. "No bra? Ice water?"

"Oh, shit." She yanked her vest back on faster than a marmot hiding from a fox. "I forgot how tight my shirt is."

"You know, you look beautiful today," he said, moving close enough to slide a hand under her shirt without being seen. "And I'm enjoying your lack of a bra." Although his cock had turned hard enough to break bricks.

"I'm surprised you even noticed. You know, life just isn't fair, giving me tiny breasts and a fat butt. That's—" Her mouth dropped open as she stared up at him. "I cannot believe I said that to you."

He didn't even try to keep from laughing.

She grinned. "You're such a jerk. It's not funny."

He lifted her chin and frowned into her lovely dark eyes. "We're not playing tonight, but I am keeping track of the insults you've given your dom. I will deal out your punishment accordingly."

Hearing her soft inhalation and seeing her lick her lips shook his control. What was there about a submissive's nervous anticipation?

Staring up at him, obviously reading the change in his face, she swallowed slowly.

He chuckled and pulled her against his chest. "Sugar, I don't think you understand men. We might prefer various sizes and shapes, but that's less important than liking who we're with. And being guys, if you have breasts of any size or shape, we're gonna like them." Concealed by their bodies, his thumbs caressed her nipples before he slid his hands down to cup her ass.

"However, it so happens that your ass is just the size I prefer." He squeezed, heard her muffled squeak. "Soft enough to cushion me, big enough to grip hard. It jiggles too—and when it's up in the air and I'm pounding into you, that jiggle is the sexiest thing I've ever seen."

He squeezed again and then nudged her back. "Those breasts are mine to appreciate. Go change."

How many times tonight could he put that red tinge into her cheeks? He grinned. As he turned away, he saw Wyatt and Morgan staring down at him from the deck.

* * *

After Kallie put on a bra and another shirt from Rebecca, she brought out more desserts for the table. She glanced around for Jake, trying not to appear too obvious. His low laugh drifted up from the grassy area, and she spotted him, surrounded by children, collecting the water pistols to store away. His wet shirt clung to his broad shoulders, outlining his contoured muscles as he ruffled Tyson's hair. The little boy grinned up at him, leaning against him as they unloaded guns together.

She set down Mrs. McCaffrey's three-layer chocolate cake, deliberately getting her finger in the chocolate-fudge frosting. As she sucked it off, she glanced at Morgan. "Need any help?"

He slammed the barbecue shut and scowled.

"What?"

"What do you think you're doing with Hunt?"

"Just what I want to know," Wyatt said from behind her.

She turned, keeping them both in her gaze. This two-against-one business annoyed the hell out of her. "Nothing much."

"Looked like much to me," Wyatt said. "He had his hands on you."

Had everyone at the party noticed? "It's… We're…"

Wyatt shoved a hand through his hair. "Cuz, I don't think you realize…Jake's, well, he's got a reputation."

"I know, Wyatt."

"You can't possibly have any idea," Morgan broke in.

"But it's more than…that," Wyatt said with a warning look at his brother. "He's messed around with every woman in town. Dates and dumps."

"I can handle myself." This was why she never brought a date home.

"Uh-uh. You don't have the experience to deal with someone like him. Or the stuff he—" Wyatt flushed. "You're not…experienced, and he…is. He's just the wrong kind of man for you. You're a good girl."

Oh, honestly. She rolled her eyes. "I'm not a girl anymore, you know, and I *have* dated men in the past."

"Not like him. Hell, we should never have let you go to the lodge, no matter how tough you are." Wyatt glanced toward the yard with a disgusted look. His face softened when he turned back to her. "He'll break your heart, Kallie, and I won't put up with that. If he keeps bothering you, we'll teach him to keep his distance, and if it costs us the lodge's business, so be it."

"What? You can't do that." Throw away clients because of her?

"He's playing you, Kallie." Morgan gripped her shoulder.

Wyatt shook his head. "I know you're having fun, but he'll hurt you. He's already messed with your head. Look at your clothes." He motioned at her shirt, and the disapproval in his eyes shook her. "You've never dressed like this before. I think you should stay away from him."

Morgan nodded.

"We're really worried here, cuz." Wyatt pulled on her hair lightly. "Don't do this to us, okay? We just want you to be safe."

A hand seemed to have gripped her around the chest,

constricting until she hurt with every breath. "I'll think about it."

Even though Morgan smiled at her, she could see the concern in his face. "I know you'd never let us down. You're a good girl."

As the two walked away, she whispered, "I'm not a girl."

Maybe she should move out. Find a house for herself. She looked around at the deck and yard filled with people, at the pastures with horses—her horses—and the mountains circling the green valley. Her sanctuary was up that trail. How could a quiet apartment of her own compete with grumbling men in the morning, fights in the hay barn, and the joy of cold beer in the evening as they compared trail stories and cop complaints?

I don't want to leave. But she didn't want to disappoint them either. And if she made them unhappy enough, they'd push her away completely.

But *Jake*. Thinking of him made her long to fling herself in his arms—however, he considered her just a short-term lover. Sure, he'd kissed her today, but she knew men, and he'd simply reacted to the red-shirted guy coming on to her. Could seeing Jake only another time or two make up for losing her family?

Her stomach coiled into knots, and she swallowed, tasting bile. Arms hugging her waist, she inhaled slowly, then again, forcing herself to be calm—to enter the quiet, white space for keeping silent when she needed to scream or fight or cry—when what she wanted had to take second place to not causing trouble and being a burden. Her stomach gradually settled.

The children milled in the yard, happily shouting "hurry ups" to Wyatt. They knew what to expect next.

Usually she helped. Today she perched on the far railing as Wyatt pulled open the big box. He looked around for her, realized she didn't plan to join him, and just looked unhappy. Unhappy, not his usual of blustering and raging. Pain lanced through her; she'd hurt him.

He turned back to the children and yelled, "Red." Several hands went up.

"What's he giving them?" Logan asked. He leaned a hip on the table, motioning with his beer to the excited boys and girls. "Looks like a pack of sharks in a feeding frenzy."

Grateful for the diversion, she said, "Those are glow sticks. Since fireworks are prohibited and dangerous in a dry forest, we light up the night in other ways."

Just then the children started bending the sticks, letting the chemicals mix inside, and a myriad of colors went streaming through the darkness as they broke into little groups, dancing and waving the fluorescent sticks in the air.

"That is brilliant. Look at them move." He shook his head in disbelief. "You go all out, don't you?"

"We're too far out of town to bother decorating the yard for Halloween or Christmas, so we splurge on this party. We've had quite a few years to accumulate everything." He seemed so much like Jake. A little rougher, perhaps, but friendly in a quieter way. She'd noticed he had fewer lines of care worn into his face, and she had to wonder why. Setting the question aside, she smiled at Logan. "Did I mention we're glad you came?"

His grin flashed. "I'm beginning to regret that we missed so many years. My Rebecca"—the way his voice softened squeezed Kallie's heart—"is showing us how isolated we've become. There're always people at the lodge, but that's not the same as belonging to a community. We'll work on changing that."

As they watched the children play, she thought how much he seemed like Virgil too. A comfortable companion if you didn't mind silence.

"What's doing?" Jake sauntered across the deck with his easygoing walk, and somehow his sociable nature barely hid the dominance shimmering right underneath the surface. Logan took after a wolf—she tilted her head—and Jake was like Gary's Great Pyrenees, greeting visitors with a waving tail, but bother the lambs and the giant dog would rip your throat out.

Her smile disappeared when Jake put his arm around her.

Acutely conscious of her cousins nearby, she sidled away. Jake dropped his arm, and narrowed his eyes.

She swallowed, glanced at Logan, and received the same focused look. It felt like being stripped bare. "I—"

"Shove off, bro," Jake said, never taking his gaze from her.

As Logan silently walked away, Jake set his foot on the table seat and leaned his forearms on his thigh. "What's wrong, sprite?"

When she averted her eyes, she spotted Morgan and Wyatt staring at her from across the deck. She winced.

Jake turned, following her gaze. “Ah,” he said in a hard voice, straightening. Just like Gary’s guard dog, ready to rip and tear. “Are they giving you grief?”

“No!” She grabbed his forearm, and his muscles were taut, ready for action. “I don’t want trouble, Jake.”

“My touching you would cause trouble?”

“I… Yes.” And yet, she wanted him to hold her, to touch her, to be with her so badly that her voice shook.

“Enough to tell me to stay away?”

The ache in her chest must be ignored. “I don’t cause trouble. This isn’t my home or…or my family. I don’t rock the boat.”

He studied her for a long moment. “Don’t you live here?”

“Yes, but…”

He watched her with no expression on his face, and she felt a surge of anger. How dare he judge her?

“Listen, Hunt, you haven’t wanted to be with me except for sex, and you’ve made that perfectly clear. In fact, I’ve heard your ‘one night only’ rule so often, it’s coming out my ears.” She hauled in a breath. “Well, it’s my turn. This isn’t the night.” There might never be a night, but she could explain that…later. Not now, when every word seemed to slash into her throat.

“I see.” His eyes never left hers. “I’m not sure your perception of your cousins is accurate, Kalinda, but I know you believe what you’re saying.” He nodded politely. “Enjoy your night.”

As he walked across the deck, her throat tightened, and

she spun around, staring past the flickering lights, out to the dark pastures. Dammit, she couldn't feel abandoned—she'd told him to go away.

And he had.

Chapter Eight

As his Search and Rescue group hiked up the trail, Jake tuned out the low chatter about the young woman who had disappeared from a campground before the Fourth.

The conversation with Kallie two days ago still clung to him like a pit bull with a good grip. He couldn't call the sprite a coward. She was competent in what she did, brave enough to defend friends from a roomful of drunks, smart enough to have a college degree. She knew herself enough to know she enjoyed submitting and was confident enough to do it. But the disapproval of her family had somehow pulled the ground from under her feet. He'd seen the pain in her face when she'd pushed him away, but she'd still done what her cousins wanted.

As the trail branched, two SAR members veered off to follow the smaller path. The others continued on, eyes constantly moving, watching for any signs of the missing person.

Kallie had the right to end their relationship—if that's what they had—although he'd felt surprisingly disappointed, not just at the lost evening but in not seeing her at all. He frowned. Perhaps he should be grateful for this clean break. One she'd requested.

But seeing such a strong woman go belly-up bothered him. Did she really think her cousins wouldn't love her if she—*how did she put it*?—rocked the boat? Considering Virgil's concern over Kallie, Jake figured she could probably tip the entire boat over without causing a ruckus.

The little sub definitely had a problem with trust, didn't she?

As he stepped over a downed log, he wondered if her phrasing of "*this isn't the night*" implied she wanted to see him on other nights, when her family didn't surround her. And the thought raised his spirits. *Pitiful, Hunt.*

When the trail branched again, Jake held up a hand to indicate he'd take it. As he veered onto the side path, his partner, Eric, fell in behind. The forest was silent except for the regular shouting of the SAR team: "Abigail!"

The uneasy feeling in the pit of Jake's stomach grew. No one had seen this hiker for three days.

Abigail Summers had stormed out of a campground after a fight with her boyfriend. Leaving the car for her, the guy had hitchhiked to town and caught a bus home. Due to the holiday, no one had missed Abigail until a family reunion. Eventually they'd discovered her car still parked at the campground. Going by the disarray in the tent, she'd never returned from her hike.

The boyfriend had shown SAR the trail that Abigail had taken. While Jake and Eric and the other teams conducted a hasty search in the most likely areas, others would round up dogs and helicopters. Unfortunately the main trail branched off several times, vastly increasing the search area.

When Eric paused to catch his breath, Jake gave him a

careful look. "Doing okay?"

"I'm good." After a minute, the college student straightened, settled his daypack, and moved out. The dry pine needles didn't leave much sign behind, and so far they'd found no evidence that Abigail had chosen this trail. Jake kept his eyes moving, looking up, looking back. No tracks leading off, no threads or cloth from the purple top or jeans she'd last been seen wearing. Each time the alarm on his watch sounded, he stopped to shout and listen. "Abigail! Abigail, are you here?"

No response other than the high call of an eagle and the faint wind in the pines. Hell. His gut cramped until the muscles hurt. Logan thought Jake should quit SAR, said it brought back too many memories. And it did, dammit. People had searched for Mimi for days before finding her broken at the bottom of a deep ravine. He'd seen her when they carried her body out of the forest.

But unlike this hiker, Mimi hadn't gotten lost, and she hadn't fallen. She'd set her pack neatly to one side. No marks on the steep trail's edge indicated that she'd slipped. In fact, her body had fallen so far out that she would have had to deliberately run off the cliff.

Suicide. Because of him.

He shook his head. *Let it go.* Right now, someone needed his full attention. He hadn't found a way to help Mimi, and the thought of her dying alone, that she might have suffered, still cut sharply. But maybe he could save someone else.

They left the forest, climbing to where the narrow trail had been carved out of the cliffside and required careful attention to the footing. Falls were a leading cause of death in the Yosemite area. Using binoculars, Jake checked over the side every few feet.

A long way down, a stream at the bottom turned the tiny gorge green with vegetation. He pressed the binoculars closer to his eyes. A long brown mark showed on the verdant slope—possibly exposed dirt from plants being ripped away. An ominous feeling bowed his shoulders.

"Eric. Look over the side. Can you spot anything below that brown patch?"

As the kid dropped to hands and knees, Jake moved another few feet, searching for any other sign. He spotted a splash of color between two trees.

"Hey, I see something. Purple, I think." Eric pointed.

"Good eye." Jake tied red and white flagging to a sturdy pine growing out of a crack in the rock, and noted the GPS point in the log. When Eric joined him, he pointed out visual references to the young man. "Do you remember how to radio it in?"

Eric nodded. The freckles stood out on his face as he swallowed. "Do you think…?"

"Don't think, Eric. We follow procedure." Jake paused, his gut aching as he added, "Yes, it's probably her."

"Oh."

"I'm going to try to climb down. Radio and then stay up here on the trail and direct me in."

The hike to the bottom of the cliff seemed interminable. He forced his way through the vegetation as Eric shouted directions from above: "More north. To your left."

And there she lay.

His shoulders tightened when he reached the crumpled remains of the young woman. She'd probably fallen to her death on the same day she'd fought with her boyfriend. He shoved his hands into his pockets to keep from touching, from trying to make it better. *She needs help, dammit.* But the blank, open eyes said rescue had arrived too late.

He still watched, wanting with everything in him for her to take a breath.

Too small. Tangled brown hair. Pale skin. So battered. He swallowed hard. Mimi had probably looked like this when the searchers found her. Sweat trickled down his back, the sun slicing through the thin air with unholy glee. A tree and shade waited only a few feet away, but he couldn't move—as if standing over her would somehow make up to her that her life had been cut short. That someone should have protected her.

As he tried to do.

And hadn't succeeded, had he? Mimi, his sweet, quiet submissive, who'd depended on him for everything and had cried when he'd uncollared her—she'd ended up just like this.

"God, I'm sorry, sweetheart," and he wasn't sure who he was talking to. Mimi or this poor young woman. Too young. They were too young to have died.

Legs braced, throat clamped shut, he stood vigil for them both.

* * *

Kallie took a long, slow breath. Like deep water, the air had a warm layer with the fragrance of dusty pine needles, and a cool, tangy layer from off the snowpack. The late afternoon sun scorched her shoulders as she led her group through a green mountain meadow. On the far side, a gurgling stream curved snakelike through the grass and then flowed across granite outcroppings in a series of miniwaterfalls. The fine spray moistened the air.

She turned to watch the Lowerys, a family from Serenity Lodge, so apparently the Lodge also booked *normal* people. The wife, Laura—a bouncy brunette in real estate sales—led the small pack, then her blond, gangly husband, Mark, a software engineer who specialized in gaming.

Their children followed. Ten-year-old Cody, who stopped to investigate something in the grass. A budding scientist.

Like a big-footed puppy, Tamara ran across the meadow to the stream and started to climb down to the lower falls.

Bringing up the rear with the packhorse came Ryan. At twelve, he was the image of his father and horse mad. Kallie sympathized. After she'd been dumped on Uncle Harvey, she'd practically lived in the stables for months.

As the horse and boy approached, Kallie took the lead. "Go play. Coco will still be here when you're done."

Ryan gave her a shy, sweet smile before darting away. With a forlorn look, Coco turned his head to watch. The Missouri Fox Trotter doted on children.

Kallie laughed and slapped his neck. "C'mon, old boy. Let's get this stuff off you. He'll be back soon enough."

An hour later, Kallie had the tents set up near the edge of the forest: one for the parents, one for the children, and hers, located a little distance away. While the kids gathered firewood, arguing over who'd found the most, she set up the stone-lined cook area. Steak and biscuits for supper. Much nicer than the freeze-dried foods needed if there wasn't a packhorse.

She rose and stretched, then checked her clients. Part of guide service was figuring out what each individual wanted—whether to be left alone for romantic moments, or to have thrills and challenges, or education. Right now, Laura and Mark sat on a sunny rock, their feet in the water. Holding hands. They'd been married almost twenty years and still held hands.

Kallie bit her lip at the pang of loss. After the Fourth, Wyatt and Morgan had watched her as intently as Mufasa guarded a gopher hole. They'd tried to entice her into poker games, fishing at the creek, even chick flicks—doing everything possible to keep her occupied. They needn't have wasted their time, considering Jake hadn't called. Her two cousins eased up when they decided Jake's interest in her had died.

Apparently they were right. Why would he want someone who told him to go away? The man could have anyone he wanted, after all. She'd spent most of last night fighting back tears because of him, and dammit, she never cried. She kept wondering what else she might have done, how she might have managed to see him without upsetting her cousins.

If Jake had really wanted her for more than sex—if he'd

wanted to date her—would she have told Wyatt and Morgan to stuff it? *Maybe.* And yet the thought of disappointing her cousins or having them pull away wrung her insides until her stomach went queasy.

She sighed. She wished to see Jake so badly, to hear his rough voice and snuggle against his side. She gave a short laugh, knowing she definitely wanted more than just sex from him. Even if he'd been in a wheelchair, he'd attract her with his honesty, with that idiotic bravery that had him jumping into a flooding river to save an old drunk, with his ability to talk with anyone. How he'd wholeheartedly played the game on the Fourth, then enjoyed teasing the children afterward.

Damn him for being someone she wanted in her life, and for not wanting her back.

So she didn't really have any decision to make, did she? She brushed the dirt off her jeans and went to check on the children. While Ryan and Tamara raced twigs down the stream, Cody pored over a field guide, trying to identify the tiny wildflowers. Lots to keep a guide busy and not thinking about "might have beens."

* * *

Jake stopped at the edge of the meadow. *There she is.* His chest constricted as he watched Kallie play with the Lowery children. Had he ever known anyone so beautiful? So full of energy?

He rubbed his face, trying to forget the body of the young woman they'd found yesterday, the way her open eyes had stared, seeing nothing.

But Kallie was alive—in fact, she seemed more alive than anyone he'd ever met. He smiled as she teased the two boys, then picked up the little girl and turned her upside down. His muscles eased as he listened to the giggles turn into delighted shrieks when Kallie slung the child over her shoulder. Strong little sub and so vibrant she seemed to glow.

He needed to hold her.

After returning from the search yesterday, he'd felt eviscerated. A quiet evening talking with Logan and Becca hadn't helped. The silence in his rooms had only increased the feeling that he'd turned to ice all the way to his bones.

Watching Kallie now was like stepping into the sunlight after sleeping in the snow. So much for his intent to stay away.

Jake shook his head. He should be at the lodge, doing his job, but he'd needed to see Kallie. To touch her and hear her laugh and watch her dark eyes turn soft when he kissed her. He'd had women, had loved before—bright, enjoyable loves—but he'd never had this...need...before, as if a part of him had gone missing.

Logan had grumbled about taking Jake's place escorting a vanload of guests to Yosemite. But Rebecca had told Jake, "*I like Kallie. And you need... Well, I think joining Kallie is a wonderful idea.*" She'd kissed his cheek—soft woman, soft heart; Logan was a lucky man—and said, "*You've beat yourself up long enough. Move on, Jake.*"

She hadn't meant the search-and-rescue trip; she'd meant Mimi. But he couldn't deal with that now.

He smiled when Kallie shooed the children back to their games and picked up a towel from the grass. Probably heading toward the lower falls. Jake debated following her. No, he'd best be polite and let the Lowerys know of his arrival. He crossed the meadow and detoured to pet the old horse cropping grass in the shade.

"Hey, it's Jake!" Tamara gave a shriek like a miniature cougar and ran to him, splashing through the stream. Little brown-haired imp. Kallie had undoubtedly looked like that as a child and had probably had the same energy level too. He swung the munchkin up with a laugh, tucked her under his arm football-style, and carried her to her parents.

"I was in the area and thought I'd drop in," he said. "Help Kallie with setting up and cooking."

From the smiles they exchanged, he hadn't fooled them with that excuse. Either he was more obvious than he'd thought, or they noticed he had only a daypack and no tent. Mark grinned and pointed downstream. "She was planning to wash up."

Wash up… Bending over, splashing her face with water. He could almost see how she'd have her ass up in the air. He remembered how it felt to hold her hips and drive into her heat. Bury himself deep and take his pleasure.

Hell, now he'd grown hard as a rock. He shook his head. "Be good parents and keep your children here."

As Mark laughed, Laura snickered and said, "We can do that. Have a nice time, dear."

"Oh, I will."

* * *

Enjoying the peace, Kallie stripped and dunked in the stream. Such cold water. Goose bumps formed on her skin, and her nipples peaked. With a happy sigh, she settled onto the seductively warm, flat granite to sunbathe. Overhead the sky was a clear, blue bowl. Bees buzzed happily, and a dragonfly flitted at the edge of the water. Legs stretched out in front of her, she leaned on her hands as water trickled from her wet hair down her back.

A rustling sound came from the trees a few feet away. She lunged for her clothing…and Jake stepped out of the forest.

Jake. Her heart did a somersault. A painful one. *He's here. Here, here, here.*

So tall and lean. His shoulders military straight. His prowling gait said, *Attack me and I'll kill you. Until then, I'm going to enjoy myself.* In faded jeans, hiking boots, and a white T-shirt that set off his darkly tanned skin and curved over every muscle, he looked like sex on the hoof.

Her body woke as if someone had plugged her into an electric socket.

He spotted her, and his smile blazed in his face. "Well, what have we here?" As his easy gait changed to a stalk, the fire in his gaze made her insides melt.

She took a step back, not exactly sure why, but hell, she wasn't dressed…at all.

"I planned to sit and discuss your concerns first. But then I saw you." As he stopped in front of her, the sun lines at the corners of his eyes deepened with his smile. "Do you realize you're naked?"

"Um. Yeah?"

He took her hand and set it on the thick bulge in his jeans. "Talking can wait."

He only wants me for sex. That's all. Well, maybe that was enough, she thought, although her heart squeezed in disagreement.

His brows drew together as his eyes narrowed. "Then again, perhaps we should talk."

Like that would settle anything? He had his rules and wouldn't change them. So maybe she'd make a few of her own. Yeah. Like they'd have a clandestine affair, never be seen in public together. Very James Bondish. Her laugh almost sounded natural. "We'll talk later."

The feeling of his thick cock under her hand set up an irresistible longing to have him inside her. She started to undo his belt and hesitated, a concern pushing through the heat searing the air around her. "Children, there's—"

"Laura will keep them close." He tilted her chin up, and the scrape of his fingers seemed to sandpaper every nerve on her body.

"Okay, then—"

His scowl stopped her cold. "We're going to discuss the battle on Independence Day. My British army shouldn't have lost. We had more soldiers. Better soldiers." He frowned and shook his head. "No, the only way we could have lost was if someone poisoned my troops."

"What?" *Weren't we just thinking about sex a minute ago?*

"You're a Yank. High in their councils. You must know what was done to my men." His fingers tightened. "And I will discover everything you know, little spy."

"But—"*Spy*? Apprehension mingled with excitement as she remembered his threat from the Fourth: "*You'd best be careful, soldier. If I capture you, I'll be forced to conduct an interrogation. There are many, many ways to make an enemy talk, and I know them all.*"

"You will speak only to answer my questions. Do you understand?"

Her mouth went dry. "Yes, Sir."

"Very pretty." He curved his hand around her throat, not cutting off her air, but the sensation, the knowledge that he could, and the way her body surrendered sent a bone-shaking tremor through her. As he studied her, his fingertips rested lightly over her hammering pulse. "I might enjoy this questioning." He paused, and his voice hardened. "*You* might not. What is your name?"

"Kalinda Masterson, Sir." Her voice came out as only a whisper, and his cheek creased.

"Such a fast little pulse. By the time I'm through, it will be so loud the deer will flee." He turned his hand over, and his knuckles teased her bunched nipples.

A flush warmed her skin all the way to her scalp. "You're still dressed."

"Did you have permission to speak?" His soft voice didn't conceal the edge, and she could feel herself getting wetter.

She shook her head. "No, Sir. I'm sorry, Sir."

He walked behind her and wrapped something—smooth

like vinyl—around her left wrist, then the right, securing her hands behind her. "There. That should keep you in place while I ask my questions. Answer carefully, spy." He ran his hand lightly over her hip and whispered in her ear, "I'd hate to mar this pretty skin."

When he squeezed her bottom, a shiver ran through her. *He wouldn't.* But her certainty kept fading with everything he did.

Returning to stand in front of her, he stared down at her, his gaze unfamiliar, colder than ice. "Where were you born?"

"Washington DC."

"Ah. Right at the heart of our country. I might have known." He threaded his hand in her hair and yanked her head back. His face next to hers, he growled, "What secrets did you learn there?"

"I..." She knew it was a game, but it didn't seem to alleviate the helpless feeling growing in her. "I didn't."

"Wrong answer, little spy. You'll regret that." He pulled something from his pocket. Setting an arm behind her waist, he bowed her back and took her nipple into his mouth. And he sucked, oh, God, he sucked so powerfully she felt a whirlpool pulling her down to the bottom of a river. Apparently satisfied with how far her nipple jutted out, he fastened something on the swollen peak.

Tiny teeth bit into her areola and didn't release. "Ow!"

"Did I give you permission to speak?"

The nipple clamp pinched, sent throbbing aches through her, and somehow made her pussy pulse in unison. Her other breast swelled as if to complain as well.

And Jake bent and sucked on that breast. Her knees wobbled, and a humiliating whimper escaped. When he put on the second clamp, her legs buckled. She tried to grab him to keep from falling but couldn't move her arms. He locked his arm around her, holding her up as easily as if she weighed less than a doll.

She stared down at the clothespin-appearing silver clamps.

When she looked up, his eyes were intent on her face, studying her expression. "Do they hurt?"

"Yes." She stopped, confused. The pain felt…hot. Made everything more sensitive. "No."

The crease of a half smile appeared in his cheek. "Very good." As her nipples burned with a mixture of arousal and pain, he paced in a circle around her, hands behind his back. "We've searched the men delivering supplies to our camps, but never suspected women might be involved. Your countrymen are barbarians"—he gave a disgusted grunt—"and now you will be the one to suffer for it, not them. Kalinda Masterson, tell me where you have hidden the poison."

Her brain had trouble moving past the "*suffer*." "But…there is no poison."

His face turned hard. "You're lying."

A jolt of anxiety shot through her…even as her arousal deepened.

He strode over to a fir and broke off a branch. As he walked back, he stripped it, leaving only a whippy stick just over a foot long.

She eyed it warily, her heart rate increasing.

His cold gaze ran up and down her body. "I need to search you."

"B-but I'm naked."

Standing at her side, he tapped the stick against her mound. "Open for me."

No way. She wasn't going to—

He swatted her butt with the stick, hard enough for a nasty sting.

"Hey!"

"That was just a warning, Yankee spy." He repeated again, "Open for me."

She glared at him, and he hit her other butt cheek. Harder. The burn sizzled across her skin straight to her clit. It hurt, dammit, and how the hell could that make her want his touch so badly that she shook with it?

"Open your legs, Miss Masterson."

Gritting her teeth against the embarrassment, she moved her legs apart. The air felt warm against her thighs, yet oddly cool on her overheated pussy.

"Very good." To her relief—mostly relief—he slipped the cane under his belt. He clamped a hand around her upper arm in a cruel grip, and then reached down between her spread thighs to touch her intimately. "You are very wet. Appears you enjoy a bit of pain, little spy."

His merciless grip kept her from moving away from the slow, slick slide of his fingers over her labia. *Oh God.* Each brush against her clit sent need boiling into her veins until the air itself simmered with heat.

Suddenly he pushed his finger up into her, and the shocking, searing pleasure made her gasp. Her insides clenched around the intrusion.

"So, Miss Masterson, have you hidden anything in your womanly recesses?" His finger stroked deeper, in and out, his thumb rubbed against her clit in a way that eroded her control, and the feeling of him touching her, of doing what he wanted, was almost too much. Her head spun.

When he stepped away, leaving her empty inside, she moaned.

"I find nothing. Perhaps it's deeper than I can reach. Or elsewhere." He pulled the cane from under his belt and idly slapped the weapon against his palm in a way that totally fixed her attention despite the need throbbing inside her. "But as long as we're at this, you will now provide me with the answer to something else."

After a minute, the ominous silence registered, and she managed to pull her gaze from the stick. *Oh my…* His eyes were so blue and as clear as the sky above. The ground under her slid sideways and—

"Kalinda?"

Hellfire. She blinked and forced herself to turn toward the forest, trying to get her brain to work, but her mind had melted away with the rest of her body.

He set a finger under her chin, forcing her to meet his gaze again. "When I arrived and said we didn't need to talk…what were you thinking that hurt you?"

She stiffened as she remembered how she'd thought: *He only wants me for sex. That's all.* She bit her lip. *Uh-huh, share that thought with the nice dom. Not.* "Nothing important."

The cane tapped the outside of her left breast, just enough to sting, to startle her, to jiggle the clamp. She hissed as pain sizzled through her breast and streaked straight for her pussy. She tried to raise her arms. Trapped. The pain and the reminder of her restraints—how the hell could that turn her on like this? Her bones felt like boiled noodles.

"Kalinda, I would like an answer."

She tried to think of something adequate…and took too long.

The cane slapped the outside of her right breast, then the tender underside, and—oh, God!—right over the excruciatingly sensitive nipple already pinned by the clamp. She yelped. And yet fire seared straight to her clit.

He looked down at her, face expressionless. The utter authority in the lift of his chin destroyed her determination.

"I decided we should have a nice clandestine affair." Her words spilled out as if a dam had crumpled, but she still managed to divert the flood into a side branch. "Never be seen together in public."

"All right. I believe you had those thoughts." His jaw hardened. "But I asked what made you hurt." He closed his hand around her arm and then tapped the cane against her pussy, just below her clit, hitting her swollen labia.

She rose right up onto tiptoes at the burning, stinging pain. "Aaaah!" She tried to step away, but his grip seemed more inflexible than handcuffs.

Whap, whap, whap.

When he stopped, she panted against the pain—only was it pain? Because if he did it again—if the sadistic bastard touched an inch higher on her clit—she'd come, right then and there.

He chuckled. "You might like this too much for it to be a punishment." When he rubbed the cane against her cheek, the scent of her arousal clung to the wood. Shaken to the core at her own response, she stared up at him.

His gaze was gentle and yet...uncompromising. He wouldn't accept anything less than the truth. "Tell me, Kalinda."

Her dry throat didn't allow her to swallow. "I didn't like knowing you wanted me only for sex."

His eyes darkened, even there in the bright sunlight. "I see." The cane landed in the grass a few feet away. He ran his hands up and down her arms and kissed her so sweetly she sighed.

"Oh, sugar," he murmured and rubbed his cheek against her. "It's not just sex."

The surge of pleasure rolled through her. He felt something too. For her. Her breath stilled as she waited for more, but he simply kissed her again.

And slowly the kiss deepened as he pulled her closer, molding her against him. Her clamped, swollen breasts rubbed on his shirt, the friction sizzling. His tongue teased hers, and then he tilted his head, taking her mouth in a way that mimicked a different kind of possession. When he pressed his erection against her, her mind abandoned any thought except that of *give me sex now.*

More, more, more. She pushed back in return, grinding her hips. His iron-hard shaft jerked in response, and he muffled a groan.

Ha, she affected him just as much. She rubbed her breasts against his chest, hoping to get him to move, but the incredible feeling just drove *her* higher instead. In sheer frustration, she gritted out, "Maybe I should interrogate *you* and drive you crazy."

He stepped back and shook his head in disapproval, although a corner of his mouth had tilted up. "You should know better than to tease a dom, sprite."

When he didn't pick up the cane, she felt relieved and a little disappointed. Her whole pussy throbbed with need—much worse than before he'd tortured her with the damned stick.

Instead he released her wrists, then tossed the crumpled mess of black tape restraints onto a rock. He pointed to the flat granite spot where she'd been sitting. "Lie on your back. Arms over your head. Legs spread wide."

Her nipples throbbed with pain as she lay back on the warm rock and lifted her arms. Her back arched slightly in the position, and the clamps pinched more. Her eyes closed as excitement blurred the burning.

Silence.

She blinked and looked up. He'd crossed his arms over his chest, and the hard bulge of his biceps captured her eyes. She wanted to run her hands—

He cleared his throat.

Had she done something wrong? Oh. "*Legs spread wide,*"

he'd said. Biting her lower lip, she opened her legs a little. Despite her need, exposing her private areas to his gaze in the bright sunlight was…difficult.

He waggled a finger back and forth for more.

Oh, fuck, damn, hell. She opened wider. Her damp folds parted—again—and she could feel how much more swollen they'd become. Air brushed over her entrance, sending a shiver through her. Open and waiting for him.

"Very nice."

The bastard still wore all his clothes, she realized. And surely Laura would think they'd been gone too long. What if Mark came to look for them?

His little sub was a lovely sight in the bright afternoon sun. Her cheeks had flushed. Her arms over her head arched her back slightly. Her small breasts swelled upward to where the clamps turned her pretty nipples to a dark red color. Her hips were made for a man's hands to grasp, and she'd parted her round thighs widely enough to display the glistening black curls at the juncture of her legs. The fragrance of her arousal mingled with the dusty pine scent of the mountains. Her lovely dark eyes clearly showed her anticipation…and nerves.

Too many nerves, too many worries. She hadn't quite reached that core level where he wanted to take her.

Maybe he'd give her only a single thing to fret about rather than a multitude. He caught her gaze. "I intend to enjoy myself now, Kallie," he said. "It will please me if you stay perfectly still and make no noise."

Her eyes widened for a second, and he saw the tiny tremor that made her breasts shiver. The flush on her cheeks deepened.

He started with her delicate toes and ankles. Strong, smooth calves. Her dark golden tan lightened to cream above her knees. Moving up, he reached her petal-soft inner thighs. When he squeezed and pushed her thighs even farther apart, her hands clenched. Hands gripping high on her thighs, he ran one thumb up and down the crease of her hip and heard her breath catch. Nice.

When he'd seen her, naked on the rocks, his mind had jumped immediately to the desire for simple, thought-erasing sex. But somehow with Kallie, he always wanted more. It truly wasn't just sex—he wanted to touch her emotions, to plumb her responses, and to hear her laugh.

However, the boundaries of their relationship could wait. Right now he intended to enjoy driving her into mindless need. As he lay down on the rock between her legs, the heat of the sun-warmed granite penetrated his clothes. Less than a foot away, the stream flowed and splashed down to the next rocky level. Could a man ask for more than a sunny afternoon in the mountains and a woman spread open for his pleasure?

Resting on his forearms, he dropped his head. He'd never taken her in daylight, so he enjoyed a long, slow look and could almost hear her anticipation ratcheting up. The sun shone on the rosy pink clit barely peeking out from the hood. Her silky black curls gleamed with moisture, and the skin he could see was nicely reddened from the blows of his cane. When he finished, her folds would be swollen and fat and her clit engorged, shoving all the way out.

When he finally tickled his tongue over her labia, her whole body jerked…but then she forced herself back into position.

He chuckled. “There’s a good girl.” His cock had thickened enough that he had to shift position. Its time would come. Right now he wanted to indulge himself with torturing a little sub. So he began by running his tongue upward to tease the juncture of the hood and clit on one side and the other. Her thighs touching his shoulders started to quiver. Featherlight strokes over the very top of her nub had her hips rising for more. Suppressing a laugh, he stopped and said sternly, “I told you not to move, sub.”

When she exhaled, it sounded suspiciously like a whine. He waited a full minute to make his point before resuming.

When her clit felt almost as hard as his erection—although nothing in the world could be as hard as his cock right now—he turned his head and nipped one tender inner thigh.

She squealed like a trapped mouse, and her leg jerked…oh, at least an inch.

“Did you move and make noise?”

“No, Sir.” Her voice sounded as breathless as if she’d run up a mountain. He had to press his lips together.

“Maybe, Sir.”

“I see,” he said gravely. “That’s very poor self-control, Kalinda.”

“I… I’m sorry.”

He could almost hear the begging she forced herself not

to utter. "Well, let's try this then..." He pushed her knees upward and out. "Give me your hands." He set her hands on the insides of her knees so that she could hold her legs there. One of his favorite positions: with the knees up, her pussy would tilt, making her pretty cunt even more available to his fingers. Maybe he'd fuck her in this position. "Very nice, sugar. Stay just like that." He waited a beat. "Kalinda, did you hear me?"

"Oh. Yes, Sir. Please..."

"Don't make any noise. And. Do. Not. Move." Avoiding her clit completely, he slid a finger into her. Very slick and hot. Her pussy clenched around him as he teased the opening, moving in and out in an erratic fashion. Never enough to drive her over. Tremors had spread to her entire legs, and she clutched her knees with a white-knuckled grip. He knew she thought of nothing else now—not the heat of the sun, not the possibility of discovery, not her job—just the feel of his hands on her and her need to stay still.

Perfect.

Oh, God, she was going to die. Sweat covered her whole body, making her hands slip as she strained to keep her legs up. *Please, please, please.* Why didn't he use his mouth again?

"Seems like I remember you saying something about interrogating me. Am I correct?"

She stared at him. Talk? Now? "Yes," she bit out.

He lay so close she could feel his breath right on her clit, but only his finger teased her, circling the entrance before sliding in and out. Never enough to send her off, just enough that everything down there kept getting tighter, more swollen.

"Did I mention it wasn't a good idea to tease a dom?"

Would you stop talking? "Uh-huh." God, she ached and burned.

"Want to apologize?"

The evil bastard. Her answer came out a humiliating whine. "I'm sooorrrrry."

He didn't move.

"So, so sorry. Really sorry. Master. Sir. Emperor of the world. God of the universe." She managed to clamp her mouth shut before adding, *Fucking sadistic bastard.*

Maybe he heard it anyway—he bit her again, and the sharp pain stabbed through her, making her jerk. Her legs slipped, and she grabbed them frantically. He chuckled, and she felt his tongue on the crease between her hip and thigh, so hot and soft. *Move over, just a little, please.* Her pussy throbbed. Burned.

He pushed one finger into her, then another, the added width wonderful, and she had to fight to keep her hips still. *Don't move.* As if in revenge, her trembling increased.

"That's very nice control, sprite," he said, the approval in his voice like a stroking hand brushing over her. "I think you deserve a reward, don't you?"

Reward? She held her breath, and suddenly the fingers moving in and out of her changed, rubbing inside her, pushing against something…something that made everything inside her contract. And then he moved slightly, and closed his mouth around her clit, holding it firmly between his lips. His tongue stroked it ruthlessly—soft and wet—over and over. Inside, the pressure expanded like a balloon. With each touch of his tongue, the pleasure built exquisitely, higher and higher.

She clamped her mouth shut over her whimpers. He slowed, each drag of his tongue bringing her closer and... everything inside her seemed to gather together, petrifying her into unmoving stone until...

He sucked on her clit. Hard.

The pressure exploded outward as if the balloon had burst, flooding her with devastating pleasure in spasm after spasm. A wildfire totally out of control.

Oh God, hellfire, damn. Panting, she realized Jake's hands covered hers, helping her hold her legs up as his tongue flickered over her, sending ripples of aftershocks through her. The screams that she'd muffled swirled inside her head.

"You did well, sweetheart," he said, moving her hands away and lowering her legs. When he rose to kneel between her legs, his face appeared stern, but laughter danced in his eyes. "Your control is improving."

She considered cursing him—but then, she'd never come so hard in her life. Would every time with him be like this? So overwhelming?

With other men, she sometimes felt as if she were watching herself react, doing what was expected, always keeping a rein on her emotions. But Jake never gave her a chance to step back or be apart—his commands left no room for anything but feeling. And part of the reason she could let go was trusting that he could and would handle her.

Holding her eyes with his, he undid his belt, unfastened his jeans, and lowered the zipper. Commando. His cock sprang out as if escaping a prison, incredibly long and thick, the veins engorged and bulging. With the same slow, deliberate movements, he sheathed himself in a condom. She'd never met anyone who had such control.

He grasped her wrists and pulled her to a sitting position. "From the way you were squirming—although you did a fine job of keeping under control—I think we'd best get you off your back."

Now that he mentioned it, she could feel scrapes burning her butt and upper back.

He tossed her clothing on the rock for padding and said, "On your hands and knees now." With determined hands, he helped her turn, and her insides started to quake with anticipation. He was so big, yet all she wanted was him inside her, filling her. "Rest on your forearms, sugar." He pushed her shoulders down. Putting his hand between her legs, his palm against her mound, he lifted her butt higher, sending a thrill through her as he positioned her body, not giving her any choice in the matter.

He set his cock against her opening, sliding it up and down and getting it wet, she realized—only one second before he drove inside her in a ruthless thrust that wrung a cry from her. Her insides convulsed around the thick erection in wavering jolts of pleasure.

"Sugar, you feel incredible," he growled, "and I am going to take you hard." He lowered his voice. "Because I want to. Because I can."

Somehow her bones trickled right out of her body.

He gave a deep laugh. With an implacable grip on her hips, he rode her, hard as he'd promised, hammering into her until the driving rhythm somehow caught her like a hooked fish, yanking her arousal up from the depths. And then she was lost as each plunging thrust pushed her closer and closer. As her need increased, she tried to push her hips back to meet his thrusts.

He slapped her butt, and as her insides clenched like a fist at the shocking sting, he said, "If you want more, Kallie, I will give you more—at my discretion."

How could he talk now? She shoved back toward his cock again. A second later, she realized his meaning as he pushed her legs so far apart that she couldn't do anything.

And then he curved his hands over the tops of her thighs and yanked her back against his groin, sheathing his cock to the hilt each time. He controlled her completely, yet gave her exactly what she wanted, and the knowledge thrilled through her and exploded her into a climax as quickly as if he'd set off a bomb inside her. This time her spasms slammed into his thick cock instead of his fingers, and God, the sensation felt incredible. Her head spun. Despite her orgasm, each implacable thrust sent her even higher until her body shook with the brutal pleasure.

His hands tightened, lifting her knees right off the rock. He growled and pressed inside so deeply she felt his cock hit her womb and then the jerking sensations as he climaxed.

God, she loved the feeling of him coming inside her, knowing she'd given him that.

He eased his grip and lowered her until her knees again

rested on the rock. As he massaged her butt, he rumbled a satisfied, "I enjoyed that, sugar." A second's pause. "But seems like I heard you making noise. What shall we do about that?"

Hellfire, I'm doomed.

Chapter Nine

In camp, as Kallie started setting up for supper, she felt wonderful. As long as she didn't let herself contemplate anything other than sex, she was happy. And sex with Jake meant never having a chance to think.

By the time Jake had let her get dressed, she didn't have a tense muscle left in her body. She'd hoped no one would notice the beard burns on her cheeks and neck, but from the amused glint in Mark's eyes, her hope had been futile.

Her lips were probably swollen too, from both kisses and her punishment for making noise. She'd probably deserved it, especially when he removed the clamps and blood had rushed back into her swollen nipples. The sound she let out hadn't been a scream…quite.

He'd set her on her knees, put his hand around his shaft, ran his finger around her mouth, and waited. She smiled at the memory of taking his heavy cock in her mouth. She'd traced the bulging veins with her tongue and licked the underside of the head. His shaft had grown even thicker, and she could see him exert his control to keep from grabbing her hair and hammering into her. But he hadn't, and she'd slowly driven him crazy until he'd pulled out and flattened her on her back beneath him. He'd seated himself with one hard thrust that made her gasp, and then ridden her until she had even more rock scrapes on her butt.

Damned if she didn't want to do it all over again. The man had turned her into a nympho. With a frustrated sigh, she lit the fire.

"I'll help you, Kallie." Shifting his weight from one foot to another, Ryan looked at her in adoration. She'd made one conquest, at least.

"I'd love some assistance."

He grinned and squatted beside her. "Cool. I've never cooked over a campfire. What do we do?"

"The trick is to let the fire burn down to coals before you put anything on to cook. While we wait, we'll prepare the food."

On the other side of the campfire, Jake yawned and stretched. As the muscles in his shoulders flexed, she rubbed her fingers together in a tactile memory of warm skin stretched over granite-hard muscles.

He caught her staring, and she flushed.

"Tamara, Cody, you want to come on a hike with me?" he asked. "I know some great climbing rocks nearby."

Both of the youngsters bounded to their feet. After he pointed the way and the children darted off, he said to Mark, "Appears that I've got two kids and Kallie's got one. You two are free for a while if you want some privacy to…wash up or anything. I can recommend the downstream area." Jake pointed in the direction of where they'd indulged earlier.

Mark's eyes lit. As if he thought Jake might renege, he grabbed his wife and hustled her out of camp. Grinning,

Kallie nodded at Jake. “Good work, Hunt.”

“Seemed like a shame not to share the fun,” he commented. He strolled after his two charges.

When the parents returned, an hour or so later, Kallie left Ryan watching the fire, and went to fetch the others. As she approached the clearing, she heard Tamara’s giggles and Jake’s deep laughter. Just the sound of his voice sent a jolt through her, and she sighed. What a wimp.

As she stepped out of the trees, she stopped to enjoy the sight of him with the children. Cody perched on the top of one massive boulder, binoculars to his eyes. At a different boulder, Jake patiently taught Tamara the basics of rock scrambling.

The rock stood taller than his head, and Tamara went up it like a little monkey. At the top, she did an adorable victory dance. When Jake laughed and held up his arms, she launched herself fearlessly, with no doubt he’d be there for her. He caught the girl, tossed her up, and gave her a hug before setting her down.

And as Kallie watched him, she realized she’d thrown herself off too—right into a disgustingly squishy sentimental emotion. She loved the bastard, damn it all. This was so, so stupid. What had happened to only having sex?

As the setting sun sent shadows dancing across the small meadow, she leaned back against a tree trunk. It better hold her up since her legs couldn’t do the job. *In love? No no no.* She thumped her head on the tree, trying to knock sense into her brain. Like that would happen, because what made more sense, in a primitive way, than to fall for a strong man who would protect your future children?

Logical, but not gonna work. *Remember the 'one night only' rule*? She needed to enjoy today, one moment at a time. *Don't look any further ahead, because, girl, you know it won't last.*

Cody spotted her, and when they all looked over, Kallie sighed. With an effort, she arranged her face into a pleasant expression. Maybe she'd turned dim-witted enough to fall for Jake, but she sure knew better than to let him realize it. *Sex only, sex only, sex only.*

Jake smiled at her as she walked up. "Come to do some climbing?" Then his eyes narrowed, and he studied her for a long moment. "What's wrong, sprite?"

Good job, oh Miss Inscrutable Face. "I'm starving. It's time to eat, guys."

* * *

After one of the sprite's fine meals and the cleanup, Jake enjoyed himself entertaining the tired children with campfire tales. Beside him, Kallie whittled on a piece of pine from her pack. Jake glanced at it and frowned. It looked like a man with legs braced and arms crossed over his chest. Although she hadn't yet finished the face, the stance reminded him of Logan. Or…himself. She met his suspicious gaze, laughter in her eyes, and he had to grin. The imp simply bubbled over with mischief.

As she returned to carving, he leaned closer and murmured, "Will that sit beside your bed to keep you in line when I'm not present?"

"Keep me in line?" She snorted. "That'd be the day."

"Really?" He waited a second, then said, "Look at me," pushing some power into the low command.

Her head jerked up, and her eyes widened.

He ran a finger down her soft cheek and said very softly, "That day is today, little sub."

The flush that darkened her cheeks rewarded him, and the dirty look she gave him just added to the pleasure.

He turned back to the children and raised his voice, "So which of you has heard the story of…"

When he ran dry an hour later, he sipped some hot chocolate and then announced that he'd forgotten his tent.

The children laughed at the dumb grown-up, Mark snorted, and Laura snickered. He didn't care, not if he ended up where he wanted. "Kallie, may I sleep in a corner of your tent?"

She looked up from her whittling. "Should I assume you forgot a sleeping bag too?"

"'Fraid so."

She rolled her eyes, to the children's delight. "I don't know, Mr. Hunt. That's pretty bad, not remembering to bring the proper equipment. I should make you walk back in the dark so you don't forget again."

"But the bears might get me."

That earned him a husky giggle from Kallie, but Tamara's eyes rounded in panic. "Kallie, don't make him. Pleeease…"

"You do have a way with the women," his little sub said in a very disrespectful tone. "Well, Tamara, since you asked for him, I guess he can bed down in my tent. Just for tonight, though."

Tamara beamed and crawled into Kallie's lap. Not a shy bone in that child's body, and Jake was a tad envious as the girl snuggled close. Then again, tonight he'd sleep in Kallie's tent, and her sweet round ass would be in his lap. Or under him. All night.

And so it proved.

* * *

A few hours after everyone had retired, Jake lay on his back on Kallie's sleeping bag with her beside him. As he tried to regain his strength, he thought about the night's activities. He decided that having her under him felt great. Then again, placing her on top hadn't been too bad either—the sprite definitely had riding skills. Good thing she'd set her tent up at a distance from the others since he'd kept her in the saddle until she'd gone limp with coming.

Now she nestled against his side, her breath creating a warm spot on his chest. His shoulders stung where she'd dug her nails in the last time. Of course, his grip on her hips had probably given her a few bruises. He hadn't had so much fun or come so powerfully in…he didn't know when. Ever, maybe.

Eventually she stirred, lifting up on one elbow to stare down at him. The full moon glowed softly on the high dome of the tent, lighting her face with silver. Her eyes were dark liquid pools, incredibly beautiful despite the frown she gave him. "You know, I can't believe the things I let you do."

"Oh? What things? Like the clamps?" He rubbed his

knuckles over her nipples, still swollen from the clamps and his attentions earlier.

She inhaled sharply, and he pinned her in place as he gently teased the undoubtedly sensitive peaks. Then stopped as he felt himself harden. Too soon to take her again. She needed a break.

"You know exactly what I mean." Her lower lip actually pushed out into the most adorable pout he'd ever seen.

He laughed once, then again at the glare she gave him. "I do know, sugar. You let me do them because you want me to."

"Not hardly. I never, ever thought about putting stuff like that on myself."

"No, not clamps specifically." He tugged on a lock of her hair. "What I do—we do—isn't as important as the fact that you want to give up control. I'm honored that you trust me enough to give it to me."

Want to give up control. She'd avoided thinking about the BDSM stuff, aside from how hot it made her. Maybe because, though he teased her sometimes, he didn't try to overwhelm her when they weren't "playing." But it formed a definite part of their relationship. And since just thinking about his control excited the hell out of her, maybe he was right. Maybe. "It never worked out with the others."

"Ah, sugar. You have a submissive nature, but that doesn't mean you want to submit to just anyone or all the time. That would be like saying that someone with a passionate nature wants to have sex all day long with any man she meets. No. In your case, little sub, you probably enjoy ordinary sex, but the act of giving up control to a dominant you trust will add"—his lips quirked—"a lot to the experience."

Definitely a lot.

"Your previous times probably failed because of those two factors: either your boyfriend didn't have a dominating personality, or you didn't trust him enough to surrender control."

Made sense, and maybe that was why she'd always felt something was missing during sex. "So when did you figure out…what you are?"

"Curious little sprite." He huffed a laugh. "Years ago in college. Logan had a very kinky girlfriend who was not only submissive but wanted two men at once." He chuckled. "We discovered we both enjoyed domination, but neither of us is generous enough to enjoy sharing."

Years ago. All that experience. She hadn't had a chance, had she?

"After we'd been in the lifestyle a while, we realized our parent's relationship has a dominant-submissive dynamic, so we probably absorbed it in childhood. Not that we'll discuss it with them. Ever."

She laughed.

"Get some sleep, sprite. I intend to waken you before dawn."

* * *

Jake kept his promise and woke up his little sub before

the sun rose. Neither of them had much energy, so he showed her there was a time and place for vanilla sex. He used the last condom in his jeans. Then he pulled her ass back against his groin and slid into her from behind to enjoy the soft climb into arousal and release.

Afterward he held her in his arms and settled her head into the hollow of his shoulder. She fit well against him, he thought again. And he doubted he could ever get tired of having her in his bed, taking the control she handed over so sweetly, and driving them both to heaven.

One hand behind his head, he glanced down at her. He'd definitely worn her out, though. After brushing her silky hair from her face, he stroked her soft cheek, still warm and moist despite the cooling mountain air.

She stirred and burrowed a little closer.

"Go to sleep, sugar."

"'Kay," she murmured, obviously halfway there already. "Love you, Jake."

The words punched him right in the gut, an impossible blow. *What have I done?* His fingers had lingered on her cheek, and now he slowly pulled his hand back. *No. This can't happen.*

As if she'd heard him speak, she stiffened, waking completely. She rose on one elbow, trying to see his face in the darkness. Her voice came out strained. "Guess that wasn't what you wanted to hear."

He cleared his throat. "No. That's unexpected." Everything in him wished to reassure her and ease the strain he heard in her voice. At the same time, he wanted—

needed—to grab his pack and head down the mountain. To get away, no matter that the sun hadn't risen. "Listen, Kallie—"

She snorted. "Relax. I was half-asleep; that's all. No need to panic."

Relief warmed his veins, and he forced a laugh. "So you were thinking of some other gorgeous guy you sleep with?"

Silence.

His heart fell. He should have taken the out when she'd given him one. She'd meant it; the sprite was one of the most honest people he'd ever met. "Sprite, I'm sor—"

"I'm not going to make any demands on you, Hunt," she interrupted, her voice as cold as the air over a glacier. "My feelings are my own; they don't need to be reciprocated like a Christmas present exchange or something."

He closed his eyes, not getting anywhere with trying to see her face. But her body told him enough: from soft and sleepy to a tense, vibrating bundle of unhappiness. Dammit. He should never have let her get so involved, should never have broken his own rules. And like the insensitive bastard that he was, he'd hiked up here to see her and almost forced her into a relationship.

Now he needed to give her an explanation. "Like you said, Kallie. How I feel has nothing to do with how lovable you are."

"Yeah. I know. You don't want anything long-term. You told me. Hell, dude, everyone in town knows about your 'one night only' lecture."

Small towns. Right. He wanted to say, *This is how I am.*

But that wouldn't be fair. After Mimi's death, he'd never dated anyone seriously and never played with a submissive outside of a club or party, which meant he'd never needed to explain himself.

Kallie had changed everything. "I'd like to explain…" His mind blanked.

Shifting, she rested her forearms on his chest, setting her chin on her arms. He couldn't even see her eyes, and for a moment, his mind substituted the memory of Mimi's lifeless brown eyes, and then those of the missing hiker. He swallowed against a wave of nausea.

"Jake." Her voice—husky and not Mimi's—dragged him back. "If you want to tell me something, just spit it out." Tough little sub.

"You know I lived with a woman a couple of years ago. Mimi. She was submissive."

"The one who looked like me. I remember."

"She started dating me after breaking up with someone else. When she learned about the lifestyle, it fitted her like a glove. She wanted to be a slave. To have a master."

"So not my thing," Kallie said under her breath.

"No. You're more of a sexual submissive. You want to be dominated now and then. She wanted—needed—it all the time."

"You were her master?"

"Yes." He huffed a hard laugh. "I enjoyed it at first, having her anticipate my every need, letting me decide everything. But I'm not cut out to be a full-time master."

She made a noise. *Continue.*

"It's tiring, Kallie. I'm a sexual dominant, and I don't want to decide how a sub lives every minute of her day. I don't want to make important decisions for someone else. Advise and recommend, yes. Order her to attend college? Hell no."

"Huh. I never thought of it like that."

"When I dom, it's a balancing act, judging a sub's wants and needs against my desires. You need a good handle on both because—as you've seen—I have the right to shut you up completely. But to do that all the time is exhausting. I have friends, both slave and master, who love it. It fulfills them. It didn't me."

"But it did Mimi," Kallie said softly. The understanding in her voice shook him. Why didn't she yell? Cry?

"Yes." His stomach cramped. "When I uncollared her, she was..." *In despair.* "She needed to be a slave. I talked with her. We planned—I thought we planned—to go to San Francisco, where I could introduce her to some available masters. Simon offered to guest her and help her too. She was beautiful—like you—and had a deep need to serve. It wouldn't have taken long to find someone, but..." Darkness swathed the roof of the domed tent. The blackness before dawn. *Why had Mimi just given up?*

"*But.* What happened?"

The rest of the story. The part that filled him with the same despair Mimi must have felt. *How could I not have known what she was feeling*? He didn't think he'd ever climb out of the abyss of guilt; he didn't deserve to. "She... Apparently she didn't believe me. I don't know. She didn't leave a note. We never found out why...why she threw herself off a cliff." He hadn't gone back to that mountain since. It must echo with her voice. Her soul. *Damn me to hell. I did that to her.*

"Oh fuck."

The husky curse splintered his thoughts. "What?"

"I'm sorry, Jake. That must have been horrible—for you both."

"A little more for her, don't you think?"

"Well, no. She took the easy way out; you had to go on living."

It felt as if Kallie had slapped him. "It was my fault."

She snorted. "Did you take responsibility for all her successes too or only the failures?"

"I—" Something in that sounded important, but it didn't matter. Not to what they were talking about. "It was my fault, Kallie, and I won't get involved with anyone else. So…" *Don't love me, sprite.*

"So back off. Clear enough." She sat up, leaving his chest cold. "You know, Hunt, I'm not sure I get it. Either you figure every woman is as cowardly as your girlfriend, or you're too much of a pussy to risk anything, because—I hate to tell you, dude—nobody gets out of this life alive. There's no guarantee when somebody kicks off. Are you planning to spend your whole life alone, or are there a certain number of years you have to go before you've served your sentence?"

She grabbed her bundle of clothing and walked out into the blackness before dawn.

* * *

As she pulled on her clothes across the clearing, she heard the scuffle of boots in the dirt and saw the darkness of Jake's form against the lighter tent. He didn't call for her, didn't look for her. He simply left. As the sound of his footsteps faded, she blinked hard, forcing back hot tears. Damned if she'd act as if he meant something to her. Even if he did. *Had.*

Unable to stay in camp, she walked through the gray light to a high lookout point. As she dropped down to sit on the granite rock, the sun glowed behind the eastern mountains, turning the peaks pink with an outline of gold as if a child had run a yellow marker across the top.

Sunrise. Her favorite time, filled with anticipation of the coming day. Light winning out over darkness. New beginnings.

Dawn wasn't supposed to be for *endings.*

In the valley below, thick fog submerged the tall trees in an ugly gray. The way she felt right now, she might as well be down there, smothered in darkness. Hands clenched, she shoved the hurt deep inside her and smothered it in her own way, pulling imaginary tendrils of fog over it until the pain dulled. She knew how to handle loss. *Damn right I do.*

Wrapping her arms around her legs, she set her chin on her knees and watched the sky brighten and the day begin.

Chapter Ten

Logan had shown a hell of a lot more understanding yesterday, Jake thought as he slapped a container of worms, a six-pack of beer, ice, and sandwich fixings onto the grocery counter.

Whipple rang them up. "Fishing?"

"For a few days." Jake pulled out a couple of twenties.

"Is Kallie going along?"

The unexpected sound of her name hit him like an icy blade, stabbing upward from his gut into his chest. "No."

His face must have shown something, for a spiteful smile warped Whipple's face. "She figured you out, didn't she? Dumped you on your ass."

Not waiting for his change, Jake walked out. After putting the ice and beer into his cooler, he got in his truck and pulled away from the curb. In the doorway of the grocery, Whipple watched, still smiling.

A few hours later, Jake shoved open the door to their small fishing cabin. He and Logan had bought the place when Jeremy Ackers had a stroke and his family had forced him to sell. They rented it out now and then, and when not occupied, the lonely spot on the river was a great place to escape.

The small, single room looked dusty but clean. Jake set the cooler on the floor, tossed his sleeping bag onto one of the cheap cots and his duffel on the couch. With his rod and tackle box, he headed out the back door, down the tilted stone steps, and out onto the small floating dock. A few minutes later, he made a good cast and settled into a wooden chair white with age.

As if his ass planted on the creaky dock sent a signal to his brain, his anger eased and his jaw loosened. His chest still felt hollowed out. Probably nothing would change that except time. He'd felt like this when Mimi died. This might be worse.

Less guilt. More pain—a lot more pain.

Sunlight glinted off the treacherous center of the river, where the slow-moving surface concealed the fast current. The alder and maple trees along the bank whispered with a different sound than the tall mountain evergreens. Shallower. Perfect for a bastard who had caused a woman to die.

"*She took the easy way out.*" Kallie had been blunt, even brutal.

Jake turned the words over in his head.

And then his thoughts wandered down more familiar trails, the arguments he'd had with himself over and over. Could he have done something differently? Perhaps sucked it up and stayed with Mimi?

He shook his head. No. Their relationship had been falling apart already, the distance between them growing as she'd increased her dependence on him and he'd wanted less. He'd made the breakup as gentle as he could. Even before that, she'd known their time together had reached the end; she had said as much.

And he hadn't left her. He'd stayed with her, held her, mourned with her over the lost hopes for a life together. She'd looked forward to San Francisco—he could have sworn it. Dammit, how could he, her dom, her lover, have misread her intentions and emotions so completely?

For months afterward, he'd reexamined every tiny nuance of her words, her expressions, her body language in the days prior to her death. He couldn't—still couldn't—see any signs that she'd felt such despair.

He forced himself to take a long breath, reeled the line in, and cast again. If he could go back and change things… If she'd never met him—if he hadn't found her staring helplessly at a flat tire one day. If she hadn't just broken up with Whipple… Jake sighed and rubbed his cheek, felt the stubble of a day's growth, and couldn't seem to care. If she'd never met him, she'd probably have met someone, married him, had children, might have lived happily ever after. She'd be alive, not dead.

The guilt of that…

He'd never have willingly hurt her. And now he'd hurt Kallie too.

He reeled in the line. A fish had nibbled off the worm. After rebaiting the hook, he cast again.

Kallie. Honest. Blunt. He snorted. Definitely blunt. "*Are you planning to spend your whole life alone, or are there a certain number of years you have to go before you've served your sentence?*" Did he want to live his life alone?

Silence surrounded him, broken only by the rippling river and the distant cry of a hawk. He could live his life in this kind of silence...but he wanted more than that. He'd always assumed he'd have what his parents had: love, sharing, laughter, and children.

How many years before he'd served his sentence? He lay the rod down, anchored it with his foot, and scrubbed his face with his hands. A clear-sighted woman, that Kallie. He'd done exactly that, deprived himself of any relationship. *If Mimi can't have love, then I can't either.*

That was just... Had he really believed that?

Yep.

The sprite had also called him a pussy. He grinned for a second. Got in a lot of blows, hadn't she? And the term fit. The pain of loss—yeah, a man would avoid that if possible, but Jake could handle loss, although the thought of never holding Kallie again squeezed his chest like a giant's fist.

The guilt he'd felt had been the sticker.

Had been. He frowned. Past tense. The blackness was still there, true, but subdued. Manageable. The pain would never leave him completely, he knew, for somehow, someway, he'd missed seeing Mimi's intentions. He'd have tried to stop her if he'd known. But he hadn't.

He was human. He'd screwed up. He undoubtedly would again.

A small flame of anger flared inside him. Couldn't Mimi have given him a chance to make things right for her? She shouldn't have just...quit, no matter how much she had hurt.

Could you even know—trust—another person to stay

alive, to weather life's difficulties? He considered his brother, Becca. Kallie. No, they wouldn't take the easy way out. Fighters, all of them.

Pussy. He hadn't thought of himself as being gutless, yet a person could find more than one way to step back from life. Refusing to live it—to participate, to love—was as craven as taking it. Why hadn't he seen that he'd been a coward?

He looked up toward the wide bowl of sky where heaven was located; his great-grandmother had told him that, and she was never wrong. "Okay, Mimi," he murmured, his gaze going past the few clouds and on farther, to the unknowable. "You've gone on ahead. I can't fix what happened, and it's time for me to go back to living." His throat tightened. "We weren't meant to be, but I did love you, sweetheart, and I hope you'll give me your blessing from wherever you are now."

His eyes burned, and he swallowed painfully. Okay. That was done.

He took a deep breath and another. On the far bank, a deer and her spotted fawn ventured down to the water, and he remembered how he'd always thought of Mimi as a young deer. He watched as they drank, ears swiveling to catch any sound, then bounded back into the forest.

Jake shifted his weight and frowned. He had a notoriously bad-tempered sprite to confront. What would he tell her?

As the river flowed past him, heading inexorably toward the sea, he pondered. He wanted her. In his bed. In his life? No. *You being a pussy again, Hunt?* Face it, he cared for her. Cared too much—for a cowardly pussy—but facts were facts.

The thought of losing her had driven him to take a long look at his actions.

Pussy. He snorted a laugh.

And now he'd have to go back, manage to keep her from belting him, and talk about their relationship—and they damn well *did* have a relationship. He rubbed his chin. Charging into battle might be less dangerous than facing Kallie in a rage. But somehow he'd simply get her to stand still long enough for him to explain.

Dream on, Hunt.

* * *

If the Lowery family noticed Kallie talked less today, they didn't say anything. She had tried to keep them too busy to talk: a mountain lake, a ridge overlooking the basin, a talus slope filled with whistling marmots. That afternoon, she returned them to Serenity Lodge, where they'd stay for another night.

After unpacking their personal gear from Coco, she helped carry it into the lodge. As she set down the packs, she noticed a man talking to someone in the kitchen. Tall, broad-shouldered, dark brown hair. Kallie's heart lifted far enough to clog her throat and started to pound.

"Jake!" Tamara tore across the room. "Why did you leave so early? I wanted to—" The man turned, and the little girl skidded to a halt on the wood floor.

Logan, not Jake. He smiled down at the child. "Sorry, kitten, Jake is out of town for a while."

"Oh." Tamara backed up. Logan lacked Jake's easy

manner, his sheer enjoyment of people, and the girl undoubtedly sensed that. Pouting, she trudged back to Kallie.

Yeah, that's how I feel too. Kallie gave the munchkin a hug and then looked up. Arms across his chest, Logan leaned against the door frame, studying them—studying her. She turned her back on him. Casually. *Nothing to see here, dude.*

She exchanged good-byes and hugs with the Lowerys. When Ryan started to awkwardly shake her hand, she pulled him in for a hug. "I had fun cooking with you," she whispered. "Coco is going to miss you."

His grin eased her heart. For a minute, at least.

She escaped outside before she tried to kick something. Jake had gone out of town, huh? He didn't think it was adequate to dump her, but he had to flee the territory too, like she'd turn into some deranged stalker. Like she couldn't take a hint—well, hardly a hint, more like, *Get lost, Kallie.* After untying Coco, she led him over to the horse trailer in the bush-concealed parking area and worked on unpacking the rest of the gear.

The chestnut turned to inspect her work, then lowered his head to crop a long tuft of grass.

"Yeah, at least one of us is having a good day, buddy." She patted his neck and picked up the leftover food supplies. The crunch of gravel drew her attention.

Logan had followed her out of the lodge. *Oh wonderful, just shoot me now.*

"The Lowerys were very pleased with your expertise." His voice—so familiar—made her heart pick up, and turned her mouth down. Jake's sounded a little smoother, a little deeper, but otherwise…

"Thanks. Good to know." She tossed the supplies into her Jeep and went back for more.

Not taking the hint, he walked over to Coco to rub the horse's forehead. "Jake was in a bad mood this morning."

Kallie stiffened. "Well, that's not my problem, is it?"

"Just surprising. He'd been damned gung ho to join you on the mountain yesterday."

And gung ho to run back down. Her ribs compressed her lungs painfully. She started unfastening straps. Damn Logan for making everything worse. Her first few choices of response, like *fuck off*, seemed too rude to use on a so-called business associate. "Butt out, Hunt."

She kept working on the straps. No noise of him leaving. God, she wanted to cry. She wouldn't—it never did any good—but why didn't he leave? When she ran out of buckles, she turned.

His blue eyes, grayer than Jake's but just as intent, examined her face. And then he sighed and shook his head. "You drive carefully, sugar," he said gently. He squeezed her shoulder as he walked past her to the lodge.

"I will," she muttered to his back. After she unclenched her hands and pulled her composure into place, she scowled at the tall figure climbing the steps. Did he think she'd drive off the road because she'd lost a…a bed partner? Not hardly. Maybe nobody ever stayed with her, but she wasn't the type to jump off some mountain like that girlfriend who'd screwed him all up.

She coaxed Coco into the trailer and headed home,

driving carefully just to prove Logan's worries were wrong.

To top off a lousy day, Virgil's police car sat by the house. She scowled. Talking to another overprotective male was more than she could handle right now. The gravel she kicked at his car made a satisfying *plink* as the stones hit the hubcap. Probably a criminal offense, attacking a cop car.

She brushed Coco down and put him into the pasture. She put the gear away. She cleaned the messy shelves, fixing everything to her satisfaction as if straightening up would put the rest of her life under control.

It didn't work, but at least the tack room looked pretty. She glanced at the house, craving one of the soft drinks in the refrigerator. Maybe Virgil would be in his room.

God hates me today. Her cousin sat at the kitchen table, eating supper. He'd stacked several burgers left over from the Fourth into a massive sandwich.

She nodded at him and grabbed a diet soda.

"Hey, little bit, how was your hike?"

"Okay. Cute kids." She popped the top and drank, the bubbles scouring the trail dust from her throat. "I'm going to shower."

His hazel eyes narrowed. "What's wrong?"

Did she have a sign on her forehead that read: KALLIE GOT DUMPED? "Nothing."

"Uh-huh. You seen Jake recently?"

"None of your damned business," she snapped.

His face set into stone, and his eyes turned glacier cold. She tried not to flinch. Last time she'd seen that expression, he'd punched an abusive husband so hard the guy probably still sucked his food through a straw.

But his anger wasn't directed at her. She sidled toward the door.

"Hold up. I need to talk to you." His brows drew together into his worrywart expression, the one he got whenever she did something he considered unsafe: dating, drinking, working in Alaska, mountain climbing, drinking, dating…

Waiting for the lecture, she rubbed her shoulder on the door frame and then frowned. With dark circles under his eyes and deep lines around his mouth, he looked like roadkill. "Are you okay?"

"Just tired. SAR found a hiker's body two days ago. A woman."

"I heard." Poor Jake. She could hate him and still feel sorry for him. "Fell from the trail."

"No, honey, that's the problem—she didn't fall. Someone murdered her. And others over the last couple of years." He rubbed his eyes as if it helped the lack of sleep. "We've got a serial killer in the area, and it looks like he targets short, dark-haired women."

Kallie blinked. "Others? Nobody happened to notice there were little dead brunettes lying around?"

"Nobody put it together—thanks to a coroner who can't tell which side of the scalpel to cut with." He muttered under his breath, "Fucking incompetent bastard."

"But he finally figured it out?"

"No. The hotshot new coroner who replaced him did when she autopsied the last hiker." Virgil's mouth tightened.

"Too many of the contusions were the same size and—wrong somehow for a fall. Someone beat that woman to death with a heavy branch."

"Oh God."

"Yeah. The coroner started checking older records. And then she called the sheriff's department. And they alerted all the police departments in the area." He moved his shoulders as if to get the knots out. "I doubt anyone got any sleep last night."

"Surely even an incompetent coroner would have realized—"

"The murderer tosses the bodies off steep trails so it appears as if they fell."

"That's…ugly." A creepy feeling started in her spine and worked upward. *I'm short and dark-haired.*

"Yes." Virgil's gaze rested on her black hair, and he gave her a hard stare. "Until he's caught, you don't go anyplace in the forest alone."

She opened her mouth to protest, caught the determination in his gaze, and rethought. *Don't be stupid.* "Fine. Nothing's booked for me until next week anyway. Catch the bastard quick, okay?"

"We're trying, little bit. We're trying."

* * *

That evening, Jake drove his truck slowly into Bear Flat, trying to decide whether a bribe of chocolate would help sweeten Kallie's temper. Flowers wouldn't get him far with his macho sprite, but she'd had chocolate ice cream in her grocery basket a couple of weeks ago. He glanced at the dashboard clock. The grocery store kept tourist-season hours and would remain open for another hour or so. He turned toward downtown.

Whipple and the delivery guy stood talking on the boardwalk. The soda truck blocked the spot in front of the store. Jake U-turned, parked across the street in front of the police station, and stepped out of his pickup. Whipple did a double take and scowled. Jake snorted. If the grocer's glare were an M16, Jake's body would be spattered all over the concrete.

As he started across the street, he heard, "Hunt, hold up a minute." Masterson stood in the doorway of the station. "I need to talk with you."

The guy looked like he'd aged a decade in two days. I need to talk to your cousin, not you, Jake thought, but he didn't want to piss off Kallie's relatives more than they already were. "There a problem?"

"In a way. Let's walk." The cop wasn't in uniform, and as he started off down the boardwalk, he stuck his hands in his pockets.

"Spit it out, Masterson. I have things to do." Like getting some food to go with the ice cream. Having a picnic with Kallie. He hadn't eaten all day; had his sprite?

"Then listen up." Masterson started talking, and within five minutes, Jake's appetite disappeared completely. Their boots thudded on the wooden planks of the boardwalk as he tried to take it in. *A serial killer*? Around here? "He's been killing women—brunettes—for over two years?"

"Yeah. I warned Kallie to stay close to home."

At the thought of Kallie in danger, Jake
But she'd take precautions. Wouldn't she? He
ensure she did.

"If she—" He realized Masterson's eyes had filled with pity. *Pity*? "Spit it out, Masterson."

"We think your...friend...Mimi Cavanaugh, might have been one of the first."

The words floated past him and then rebounded, hitting him right in the gut. "Mimi." His voice went hoarse. "Murdered? She didn't kill herself?"

Virgil's attention turned to the street as they crossed to the other side. His jaw tensed for a moment. "Her death fits the pattern. I'm sorry, Jake."

Mimi. Soft brown eyes, high, light voice, so very sweet. Some bastard had hurt her? Rage welled up inside like a forest fire, and Jake fought it back. The sun burned his shoulders, but the sweat trickling down his back felt cold. "You got any suspects or leads or whatever?" *Someone to kill?*

"The sheriff's office is working the information and narrowing the list. It's pretty much a given that he'll be a single, white male who lives in the area. Since serial killers often begin with friends or family before escalating, they're looking at the earliest victims and their relationships."

Relationships. "You telling me that I'm a suspect?" No real surprise; cops didn't like the notion of BDSM. He stepped up onto the boardwalk on the other side of the street.

"How's it hanging, Hunt?" The old geezer who warmed

the bench by the feed store gave a token salute.

"Good enough," Jake answered.

Masterson nodded at the old man as they walked past, and continued, "No, you're off the suspect list. Last year there was a murder in early spring; you and Logan weren't even in the country. In fact, that one eliminated most of the seasonal workers."

"Seems like there'd be far too many suspects."

"God, yes." Virgil rubbed his face. "Our station is interviewing the ones around here. If we get any dings, we'll pitch it to the county detectives—or the FBI, who'll probably descend like a bunch of locusts."

"Ah-huh." Cops shared their territory about as well as schoolchildren with candy, and they sure didn't hand out information for fun. "What do you want from me?"

"Cynical bastard, aren't you?"

"Realistic."

"The chief needs to interview you about Mimi's death. What was going on, who was around...that sort of thing." The cop glanced across the street at his station. "He's got interviews lined up for most of today, but I figured knowing ahead of time might let you give it some thought first."

And would let him get over the shock of hearing about Mimi. A good notion. And he appreciated the news from someone who wasn't a stranger. "Got it. And thanks."

"No problem."

"Hi, boys." Mrs. Reed smiled, then resumed snipping dead blossoms off the yellow flowers in the half-barrel planter. She and Vanessa of Vanessa's Antiques kept the boardwalk barrels filled with blooms all summer.

"Mrs. Reed." Jake nodded, then stopped in front of the grocery. Should he still go see Kallie?

Masterson halted also, and the assessing gaze he gave the store startled Jake.

"You can't possibly believe Whipple is a killer."

The cop didn't answer.

"Why the hell would you think that?"

"He dated her before you. Apparently smacked her around?"

Jake nodded. Searching for a dom without knowing it, Mimi had confused violence with dominance. Jake had taught her that submission didn't have to involve getting the crap beat out of her. "He was pissed off when she broke up with him."

"He's been busted twice for drugs. Then again, he's only one of far too many possibles." Masterson shot him a dark look. "But when you're thinking back, try to remember anything your girlfriend said about Whipple."

"I'll do that." Nonetheless, he couldn't quite visualize the geeky Whipple in the role of murderer. As Masterson turned away, Jake grasped the knob of the grocery store and saw a CLOSED sign in the window. *Already*? He checked his watch. The place should stay open for another hour at least.

"He's closed," Mrs. Reed said, looking up from her flowers.

"I didn't think he ever shut down early."

Mrs. Reed pressed the dirt around a small plant. "Never happened before."

Whipple hadn't locked the door, so Jake stepped inside. Maybe he could grab some ice cream and leave a few bills on the counter. Most of the lights were off, and Jake paused to let his eyes adjust. Someone taller than Whipple was stocking the shelves at the far end with soft drinks.

The man straightened. "Store's closed."

A shaft of light tinted his hair red, and Jake recognized the delivery guy who supplied the lodge. "Hey, Secrist. Where's Whipple?"

"Dunno. He took off a bit ago like a cat with its tail on fire."

Masterson blotted out the light from the door as he came in. "Was there an emergency?" the cop asked.

"Naw. We'd been talking outside." Secrist hitched up his camo pants. "He was planning to visit his girlfriend after work. Said she was free or something. But all of a sudden, he goes, like, nuts. Shoves the paperwork in my hands and tells me to have Mrs. Reed lock up when I'm done."

A girlfriend? Jake's mouth tightened, remembering Whipple's arm around Kallie in the bar and his gloating expression when Jake said he'd be out of town.

And his fury when Jake returned to town.

A serial killer in the area. Whipple had dated Mimi too—had been obsessed with her. Jake spun on his heel and strode out of the store, knowing he'd jumped to unfounded conclusions. Whipple didn't have the guts to murder anyone.

So why didn't that loosen the knot in his chest?

* * *

As the evening sunlight slanted through the barn door and Mufasa sprawled in the clean straw, Kallie started cleaning stalls. Yeah, she was pooped, but the mindless work of mucking out felt good. Felt orderly as everything else in her life fell apart. She'd lost her not-quite-a-boyfriend. A murderer ran loose in the area.

A murderer. How strange. She tried to remember if anyone from Bear Flat had died on the trails, and an icy thought slid into her mind. Jake's girlfriend had committed suicide…by jumping off a cliff. They didn't know why. What if something else had occurred?

Would it make any difference to Jake?

She shook her head and flattened the hope. He was too much like Virgil, taking personal responsibility to whole new heights. Even if someone had murdered his Mimi, Jake would decide that was his fault too. For whatever reason. Kallie might as well face the fact that the man couldn't—wouldn't—move past his old girlfriend.

I'm not enough for him. That hurt. Needing something to hold, she gathered Mufasa into her arms. The hefty twenty pounds of soft fur and purring didn't fill the echoing space in the center of her chest, but it helped. *My cat loves me, and how pitiful can I get to need to know that?*

She slid down into the fresh straw, leaned back against a post, and cuddled the cat in her lap. "I'm tired," she whispered.

Mufasa's ears flickered.

"And I hurt." Everywhere. Her chest, like someone had wound rubber bands around it. Her stomach muscles, the muscles at the juncture of her thighs, her inner thigh muscles. Well, she knew why her lower half hurt, and she wasn't going to think about any of the reasons why, like the last time when he'd put his arm under her knee, pulling her leg up so he could get deeper and—

Damn him anyway. Her eyes prickled, and the lump weighing down her stomach grew heavier. She laid her cheek on Mufasa's furry head and gave an unhappy sigh. She'd given up on having a family love her, but was she asking too much to have a guy want her? Even if he didn't love her? Other women managed it... *why not me, dammit?*

She didn't find an answer—she never had.

Instead she stroked the cat and thought about Jake's reaction in the tent and how he'd so carefully avoided entanglements since his girlfriend. "Mufasa, I can't fight this one. Even if I hadn't blurted out...that...he'd still have dumped me sooner or later."

She'd gone into the affair with her eyes wide open—no one could say Jake had lied to her—but her feelings had changed. Jake had made it clear that he didn't want her love, and she wouldn't—couldn't—play up-and-down games with her emotions. She rubbed her chest. How many times could she survive being turned away by people she loved?

The sound of a vehicle's wheels on the gravel brought her head up. Jake? As Kallie's breath caught, Mufasa flowed out of her lap to stand in the doorway and peek out. Kallie pushed to her feet, heart pounding, and paused. *No, I'm done with him.* Even if Jake had come, she wasn't going to roll over like an idiot dog who'd love a person no matter how badly he treated it. She stopped beside Mufasa. "I'm no dog—I'm a cat. Kick me and I'll walk away, right, Mufasa?"

A furry head butted her leg in agreement.

She stepped out of the barn and saw a car, not a pickup. A man got out, and she recognized the sandy brown hair and stocky frame.

"Hey, David," she said unenthusiastically. "What brings you up the mountain? You making deliveries now?"

Without speaking, he walked over to her. His brown eyes looked...odd. "Kallie. I came to you when I saw..." His face darkened. "I closed the store early to come out here."

He never closed early. "Why?"

"I had a chat with Jake this morning."

Jake? Her back stiffened, and she resorted to the tone Aunt Penny employed with rude salespeople. "Excuse me?"

"You're not with him anymore, are you?"

"That's none of your business."

"Oh but it is." He gripped her shoulder with one hand, and gave her a shake. His mouth worked for a second like a landed trout's. "The bastard isn't right for you. You're too fine for him. No"—he shook her again—"it's us. We're meant to be together. You belong with me."

Was the man out of his flipping mind? "Listen, David, I'm flattered that you—"

"You can move in with me," he interrupted her, his words now tumbling out almost too fast to follow. "You shouldn't be living here with a bunch of men anyway, even if they are your cousins and"—the way his expression changed so quickly, from pleasure to anger, set her nerves to twanging—"I don't like that partnership with the Hunts at all."

"You're moving a little fast for me. We only dated twice." She tried to ease away, but he didn't let go.

"That's okay. We'll get to know each other real well." Again that shift, as if his emotions controlled him.

The flush in his face and the way his gaze lingered on her breasts sent alarm through her, and her skin chilled despite the evening's heat. Enough was enough. She didn't want to have to punch him, so she shoved his hand off her shoulder and took a step back. "I like you, David"— *and I'm rethinking that right now*—"but I'm not interested in having a new guy. Not any guy, really, for a long, long time. I just am not going to—"

"It's because of that bastard Hunt. Because he hurt you."

Hurt me? Ripped my heart right out of my chest. "I don't want to talk about it. Just—"

"He left town, you know." He reached for her, and she retreated again. "Yeah, got groceries for at least a week. He went fishing. Without you. He—"

As his words slashed at her, she stumbled back another step. The pain knotted her throat closed until the only words she could force out were: "Go *away*."

"Kallie, you need to stay away from Hunt. He hurt Mimi's heart too. My pretty, pretty Mimi."

Even as fear trickled up her spine, he grabbed her arm.

Chapter Eleven

By the time Jake hit the turnoff, his fingers had dented the steering wheel cover. He turned the truck onto the Masterson road without slowing, and gravel splatted across the foliage. Another car turned off right behind him—Masterson's police car.

As his pickup entered the graveled yard, Jake spotted the two figures by the barn. Whipple had Kallie by the arm. Rage welled up. So Whipple *was* the one. *Fucking murderer.*

His truck skidded to a stop right beside them, and Jake charged out the door. He grabbed Whipple by his shirtfront and shook him, then threw him across the yard. He started after him. "You bastard. If—"

Masterson got between them and slapped a hand on Jake's chest. "Ease up, Hunt. My job."

Jake stopped. The gravel seemed tinged with red as he rode the anger like a bucking horse, trying to get it under control.

Masterson yanked Whipple up. "What the hell were you doing, Whipple?"

Seeing the cop's hard grip on Whipple's arm, Jake turned to Kallie, looking her over carefully. Clothes intact, no bruises or cuts. "Are you all right, sugar? Did he hurt you?"

"No, of course not, and I sure didn't need your help." She stared as Virgil pushed Whipple into the cop car. "What the heck is going on?"

"Didn't your cousin tell you about the killer?"

Her face went white. "David?"

"Maybe. Looks like." Whipple might have murdered Mimi. Jake still couldn't get his mind around that, but the bastard had put his hands on Kallie, and that infuriated Jake all over again. "He could have killed you, dammit." He curled his fingers around her shoulders, needing to hold her.

She started to move forward into his arms, then wrenched away. "Back off."

"What?" *This morning. Our fight.* In his worry for her safety, he'd forgotten all about it. "Kalinda, I'm sorry. Let's go—"

"Stop." She retreated, looking at him as she had at Whipple. "I don't want to hear anything you have to say, and I don't want you near me."

The ground shifted underneath his feet at the ice in her voice and the pain in her eyes. Guilt swamped him. He'd worried about hurting a woman again, and yet he'd done exactly that. "Kallie—"

He heard the crunch of footsteps, and then Masterson shoved him away from Kallie. His voice sounded as cold as his cousin's. "You're leaving now, Hunt. Get in your truck."

"Kallie and I need to talk."

"No. You don't."

Jake paused, considered Masterson's determined stance, and gave up. Might take him, but fighting a cop—and Kallie's cousin—was a no-win situation. He tilted his head in acquiescence and took a step back.

Masterson's voice softened. "Little bit, are you all right?"

Jake heard the shuddering breath Kallie took and then the lie. "I'm fine."

"Hell, honey, I wish I could stay, but—"

"No, cuz." She glanced at Jake, and the lifeless look in her eyes cut like a blade through Jake's heart. "In fact, I won't be here. I'm going to head up the hill and sit by my stream."

The cop frowned. "I'd rather you stay put. We still—"

"I want out of here. Let me out!" Inside the cop car, Whipple banged his shoulder against the door.

"Go," Kallie said.

Masterson gave her a frustrated look and jerked his chin at Jake. "Move, Hunt. I'll meet you at the station."

"Kallie—"

"Go away, Jake. Just...go away." Her voice was flat—no anger, no warmth, no life.

* * *

The aching knot in her chest stayed with Kallie as she hooked a water bottle onto her always-ready-to-go backpack. It stayed as she patted Mufasa, as she checked the horses in the corral. Wyatt and Morgan would return around dark, so the animals would get fed. All she wanted was to escape.

The pressure eased a little as she moved up the trail. The

scent of pine surrounded her, and the hateful words she'd almost yelled at Jake faded into the quiet.

Up and up. Her breath came harder as her muscles strained against the steep climb. The effort of hiking around dead timber from the last storm, climbing over rocky outcroppings, and dodging low-hanging branches occupied her. Perhaps they should work on trail maintenance this summer. But no hurry. No need to keep a private trail groomed like the ones at Serenity Lodge.

Her mind fled from memories of the lodge as if she'd stepped on a yellow jacket nest. *Don't think of him.* Let it all wait until she reached her special place. If she started crying now, she wouldn't be able to see the path. *And just look what that bastard did to me—I don't cry, dammit.*

Reddish rays glinted through the trees as the sun hung over the western mountains. Sunset. It would be twilight when she arrived.

The thought of her peaceful sanctuary comforted her. Soon after she'd moved in with the Mastersons, Uncle Harvey had taken her up the mountain. He'd said each boy had selected a private campsite for their very own—a place to conquer their demons, their angers, their sorrows. He'd told her to find a spot for herself, saying she'd need a place to escape from a household of four butt-headed men. She smiled, remembering how he'd called them that. She'd used her forest sanctuary often those first few years.

There. White river rocks marked the turnoff to her spot. She paused on the ridge to catch her breath and let the breeze cool the sweat on her face. The trickling sound of her tiny stream called her. *My place.* In weary relief, she left the trail and headed to her sanctuary.

* * *

The bastard Masterson tailgated Jake all the way back to town, giving him no chance to turn around. So when they arrived in Bear Flat, Jake parked across the street in front of the grocery store behind Secrist's delivery truck, then walked over to the police station like a cooperative little citizen. Masterson nodded approval.

He waited until Masterson had hauled Whipple out of the back and had his hands full with the furious man. Then Jake turned and headed straight for his truck. He'd make Kallie listen to him whether—

"Hunt, hold up a minute," Masterson yelled. *Hell.* Jake checked his six for what had happened behind him. A uniformed officer marched Whipple into the station as Masterson strode across the street after Jake.

To hell with this. Kallie *wasn't* fine like she'd said. She shouldn't be alone. A few feet from his truck, he turned and faced the cop. "Either arrest me or back the hell off."

"No arrest, Hunt. I'm on break."

"And?" Jake glanced at the mountains, where the sun almost touched the peaks. He needed to leave.

"And this." The cop punched Jake so hard he staggered back.

Jake's jaw flared with pain. What the fuck? For one second, he stood, stunned; then fury poured through his veins. *Been a hell of a day. Didn't need this kind of shit.* He slammed into the cop and shot a fist right into his gut.

Jake caught a punch in return and blocked another. Stepping to one side, Jake almost tripped over stacked pallets of drinks and saw Secrist's shocked face. Poor delivery guy acted like he'd never seen a fistfight before. *Just watch, buddy. You'll see plenty.*

He caught Masterson with a punch hard enough to knock him back against the pickup. "What the hell is this about?"

"You fucking bastard." Masterson wiped blood off his chin. "I warned you not to hurt Kallie."

Oh, hell. When Jake faltered, Masterson nailed him with a short one to the ribs.

Fuck this. Jake struck before Masterson could retreat, belted him in the mouth, and followed with a gut shot that folded the cop in half.

As Masterson straightened and his fists came back up, Jake stepped out of reach. Kallie would probably beat the crap out of him if he put her cousin in the hospital. "I know I hurt her. Dammit, Masterson, I want to make it right." He scowled. "If I can get her to listen to me. Is your whole family pigheaded?"

"Yes." Masterson hadn't moved, still in fighting stance. "Make it right how?"

"Whatever it takes." Jake fingered his throbbing jaw. "Nice punch, you asshole. I love her, you know." The words slipped out and stunned him into silence. What the hell? Yet the undeniable rightness flooded through him—and then slammed him hard enough that he felt as if he'd taken a .44 Magnum in the chest. "Damn," he said, and the curse came out sounding like the wheeze of an old geezer.

Masterson huffed a laugh. "I bet that hurt more than my fists."

No shit. Jake slumped against the side of the pickup next to the cop. "It did, you bastard. And I figure I'll hurt a lot more before she's through."

"Hunt, she's going to rip you to mincemeat and leave you bleeding in the dirt." The cop appeared pretty damned happy about that.

Jake swiped the blood from his mouth. "Thanks a lot. Now if you'll let me—"

"Nope."

"What?"

"Sorry, but the chief wants to see you now." The cop nodded toward the station, then glanced up at the darkening sky. "Besides, Kallie might well spend the night in her special spot by the creek while she calls you every filthy name in her vocabulary. Best if you give her till morning to cool off."

Wait until morning? Far too long. Jake considered. He had a flashlight in the truck, and he'd hiked trails in the dark before. "You only have the one trail, right? Just to the west of your cabin?"

Masterson frowned and then nodded.

"How do I find this place?"

The cop crossed his arms over his chest. "You'll come and answer questions first."

"Deal."

"Her retreat is by a creek. About half a mile up the trail. Watch the left-hand side for her name marked in white stones. A tiny path leads downhill to the stream." Masterson frowned. "You know I still don't like your…hobby."

"Didn't ask your opinion." Jake rubbed his aching ribs. "If you want mine: anyone using the missionary position twice in a row should serve time."

Masterson choked on a laugh.

* * *

The bitch. He should never have let her live. Now see what had happened—her evil had spewed over two good men, two brothers, until they came to blows in the street. And Hunt planned to crawl back to her. Even after the men had left, the cop's words rang in his ears: "…*Leave you bleeding in the dirt.*"

His stomach heaved, and he fled into the store, barely making it to the small bathroom in the rear before everything spilled out of him. He vomited over and over, his stomach in knots. Fear slimed his skin. Had he taken in some of her evil?

Eventually the sickness passed. After, he wiped his mouth and used a paper towel to wash the sweat from his face. His hands shook as if he had Parkinson's like old Gus, and terror halted his breath. Was he dying now? Deliberately poisoned by demons so he couldn't complete his duty.

He couldn't let them win. He exhaled slowly, forcing calmness, and the trembling slowed. Poison hadn't caused his sickness then. He shook his head at his weakness that had let his past overwhelm him. Seeing the fight had brought it all back.

Ugly memories… Even after he realized everything was

her fault, that she was evil, he'd still crawled back to Gloria one last time—after so many times—and begged her to return to him. Crying, he'd touched her silky, black hair.

She'd laughed at him. Her dark eyes had flashed, filled with malice. Her voice had cut through him, tearing pieces of his soul away with each word. "*You're such a loser. You can't even get it up. Bug off and leave me alone.*"

She'd started to turn away as if he were nothing, and then...right then he'd seen his first demon. How it appeared in her eyes and reveled at his pain. His hand had risen—by itself, not under his control—and his fist had hit her over and over. The shrieks of the dying demon scraped across his ears until he thought he'd die from the pain. But when the evil had died, the silence had filled him with power until he felt invincible.

And he had been a man again.

With the memory of how he had hardened, how he had taken a man's due, strength flooded through him. The shaking disappeared. He examined his hands—big hands and strong, capable of doing what must be done. He rose to his feet.

Andrew wiped the sink and the toilet, leaving the bathroom clean and tidy. He closed the door. As he walked out into the gray twilight, he noticed the remainder of the pallets sitting on the boardwalk. He should finish his work here. But urgency pulsed like a drum within him.

He should never have left her alive, there on that deserted road. And because of his uncertainty, his weakness, she had destroyed a brother.

But she would be alone now...right now. Holed up in

her special area, she'd undoubtedly gloat over her victim, while evil surrounded her and covered the forests with filth. He couldn't wait; he needed to act now. That was his job.

He stepped around the stacks and got into his truck, turning on the headlights as darkness spilled down the mountain.

* * *

Jake had never visited the Bear Flat police station before, and he wasn't much impressed. The place appeared even smaller than the main room at Serenity. One puny-sized room with a table in the center and a couple of desks shoved into corners. Bulletin board, whiteboard for scheduling, phones everywhere. The chief of police had an office the size of an outhouse.

In there, Jake impatiently answered the questions put to him by Chief Jackson and Masterson. When had he seen Mimi last? Did she talk about Whipple?

Had she ever looked hurt?

"Only once," he answered the tall, gaunt chief. "When she broke up with Whipple, he smacked her around." Jake's jaw tensed as he remembered the bruises on her smooth skin, her swollen lip and black eye.

"Knowing you, I'm surprised you let that pass," Masterson said from his position by the door.

Jake kept his trap shut. Tell a cop that he'd beat the hell out of a local citizen? Nope.

Amusement glinted in Masterson's eyes.

"A couple more questions, Hunt, and I'll let you go,"

Jackson said. "When Mimi—"

"Chief." A cop who looked too young to even drive came in. "Sorry, Chief. Appears the only thing we can charge Whipple with is being coked up, and he even admitted that. Seems to think snorting cocaine helps him be more...assertive...with women." He grimaced in disgust and handed the captain two sets of papers. "Unfortunately he has a strong alibi for one of the murders."

The chief flipped through one set of papers, and his mouth flattened into a thin line. "Give him a warning—a serious one. And spring him."

As the cop left, leaving the door open behind him, Chief Jackson told Masterson, "He was best man at a college roommate's wedding. The family confirmed and faxed photos as well."

Masterson scowled. "He might have slipped out and done it, then gone back."

"The wedding happened in New York," Jackson said in a dry voice.

"Dammit!" Masterson slammed the wall with an open hand. He bowed his head for a second and then straightened. "All right. On to the next one."

"Hold up a minute." The chief scanned the other set of papers and frowned. "New information from the sheriff's department. Says they correlated information from the victim's families and friends." The chief pinched the bridge of his nose. "All the victims argued with a boyfriend or husband the day they disappeared. Nasty fights. In public."

"Wait a minute," Jake said. "You're saying the murderer

killed them because of a fight? With someone else?"

"Could be. Serial killers exist in a different reality, and they'll kill for the damnedest reasons." Chief Jackson tilted his head. "So, Hunt, did you ever fight with Mimi in public?"

"Never."

"I did." David Whipple appeared in the doorway. A sheen of sweat coated his pale face. He curled his hand around the door frame, and the knuckles turned white. "In my store. After she and Hunt broke up." Anger darkened his face, then disappeared as his eyes pooled with tears. "I wanted her back. I even begged."

Jake felt a moment of sympathy.

"She said no. She said she was moving to San Francisco. I yelled at her." Whipple wiped his sleeve over his eyes. "I called her a bitch. I never thought—"

"Who else was in the store, David?" Masterson asked softly. "Can you remember?"

Whipple leaned against the door, his balance obviously unsteady. "Yeah. I was embarrassed they'd heard me lose it. There were a couple of loggers. But I know them—they're gay."

The chief shook his head. "Probably not them. The victims were sexually violated after death."

The sickening information hit Jake like a battering ram to the chest. *Not Mimi.* Masterson's hand on his shoulder returned him to reality—a worse reality than before.

"Anyone else?" the chief asked Whipple.

"Those were the only men. A female firefighter. Mrs. Anderson. Samantha—she'd have been about ten." He frowned. "Oh, the soft-drink supplier—Andrew—was in the back, finishing a delivery."

Andrew Secrist? The air left Jake's lungs in an explosive gust. Secrist had watched him and Masterson fight. *A fight.*

He slammed out of the station so hard the door banged off the wall. Thudding footsteps sounded behind him. He skidded to a stop in front of the grocery, and Masterson halted beside him.

Even as fear blasted into Jake, he heard Masterson curse.

Under the dim glow of a streetlight, stacks of soft drinks still sat on the boardwalk. The delivery truck was gone.

Chapter Twelve

Unable to find any appetite, Kallie leaned against a log by her small fire. The low song of the wind in the high pine branches, the crackle of the burning wood, the gurgle of the stream comforted her—and yet increased her loneliness. She remembered other evenings when Jake's deep laugh had added to the wilderness melodies. Like two nights ago, they'd sat so close together that his shoulder had rubbed against hers as he fed another stick to the campfire. When she'd shivered from cold, he had pulled her closer, warming her with the heat of his body.

She tossed a pinecone into the flames and listened to the snapping sound as the seeds ignited, as all their potential burned to ash. Seemed about right.

Her heart ached like a torn muscle, and she had only herself to blame. Even knowing he wouldn't stay, she'd still gone ahead. Just like Serena's favorite chick flicks—the ones where the woman's friends had warned her and she still headed straight for disaster. Kallie had always wanted to slap the heroine upside the head and tell her not to be a total moron.

Moron, here.

At least she knew when to cut her losses. Even if he got

down on his knees and begged, she'd never have anything to do with him again. Not that he'd want her to. All he'd said earlier was, "*Kalinda, I'm sorry.*" Of course he was. Of course he felt bad for hurting her because, despite being a cowardly asshole, he was wonderful, caring, strong, smart, and...

With a snort of disgust, she wiped her eyes. Could she get any more maudlin? *Yes, it hurts. Get over it and move on.*

She picked up her whittling knife, pulled her current project out of her pack, and winced as she saw the carved figure of Jake. She should have taken time to find something else.

Well, maybe she'd just whittle a few pieces off him. But the thought gave her a pang. As she worked, the need to concentrate lent her peace. She carefully added the hair that hung over his face and hid his scar. Then an ear.

After she finished, she'd store it away and not look at it until she reached...oh, maybe seventy or so? Maybe someday the memories of how his hand cupped her face, how he'd nestle her against his side, how his rumbling voice sounded when he teased her and called her sprite... Maybe someday she'd manage to think of the past month as a wonderful time, without mourning that she'd not feel his touch or see him.

See him... *Oh no no no.* She'd have to see him with other women. Even her anger wasn't enough to overcome the way her stomach twisted with nausea at the thought. Oh hell, how would she ever endure that? What if he asked Gina or Serena out, and she had to hear every tidbit of what he did?

Her knife scraped down. Hard. Too hard, slicing the chin

right off the figure. Tears filled her eyes, and wasn't that stupid? As if she could hurt a wooden man.

As if she could ever hurt Jake.

"To hell with this." She flung the knife toward her pack. It landed point down in the dirt, the handle quivering. Aching inside, she tossed the wooden man into the fire.

The soft pine burned hot and fast.

Doubting that sleep would help, she pushed to her feet anyway. She hadn't bothered to bring a tent. No rain in the forecast, and this time of year, the dry forest held few bugs. She tossed her pad on the ground, unrolled and unzipped her sleeping bag, and crawled inside.

Her body felt slow, heavy. Probably PMS. She gave a bitter laugh. Because of Jake, she'd made an appointment with her doctor to get birth control pills. No need for them now. So hey, she'd found the bright side to all this; she could cancel the appointment and keep her legs out of the stirrups.

A crackle of something in the underbrush drew her attention. Probably a bear checking out the possible food situation. Poor sucker wouldn't find anything. Lacking any appetite, she'd already hung her small emergency stash from the wire that Uncle Harvey had put up years ago. She glanced at it, a small bag, black against the stars. Isolated in the night sky.

Like her. She pulled in a breath as grief pushed her down, its own kind of immutable force, like gravity. The rocky ground might feel like a feather mattress now, but around four a.m., her hips would register every lump. She tucked her hands behind her head. Tall pines speared into the night sky like dark arrows, and above them, stars filled the sky. Thousands and thousands of stars, millions...each with their own solar systems and planets.

Maybe other civilizations lived on those planets; other forms of life going on about their way. *And none of them would care that Jake Hunt broke my heart.* As she bit her lip to keep the tears at bay, she watched the stars and waited for the moon to rise.

* * *

Taking advantage of a straight section of road, Jake punched the Off button on his cell-phone speaker. He'd barely finished the call to Logan before the service gave out. The lodge was closer to the Masterson's than the town, so Logan should arrive right about when Jake and Masterson did. One more man for a total of three. A shame the other two Mastersons hadn't returned from their hike yet. He stepped on the gas to catch up with Masterson's car.

The curves started again, and the truck tires screeched as he took a corner too fast. His shoulder hit the door. They might need Logan's help if the shit hit the fan. *What kind of a police department has only four cops and a chief? And two of them elsewhere?*

Chief Jackson figured Secrist had panicked and fled, so one of the cops had headed for Secrist's house in the mountains east of town. Another went to set up a roadblock. Jake could see the logic in Jackson's actions. After all, Secrist had witnessed two men fighting, not a man and a woman. But he couldn't forget Jackson's words: "*Serial killers exist in a different reality, and they'll kill for the damnedest reasons.*" But neither Jake nor Masterson would take the chance that

Jackson was wrong. Secrist had taken off right after their fight. If he went after Kallie…

Please have run, you bastard.

Of course, cops from the Mariposa County sheriff's office were on the way…would get to Bear Flat eventually. Jake's teeth ground together. *Never a cop when you need one.*

And women were never where they should be. Kallie hadn't done it deliberately, but he'd yell at her anyway for scaring him twice today. Might make him feel better. *God, let her be alive. Safe.*

Illumined by the headlights, a deer leaped out of the forest in front of Masterson's car, and his brake lights flashed.

"Fuck!" Jake slammed on his brakes. As the cop car fishtailed, Jake fought his pickup out of the skid and then stomped on the gas again. Both vehicles surged forward, up the winding gravel road.

Concentrating only on the road, not on what could be happening…anywhere…Jake drove for what seemed forever as minutes and miles stretched into infinity. Finally the turnoff into the Masterson's dirt road appeared.

The dust from Logan's truck still hung in the air when Jake pulled up to the house behind the cop car.

Five minutes later, the three men hit the trail, flashlights flickering over stumps and branches. Masterson had his pistol. Logan had brought Thor. Jake was armed with sheer rage.

* * *

He loved the forest at night. As Andrew reached the

ridgeline, the breeze cooled his sweat-dampened skin and dissipated the poison lingering in the demon's wake. He waved his flashlight back and forth over the trail, checking the footing ahead, and studying the left side for white stones. Only a few minutes ago, he'd found his weapon in a mass of deadfall where the hefty limbs had been snapped off and scattered along the trail. One branch was the size of a baseball bat. After he'd cleaned it off, he had his cudgel—his instrument of punishment and death.

Death was the only solution. Once a demon infected a woman, it clung like a parasite until the host died.

He swung the branch now, checking the balance. Gave a nice whistling sound, felt heavy in his hand. The impact against her flesh would be satisfying. He glanced toward the east, where the moon had barely cleared the mountains. He would wait until it was high enough to give him light.

So he could watch her die.

* * *

Kallie'd started to drift off when a rustling noise pulled her awake, the tiniest of sounds, but only a fool disregarded anything in the wilderness. Part of her job included keeping her clients safe: seeing they returned from three a.m. bathroom breaks and checking they remained safely in their tents if a bear prowled through camp.

With a sigh, she rolled onto her side. Her fire had died down to sullen red coals, but the moon spilled silvery light across the clearing and sparkled on the stream. Near the trail, a shape moved in the shadows. From the size, a bear. Despite

Yosemite's policy of not feeding the wildlife, tourists inevitably did…or didn't get their food out of reach, so the animals frequently raided campsites.

As she unzipped her sleeping bag, she saw it lurch closer. Noisier than normal. She'd watched one bear steal a backpack from beside a camper's head without making more than a whisper of sound. This one crunched as if…

As if it wore boots. When the man stepped into the moonlight and hefted up a piece of wood the size of a baseball bat, terror spilled straight into Kallie's bloodstream, cold as a mountain glacier.

She tried to roll out of the sleeping bag, but it had tangled around her legs. As she frantically shoved at the bag, the man raised his weapon and stormed across the clearing.

Her legs wouldn't come free. *Oh God.*

He stood above her and brought the club down hard and fast.

She screamed.

His flashlight illuminating the trail, Jake ran, jumping tree trunks and brush that no one had bothered to remove. Next time pick a better-maintained trail, Kallie, he thought. God help him, please let there be a next time.

Thor ran ahead of them, his tail straight up, the white tip like a beacon. As the dog disappeared around a curve, Jake picked up the pace. He heard Logan's harsh breathing behind him, a grunt as Masterson miscalculated a step.

Not slowing, Jake flicked his flashlight upward and managed to spot the dog's dark fur against the black forest.

Next dog they got would damned well be white.

"Almost there," Masterson called, just loudly enough for Jake to hear. "Watch for her name."

Suddenly Thor disappeared. A whip of the flashlight revealed no dog. Turning, Jake swept his light along the side and paused at a bunch of scattered white stones that he'd disregarded. Not her name like Masterson had said. Jake sidestepped to keep Logan from plowing into him and asked, "Is this it, Masterson?"

"That's it, and he's here, dammit. Kallie would never mess up her stones. Where's the dog?"

Logan shone his flash downward. "There." Thor had already moved down the tiny animal path and stopped to wait.

Masterson said in a low voice, "It's not far."

Jake cocked his head, could hear the soft gurgle of water, and said reluctantly, "Take the lead." This was Masterson's territory.

The fear gripping his guts hadn't loosened. All the way up, he'd hoped the bastard had gone somewhere—anywhere—else tonight. An icy hand squeezed his spine. Every instinct yelled that the woman he loved—and he did, dammit—was in danger.

He had a second of thinking they should turn off their flashlights, and then a woman's scream of terror ripped through the quiet night.

Kallie frantically rolled. The club aimed at her head caught the edge of her shoulder and slammed into the bag with a muffled thud. Her shoulder flared with agony, and then she kicked free of the bag, scrambling away on hands and feet. From some instinct, she dodged left. The club grazed her thigh, a sharp slap of pain. *Go, go, go.*

She rolled, dodged one blow, shoved up.

Before she gained her feet, he struck her hip, knocking her sideways onto her back. Helpless.

"Beat the demon out of you."

Stunned by the pain, she stared up. Stocky, barrel chest. Red hair. "I know you," she gasped. "Andrew?"

Andrew attacked me? With a club? "*Someone beat that woman to death with a heavy branch.*" He's the killer. "Why…?"

"No! Don't talk!" he shouted and swung.

Roll! She heard the thud as he missed her again. He roared in frustration, and then his boot came down on her back and flattened her like roadkill. His weight was too much. Her hands scrabbled in the dirt. She futilely kicked her. He wouldn't miss, wouldn't miss…

As her muscles tensed, anticipating the blow, her hand bumped against something cold—metal. Her fingers closed around the handle of her whittling knife. She ripped it out of the ground and blindly swung up behind her back.

The impact hurt her wrist, and he screamed like an animal, the sound terrifying. She gripped tighter and yanked downward against the resistance of jeans and flesh.

He staggered sideways, and the weight lifted off her spine.

She shoved away, gained her feet, and darted for the

trees. Fast. Faster. Dodge left, right, left. Into the shadows.

Too dark. She tripped over a log and landed on her hands and knees. *Stop.* He'd track her by the noise she made. Hunkering down behind a patch of brush, she tried to silence her gasping breath. Her heart hammered so hard she couldn't hear anything past the pounding of her pulse.

An outraged bellow ripped through the night. Beyond the trees, sparks flickered upward like fireworks. He was taking his frustration out on her camp, she realized.

Then his footsteps headed straight for where she'd entered the forest. "Come out, demon." An eerie note tinged his voice. He didn't sound like the delivery man she'd met. He didn't sound entirely human. Or sane.

Light flickered through the trees. *Oh God.* He had a flashlight, and the full moon had risen. She couldn't hide long in the too-open forest. *I can fight him.* But if he caught her squarely with that club, she'd never get back up. *Hide. Fight if I have to.*

An explosion of crackles and a curse broke through the silence. She realized he was hitting the underbrush at the edge of the clearing…and working his way closer.

She shoved her hand against her mouth and bit down to muffle her breathing.

Barking came from the clearing, and Kallie's head jerked up. A dog? Help?

Andrew stopped. His footsteps retreated. "Demon dog. Hellhound," the unnatural voice called.

A growl ripped through the silence, and the killer yelled. A yelp. *Oh, God, the dog.*

Kallie almost stood up, then forced herself down. Jumped back up at a shout—Virgil's voice, "Put it do—"

Another yelp and a grunt. The roar of a monster, sick with delight.

No! Terror filled her, and she ran, bursting from the protection of the forest into the clearing and straight into a nightmare.

Virgil on his back, unmoving. Andrew on one knee beside her cousin, holding her whittling knife up with his head cocked as if he'd never seen a blade before. He spotted her and laid the edge across Virgil's throat.

Kallie stopped so suddenly she almost fell.

Virgil lay terrifyingly still. Blood streaked his head, almost black in the moonlight.

No, please God…not Virgil. Don't touch Virgil. "Andrew!"

Andrew turned slightly, his eyes unfocused, the knife still there…

The blade filled her vision as it lay against her cousin's neck. She had to get the monster away from him. *Beg*? Her thoughts came too slowly; why couldn't she *think*? Every inadequate breath seared her throat. She stepped a little closer. *Think, Kallie, think.*

Begging won't work. He'd killed women—lots of women. They'd probably begged too.

Make him mad? But if he hurt Virg instead of her? Her stomach knotted with fear.

Lure him away from Virg? Yes. Give him something better. Her hands fisted. "Hey, Andrew. You wanted me, right? Female?"

He turned a little farther.

"Yeah. Me." *Dammit, move, you bastard.* "Hey, I've even got dark hair. Isn't that why you wanted me?" She shook her head and ruffled her hair mockingly.

She stood close enough to see the way his eyes changed, and the wrongness in them raised the hair on the back of her neck. She forced her feet to stay in place, fought against the need to run. *Get him away from Virg.*

Andrew didn't move. *Why isn't he coming after me?*

Near the trail, Logan stepped out of the forest. "Let Virgil go, Andrew. Let him go, and we'll let you leave."

"No." Andrew's mouth flattened, and he looked down at Virg.

No, don't look at him, don't pay attention to him. "Andrew, why? Why are—"

"Don't speak to me, demon!" Andrew shook his head, and rather than letting go, he wrapped his hand in Virgil's sandy hair, ensuring the knife would stay put. "I have your claw. I can kill your servant."

Kallie's heart missed a beat. *I made it worse.*

Andrew watched a river of black spill from the black-haired female, filling the clearing. He must kill her and get away before the poison entered his veins, penetrated his mind. When she died, her blood would sink into the earth, taking the evil with it—scorching the ground horribly, but the forest would eventually heal, unlike his brother, whom she'd ruined.

He must destroy her. He judged the distance. She could move fast; he'd seen that. She might run into the forest and escape him.

His leg burned like fire. The demon's claw had ripped through his flesh, and he knew, knew at this point, he had nothing to live for. The mark she'd put on him would slowly take over his skin, his muscles, even his bones, blackening his body like a burned corpse even while he lived, and then would steal his bright soul with it. Tears spilled from his eyes. *Destroy her.*

"Come closer," he gritted out.

She shook her head. "Come and get me. Leave him, and come for the one you wanted."

Kill him first.

"No!"

The man's shout rang through night, and Andrew jerked…realized he'd spoken aloud. The darkness had lured his mind into confusion. Time was running short.

Logan stepped farther into the clearing. "Put the knife down, Andrew, and you can go. If you hurt him, I'll rip you to pieces."

If he died now, with her foulness inside him, he would descend to the depths, screaming in agony, his mission unfinished. The stench of her filled his nostrils until he gagged. No hope, no—he pressed and watched the claw cut into her minion's throat. A trickle of blood, black as her heart, ran down to burn its way into the innocent earth.

She made a sound, and he looked up, hope scrabbling to the surface of his mind. Tears streamed from her dark eyes, and he knew he had the key. If she died first, her evil would wash out of his body. He could still die, but his soul would escape the black abyss of hell.

She took a step closer. No. A demon might care for her slave, but not enough, never enough. "You're trying to trick me." His words slurred, his tongue stumbling. The blackness surged through him in waves.

"No trick. I'm right here," she said. He blinked, bringing her back into focus. She'd moved closer, clawed hands in front of her. Empty. Pleading—with him.

"No, Kallie!" her other servant shouted.

Chapter Thirteen

"Oh please," Kallie whispered, to Andrew, to God, to whoever might help. She could barely see through the tears in her eyes but couldn't miss the widening red spilling down Virgil's neck. If the monster pressed harder, he'd hit the artery and…

He muttered something about demons and slaves. A sacrifice.

But he wanted her, not Virgil. "Andrew, take me."

Andrew's head jerked up. He stared around him, horror filling his face as if he saw something other than the clearing. His gaze finally came to her. "Demon, don't speak to me. Demons don't die. Cling to life."

"I don't." She took a step closer. "There's nothing for me here. No one. You can kill me, and they'll be sad for a minute and then move on."

"Your lover won't." His fist clenched, and the knife moved an infinitesimal amount.

Her heart hammered frantically. "He left me." Andrew's muscles slackened as Kallie edged closer. "He won't care—I wasn't who he wanted." The hurt of that must have entered her voice, for the knife moved, a half inch…an inch…from Virgil's throat. "I don't belong anywhere." Just two steps out of Andrew's reach, she dropped to her knees.

"Dammit, Kallie," Logan shouted, panic in his voice. She glanced at him. Too far away to help her, but when the monster attacked, Logan could save Virgil. Fair trade, her mind and heart said, though her hands shook, everything inside her shook, every nerve screamed, *Run!*

Doubt showed in Andrew's face. He glanced at Virgil, then at her.

Almost, almost. Bowing her head was the hardest thing she'd ever done.

She saw the knife drop into the dirt, and jerked her eyes up as, in one move, he grabbed the club. As the weapon swung up, Kallie lifted her arms to cover her head, even knowing her bones would break like dry twigs.

Something hit Andrew from the side, knocking him away. She felt the wind, the swish as the heavy branch whipped past her face. The shock—she was still braced for pain—stunned her. *I'm alive?*

She stared at the struggling men and panicked. *Nooo, not Jake.* Her Jake against that monster? She scrambled to her feet, snatched up the knife, and—Logan grabbed her, dragging her across the clearing and away from the fighting. He locked his arm around her when she tried to get free.

"Let me go!" She fought him, yelled at him. Logan's hold didn't loosen.

She saw the club come up and swing down brutally, and she moaned, cringing in anticipation of seeing—Jake dodged, but the weapon hit his shoulder in a glancing blow. Jake stumbled back, and Andrew swung, and again Jake dodged.

He stepped in quickly and punched Andrew hard in the face.

Andrew staggered and recovered too quickly, forcing Jake to evade the backswing.

"Fuck, Jake's screwed. Secrist is madman strong." Logan charged across the clearing as Andrew swung again.

"No no no." Kallie threw her knife.

It hit Andrew in the back, too small to do any good, but Andrew screamed as if it had impaled him. His arms spread wide.

Jake stepped in and kicked, his boot hitting the monster's bloody leg. Andrew shrieked and stumbled forward.

Jake ripped the heavy branch away. Holding it in two hands, he spun around like a discus thrower. One turn and then the club smashed into the monster's head with a crunching sound that Kallie would never, ever forget.

Andrew catapulted back with the complete flaccidness of the dead, even before he hit the ground.

Chest heaving, Jake stood over him. Logan stepped beside him and set his hand on his brother's shoulder.

Kallie stared at Jake. *Alive.* Blood streaked his face, gleaming wet and dark in the silvered light. His shirt gaped open from a long rip across the shoulder. When he moved, he limped. But he was all right. *Thank you, thank you, God.*

After one last reassuring look, she dropped to her knees beside Virgil. Relief flooded through her as he groaned and struggled to a sitting position. He held one hand across his ribs. "What the hell did he hit me with?"

"Something Goliath might carry," she said, laughing—

she thought she was laughing, but tears blurred her vision. "You asshole, he might have killed you." She ripped a sleeve from her shirt and pressed the fabric against his neck. But the cut had almost stopped bleeding.

Virgil touched his forehead and winced. "Good thing he didn't get in a solid hit." Then he grabbed her shoulder and shook her hard. "I heard you. What the hell were you thinking? He—" He choked and muffled the rest of his increasingly foul curses.

He was definitely alive. Her vision blurred again as she smiled at him. A second later, she felt a soft touch on her head and looked up, but Jake had already moved away. He walked over to where his brother knelt in the grass.

Logan glanced up. "Considering your lack of grace, that was a nice job of getting up close and behind him."

"He wasn't paying attention to anything except his *sacrifice*." Jake shot Kallie a furious look that made her wince, then bent down. "How is he?"

A whine. Kallie's heart clenched as Thor struggled to his feet. The yelps she'd heard…

Logan ran his hands over the dog's body. "Gonna be sore, but doesn't feel like anything's busted." His voice roughened with anger. "Why the hell didn't you shoot the bastard, Masterson? You drop your weapon or something?"

"Or something. He threw your damned dog at me. That's a fucking heavy dog, Hunt. He knocked me on my ass." Virg snorted in disgust. "I should have shot through it. Couldn't."

Silence. Logan's hand paused on the dog's fur, and then he sighed. "It's hard to fault you for that. Thanks for not killing him."

"No problem." Virg looked over toward Andrew's body, and his mouth thinned. "Worked out. Good job there, Jake."

Jake grunted acknowledgement—*why do men do that?*—and glanced at Kallie. "I had help. Nice throw."

She stared at him and couldn't think of a thing to answer, not with the memory of the club swinging for him.

Jake knelt beside the dog. "Stupid beast. Learn to dodge better." His arms around the whining dog belied the cold words. The wagging tale said Thor knew better than Kallie did how a man expressed his love.

Hell, her eyes had blurred again. Had she gotten struck on the head?

With a few more curses and still holding the ribs on his left side, Virgil struggled to his feet. "It's going to hurt like hell to laugh for a few days," he muttered. "You tell any jokes, little bit, and I'm going to thump you."

Yeah, he was all right. The surge of relief made her dizzy. "So, cuz, what did the prostitute say to the priest?"

He barked a laugh and groaned, then pushed her over with his foot.

Right onto her aching hip. Her yelp of pain sounded like Thor's.

Not a second later, Jake shoved her cousin to one side. "Bastard, she's hurt," he growled and knelt beside her. "Let's see the damage, sugar."

With those words, the same words he'd used in the ClaimJumper so long, long ago, her defenses shredded, and a sob ripped out of her.

He wrapped his arms around her and pulled her against his chest, and she knew—no matter how many other civilizations thrived out there among the stars—his embrace was the safest, warmest place in the universe.

Dammit. Jake had tried to stay away and let Virgil care for her. She trusted her cousin. Not Jake. Not anymore. He'd have to regain her trust somehow, but right now she didn't need any more emotional upsets.

He really had tried to stay away. But now, as she clung to him, he knew he'd break Virgil's face before he let her go.

"Is she…? Kallie, I didn't mean…" Virgil bent and touched her shoulder. "Come here, little bit. Let me check you—"

"She's mine," Jake snapped, then amended, "I mean, she'll be all right."

A corner of Virgil's mouth turned up. "Got it." He straightened, hunted and found his pistol in the grass, then walked over to check Secrist's body.

Jake returned his attention to what was important in his world. "Shhh," he murmured, her sobs hitting him harder than the cudgel had. He gathered her closer, so tiny and so brave. She'd terrified him, walking out of the forest to plant herself in front of a murderer twice her size. His little Toto, growling and never backing down. How could a man feel so much pride and fear all at once?

"Don't ever do that again," he murmured and rested his cheek on top of her head.

She cried a little longer, and then—all too soon, in his

opinion—shut down her tears. Macho sprite. But she couldn't stop the shivers racking her fragile bones.

Virgil had kept an eye on Kallie, and when she sat up and wiped her face, he walked back across the clearing. "I don't think I've ever heard her cry before," he muttered to Jake, his face strained with more than pain.

Jake understood completely. She needed to cry, but each sob had stabbed through him like a knife.

Virgil offered Jake a hand. "Let's get out of here. I'll send a team up for the body."

The narrow trail demanded they walk single file, and silence reigned on the way down the mountain, except for the occasional curse when the bad footing jarred an injury. In an emotionless fog, Kallie marked that Jake swore less than the others, probably because of her presence. Virgil groaned more. Logan was the only uninjured one, she thought, until she realized he limped as badly as Jake.

"Logan, how'd you get hurt?" she asked, her voice startling her.

Logan glanced back at her and huffed a laugh. "In case you haven't noticed, my brother has the grace of a hippopotamus on drugs. He tripped over a log right in front of me, and I piled into him. Wrenched my knee. Then we had to untangle, find the flashlights, and locate the trail again. It's why we didn't all get there together."

"Well, bro, if you hadn't been trying to run up my ass, you'd have had time to stop." As he'd done all the way down, Jake turned to help her over a log, and she took comfort from each time his warm hand closed over her cold one.

A few minutes later, a couple of deputies rushing up the trail barreled into Virgil, and after some discussion, turned around and accompanied the group back down.

By the time they reached the edge of the forest, Kallie felt as if she had five pounds of mud dragging down each boot. Jake put his arm around her, and she gratefully sagged against him.

They stepped out into a world of flashing lights and noise. A short distance away, two officers blocked Wyatt and Morgan from the trail, and her cousins sounded ready to explode.

Thor gave a sharp bark, attracting everyone's attention, and within a second, far too many people converged on them. To Kallie's relief, Virgil pulled his brothers and the cops off to one side, leaving her with Jake and Logan.

Logan stopped in the center of the gravel yard, and Thor waited beside him, tail drooping in exhaustion. "You heading back now, Jake?"

Stay here. Please. Kallie took a breath and released it slowly, then tried to move away. *He should go. Don't start this all over again.*

Jake tightened his arm around her. "Thanks, but no. I have a few problems to deal with here."

Logan's gaze dropped to her, and after a moment, he glanced at Jake. "Understood. Call if you need anything."

"Thanks, bro." Jake's voice softened. "Seriously."

Logan lifted a hand. "Part of the brotherly job description." He touched her hair gently. "Night, sugar."

"Good night, Logan," Kallie managed. "Thank you."

She bent to stroke Thor's soft fur and whisper, "Thank you, Thor." He licked her cheek. Logan stopped to speak to Virgil briefly; then he and Thor climbed into his vehicle.

As the sound of Logan's truck faded, Virgil left the police and walked over. "You're free to go, Jake, but you'll need to come in to the station tomorrow to give a statement."

"I appreciate the reprieve, but I'm not leaving yet. I'll help Kallie shower, and then—"

Kallie's mouth dropped open even as Virg's brows lowered, and he said, "Not going to happen."

"Which one of you men will help her?" Jake glanced down at her. "I've seen her naked before, you know."

Kallie stiffened. "Jake, dammit."

Red stained Virgil's face, and he ran his hand through his hair. "Hell. Fine."

"Afterward, I'd appreciate if you could get everyone into the living room."

"For what, exactly?" Virg asked sarcastically.

"We're going to discuss some misguided perceptions and sacrificial lambs."

Kallie had lost track of the conversation as she tried to keep her legs from buckling.

Virgil said slowly, "I didn't like that either. But"—he glanced over at the other cops—"later?"

"Right now. At this time, we might be able to get through. Maybe. Not later."

"What are you two talking about?" Kallie asked, locking

her knees.

Virgil didn't answer. He studied her for a second. "I can take some time if I make a quick report to the chief. I'll leave clean clothes for you outside Kallie's door, and we'll see you downstairs."

"Good." When Jake turned Kallie toward the house, she stumbled. With a huff of laughter, he scooped her into his arms. "You're exhausted, sprite. Where's your room?"

You have to let him go. "I can get there myself."

"Nope."

As Jake hauled her across the yard, she saw Virgil intercept Wyatt and Morgan before they could get to her.

Despite his limp, Jake carried her all the way up the stairs. After setting her on her feet, he flipped on the lights in her bedroom and looked around.

She sighed. She'd left her new red underwear on the dark blue carpet, flannel shirts tossed over the desk chair, a stack of books beside the bed. In one corner, a table held her carving tools and projects...and shavings circled the area like snow. Martha Stewart would cringe. "Sorry about the mess."

"As long as the bed fits us both, I'm happy."

The thought of not being alone... She leaned her forehead against his chest. "Thank you. For staying."

He shook his head. "No thanks needed, but we definitely have some talking to do. For now, let's clean up."

"I shower alone." She caught the amusement in his eyes and glared at him.

"Uh-uh, little sub," he murmured. He pulled her against him, careful but firm. "Are you allowed to glare at your dom?"

My dom? A curl of warmth eased the cold inside her. "You're not my dom."

As if she hadn't spoken, he brushed his lips across hers. "Shower, sprite," he whispered.

In her bathroom, he looked around slowly. "Nice."

"The guys remodeled it when I was fourteen." She'd lived with them for only six months and had expected them to send her away at any time. But when her history class had gone on a three-day field trip, she'd returned to find it like this. Pale blue floral wallpaper, dark blue countertop, amazing lighting. A walk-in shower with delicate flowers decorating the tile. An oversize tub. A very feminine bathroom—they'd done it just for her. Like she was going to stay. When the four big men had beamed at her, she'd almost cried.

Over the years, she'd changed very little. In this one place, she could believe she was a woman, not one of the boys.

"It suits you, sweetheart," Jake said and efficiently divested her of her dirty, bloody clothing.

He opened the smoky glass shower door and turned on the water. Steam rose in the cool air. Jake stripped and stepped into the shower with her, never letting go of her arm.

As the spray hit her, she sighed. So warm.

Jake washed her carefully, his big hands gentle on her scrapes and sore spots. He growled at the undoubtedly huge bruise in the center of her back. She remembered the feel of

Andrew's boot, his weight on her, and cringed.

"Shhh, Kalinda, it's over." He moved on, washing thoroughly, not turning it into anything sexual, then washed her hair. Afterward he scrubbed himself down, and the fragrance of her herbal soap mingled with his masculine scent.

He dried her as carefully as he'd washed her.

"I can do it myself," she protested. "I live here, so I should be taking care of you." She tried to take the towel.

"Not this time. Your turn will come."

Ignoring her protests, he tucked her into her heavy terrycloth bathrobe and ran a finger down her cheek. "It pleases me to care for you, sprite. I came too close to losing you." His eyes darkened, and he pulled her into his arms, squeezing the breath from her. "God, that was too close."

When he released her, she clung for a moment, then pushed away and stood on her own. If only she didn't feel so damn tired. And shaky. *I need to call Rebecca and request some big-girl panties.*

Jake retrieved the black sweatpants and T-shirt that Virgil had left at her door and dressed quickly. Ignoring her objections, he scooped her up again to carry her downstairs.

She seemed to weigh nothing in his embrace and felt almost fragile. Precious. Every time he remembered how she'd knelt and offered herself to save Virgil, his anger flared, and he wanted to kill the bastard again.

The living room was empty, the silence broken only by the faint noise of people in the kitchen and the ticking of a mantel clock. After glancing around, he chose an oversize chair and then settled Kallie on his lap so she could lean against his chest.

Morgan must have heard them. He crossed the room to yell out the front door for his brother, and a minute later, Virgil came in, filthy and exhausted.

From the kitchen, Wyatt brought mugs of hot chocolate. Jake took one and set it on the adjacent table, then accepted the other and sipped to check the temperature. Just right and liberally laced with Baileys Irish Cream.

"Here you go, sprite," he said, letting her curl her fingers around the mug but keeping a grip when her hands trembled. She closed her eyes as she sipped, and her long eyelashes made a dark smudge against her pale cheeks. His heart contracted. He wanted to take her upstairs and simply hold her.

But he was also her dom, whether she'd accepted it or not. Much like intense BDSM scenes, painful, frightening events could uncover tears in the soul. Somewhere, something in her past had convinced her that she didn't belong anywhere—that no one loved her—although anyone seeing her family knew different.

Tomorrow he and her cousins might tell her how they felt, but her heart would be guarded again. Tonight, perhaps, they had a chance of getting through. Perhaps.

He felt like he was setting out poorly equipped for a mission. To try to mend such a long-held belief? He had half a mind to wait and push her into seeing a counselor. Yet was there ever a wrong time to hear you were loved?

Virgil had chosen the couch, Morgan a chair. Muttering

under his breath, Wyatt dropped into another chair and scowled at Jake. He obviously didn't like seeing Kallie in Jake's arms or the way he'd assumed control. "Listen, Hunt, this—"

"Shut. Up." Jake shot him an even look. "Up on the mountain, Kallie told Secrist it wouldn't matter if she died, that she'd never belonged anywhere." He took her cocoa and set it on the adjacent table.

Wyatt's mouth opened. Then his brows drew together. He exchanged a dismayed look with Morgan. "But—"

This time Wyatt stopped when Jake frowned.

Jake looked down at Kallie. Exhausted, fading in and out, although light tremors still shook her body. Her exhaustion had caught up. "Sprite."

She opened her eyes slowly, her gaze not quite focused. "Uh-huh?"

"Tell me where you went after you left your stepfather."

"Now? But—"

"Don't think; just tell me." To better evaluate her responses, he slid his hand between the buttons of her robe. With his palm on her upper abdomen and fingertips between her small breasts, he could feel her relaxed stomach muscles and slow heartbeat.

"I went to live with Aunt Penny."

"Why'd you leave?"

Every muscle under his hand tensed, and the hurt that gathered in her eyes tore at his heart. She shrugged. "She sent me to Teresa—got tired of me, I guess."

"What? No," Morgan said loudly enough to make her

startle. Her cousin jumped to his feet. "No, that's not true." Moving closer, he stared at her. "Jesus, Kallie, didn't anyone tell you? She was terrified Charles would hurt you."

Kallie blinked and frowned up at Morgan, unable to understand what he meant. "Charles never hurt..." Well, maybe her big cousin had slapped her once because she'd spilled her milk. "But why?"

"He's bipolar. Hell, right after you left, he beat up a kid at school so bad the kid went to the hospital. Penny said he'd just...lose it sometimes."

Bipolar? Kallie tried to think, but her thoughts tangled as if caught in underbrush. Charlie was bipolar? He'd been a teenager. Maybe he'd gotten a little...weird. Lost his temper. Threw things, usually at her. "I thought he didn't like me. I was so clumsy."

"No," Wyatt burst out.

Morgan shot him a silencing glare, then took her hand. "Kallie, he cried when you left. He'd refused to admit anything was wrong, and so had Penny. But then he hit you..." His lips pressed together. "Yeah, well, he got a psych doctor who figured out what was wrong and put him on medication. Aunt Penny bawled for—hell, forever—at losing you. But she had to work and couldn't trust Charlie to watch you after school. Not when he was so messed up."

Oh. "I didn't know," she whispered. Aunt Penny hadn't wanted her to go? Charlie had cried because she'd left? In her head, the murky picture of her aunt with a cold, hard face and her angry cousin lightened and changed until tears filled their eyes. Sadness. *Oh.*

Morgan squeezed her hand. "Let me tell you—"

"Later," Jake said, silencing her cousin. "She'll want more later. Right now, I want to hear about—"

"Who the hell do you think you are, Hunt?" Wyatt snapped, not Virgil, who she'd thought would object first. "And get your hands off her."

Kallie suddenly realized Jake had his hand flattened on her stomach, his fingers between her breasts. She shook her head at him.

He didn't move. His eyes never left hers, intent, so very blue. "I'm the man who fought a killer for her."

Her mind replayed the way he'd come out of nowhere to slam into Andrew—he could have died. She started to shake again. He shifted, holding her closer, with his hand still warm on her bare skin. She tried to push at it.

"Uh-uh, sprite," he said softly, and she gave up, too lost in the warmth of his gaze to argue.

"So," he said, his voice as easy as if they'd simply gotten together for a beer at the ClaimJumper. "After Penny, who'd you live with?"

Why did he keep asking about her past? She frowned, trying to understand why he was—

His chin rose, and his eyes hardened. His voice deepened, "You will answer me. Now."

Wyatt made an angry sound even as her words spilled out. "I went to Aunt Teresa and Uncle Pete."

"Good place?" he asked, his fingers rubbing her cheek for a moment before dropping back down to lie as warm as a blanket on her chest.

She remembered the sound of children laughing, bickering, Aunt T singing as she cooked. Pete coming home from work, roaring, "*Who has a kiss for an old man*?" Her lips curved for a second. "Yes. I loved it there."

"So what happened? Why didn't you stay?"

The hurt slammed into her like a car wreck. She tried to sit up, and the hand on her chest held her down, keeping her still. She shoved at it again. "I don't—"

"Go on, sprite. Tell me."

"They moved." She pressed her lips together as she remembered how Teresa had put her on the plane. Hugged her. Just a vacation, she'd thought. "They sent me here and didn't want me back in the new place."

"That would hurt," Jake said softly. "How come?"

The comforting tone in his voice did her in, and her eyes filled. "I don't know," she whispered. "I don't know what I did wrong. Nobody ever lo—" But no, Aunt Penny had loved her. Morgan said so. She'd cried. Kallie blinked, confused.

And Wyatt exploded. "Son of a fucking bitch. Didn't Pa ever talk to you?" He stomped over—her grumbly cousin—and glared down at her. "Pete lost his job, dammit." He inhaled slowly, and the anger faded from his face. "Cuz, he got laid off, and they had four kids and you. They couldn't pay the mortgage and had to move in with his sister. Two families in a one-bedroom apartment. On food stamps. Pa tried to give them money, but you know Uncle Pete, a real hard-ass about being a man."

Kallie stared up at him as he shoved his hands through his hair. "They had a fight with Pa over the phone. They didn't want to let you go, but it sounded like they were going to end up on the streets. Pa was yelling that he'd be damned if he'd let his niece starve."

She hadn't done anything wrong? *It wasn't me*? Her lungs constricted until she couldn't get any air. Wheezing, she grabbed Jake's hand and heard him curse. He sat her up, an arm around her waist.

"Breathe, Kalinda. Pull it in. Slower." His deep voice held her, made her listen, and there was air again, though her insides felt...wrong. Like her chest had filled with broken fragments and nothing lined up right inside.

She still gripped his hand so rigidly her knuckles hurt.

"No, don't let go." He kept her fingers in his, so strong. "Take another breath. Bad day—I'm not surprised you got a panic attack." His easy laugh reassured her more than anything else could, and she sagged back against him. And looked up to see her terrified cousins crowding around her.

Wyatt broke first. "Jesus, fuck. Don't—don't ever scare me like that again." He dropped to his knees and set his big hand on her leg. The muscles in his face were drawn. "Dammit, Kallie."

"I didn't...didn't know." She tried to smile. "I thought Teresa made Uncle Harvey take me. And you had to put up with me because he told you to."

"No wonder you were such a mouse when you got here." Virgil was on his knees now too, his face strained. "We wanted you, Kallie."

Morgan's laugh sounded more like a croak. "When Pete got a job, they tried to get you back, but you were ours."

"Pa said not to tell you about how he and Teresa had stopped talking. He said you had such a soft heart that you'd feel bad having people fighting over you." Virgil touched her cheek gently. "God, little bit, don't you know how much we love you?"

In her chest, the splinters slowly merged, pulling together into a lumpy but complete whole. "I-I..." Her lips started to quiver.

"Hell, cuz," Morgan said, his voice ragged, "the only fighting in our family has been because everyone wanted to keep you."

"Teresa finally forgave Pa when you graduated, but..." Virgil's brows drew together. "Is that why you never visited them on your vacations? You didn't think they wanted you?"

She nodded, her throat too clogged to speak.

Wyatt choked out a laugh. "Well, stupid, I guess you've got a lot of visiting to do."

They loved me. Everybody loved me. She couldn't—couldn't—A sob wrenched out of her, and she only had a second to see the horror crossing her cousins' faces before Jake turned her, holding her like a baby to cry against his strong shoulder.

"There we go, sweetheart," he murmured. "I've got you. Get it all out now, sugar."

Her chest hurt with each horrible cry, one for each year she'd felt alone. Unloved. Abandoned.

Wanted. They'd wanted her. Teresa and Pete and Penny and Charlie. Harvey and Virgil and Morgan and Wyatt. All of them. As her tears slowed, she realized one of Jake's big hands cradled her head against him; the other stroked her shoulders.

God, she loved him. She raised her head and bit the words back just in time. Hadn't she learned anything?

The pang that shot through her hurt all the more because she felt whole.

* * *

After tucking Kallie into her bed, Jake had gone downstairs and talked to the brothers, suggesting counseling to help her integrate everything that had happened, from murder to family. He remembered how Logan had benefited from help, although they couldn't perform miracles—especially with someone as mulishly stubborn as his brother.

Still shaken, the Mastersons agreed. While they were acting so agreeable, he considered pushing his claim to be part of Kallie's life and decided he shouldn't kick a man when he was down.

Not that they had time for a fight. The cops claimed Virgil, although before he left, he made an appointment for Jake and Logan to come in to the station for interviews. Outside the house, cops milled everywhere like a kicked-over ant heap. Ugly business, bringing a corpse down a trail at night, and Jake was pleased his sprite couldn't see it.

But when he ran up to check on her before leaving, she was still awake. Still trembling. So he joined her on the bed, holding her and ignoring her protests.

As the minutes ticked by, he watched over her until her breathing slowed. Deepened. A warm, soft weight in his arms.

With a sigh of relief, Jake brushed a lock of hair from his little sub's cheek. Not as pale. Her shaking had stopped. His hadn't—he still felt as if his world hadn't steadied yet. He'd loved women before, but not like this, never like this. Wanting nothing more than to protect her from everything that might harm her. Wanting to bury himself inside her and yet wanting only to have her sleeping in his arms.

He needed to hear her laugh though. Soon.

Chapter Fourteen

Jake had gone home by the time Kallie awoke, and loneliness had sheered through her so hard she almost started crying. Again. Shoving it back, she'd taken a shower, making it cold enough to wipe out any warm and fuzzy feelings.

She and Wyatt and Morgan had spent the rest of the day talking to the police and doing chores. Thank God for chores. She'd actually argued with Wyatt for the privilege of turning over the compost heap.

After the cops and all had finally left, she'd cooked supper despite her cousins' attempts to help. She might have found their bumbling efforts to show how much they loved her funny if they hadn't also made her want to cry.

Of course, all that sweetness and light hadn't lasted long, and now they were faced off in the entry, with Morgan and Wyatt blocking her escape.

Even the night air wafting in the open front door couldn't cool Kallie's annoyance. She glared at the two, then glanced to her right. "Virgil?"

He crossed his arms over his chest. "Absolutely not."

Three against one. What was fair about this? "Absolutely so."

"Knock, knock." Jake appeared in the doorway and rudely shoved Wyatt and Morgan aside so he could step in. His gaze took in the room. "Standoff at the OK Corral?"

"Something like that," Virgil said.

Jake smiled at her, then obviously noticed the backpack at her feet. Now one more person scowled at her. "What the hell are you doing?"

"I'm going for a walk."

"At night? And where were you planning to walk?"

"That's none of your—" She stopped when he raised his chin just an inch. Damn him. "Fine," she muttered. "I'm going back up the mountain."

"No, you're not," Wyatt said loudly for the hundredth time, and Morgan echoed him.

Jake didn't say anything. He studied her for a second, rubbed his hand over his cheek and chin, and then pulled in a slow breath. "Tell me why."

How could she not love him? He had all the protective instincts of her cousins—that knee-jerk need to insist she stay where she was safe—but he throttled them back and asked her why—well, *ordered* her. But he would let her explain, and he'd listen in that way of his, focused completely on her…and waiting with relentless patience.

But would he understand? "I…" She searched for the right words and tried again. "This is my home, the mountain is"— *part of who I am*—"my shelter. All the years I've lived here, that's where I went when I was upset or mad or…" *Lonely*. "But now the thought of being up there is terrifying." She showed him the way her fingers trembled. "I need to go back, to know that I can, that it's still my place. Now—at night. And before I think about it too much."

A long moment passed before he gave her a faint smile. "I'm not sure I understand, but I was raised on a ranch. Getting back on the horse that threw you is a cowboy law. But I'm going with you."

"No, you are not," Wyatt told him and then abandoned the door to loom over Kallie. "And you're going nowhere, cuz."

She ignored him. "Jake. You don't need to—"

He stroked a hand over her hair, slow and comforting. "Of course I do. Now deal with your family."

Family. Just the word sent a thrill through her heart and gave her strength enough to face them. God, she loved them—Wyatt with all his bluster, Morgan with his silence, Virgil with his strength—and they loved her. She knew that now.

"I need to do this, guys," she said firmly and held up a hand to silence Wyatt. "You can't stop me."

Virgil raised one eyebrow, and a crease appeared in one cheek.

Morgan shoved Wyatt over to glare at Jake. "Maybe, but we can keep you from going with him."

She rolled her eyes. "Morgan, did I stop you from dating that blonde bimbo with the brains of a gnat?"

He reddened.

"Wyatt, do I interfere in your life when you bring women back here? Even when you have two at a time?"

"That's different. I'm—"

"I'm a woman. And have been for a long time." She smiled sweetly at each cousin in turn. "Everyone's equal in this house, remember? What I got, you got—and vice versa. I don't interfere in your love life; you don't get to interfere in mine. I don't tell you how to dress; you don't complain about my clothes."

The deepening scowls made her step back. Her determination wavered. What if they decided they didn't love her, if they wanted—

"Jesus fucking Christ, don't look at us like that." Virgil gripped her shoulders and gave her a shake. "Yell at us and throw things, bring home every lowlife in Bear Flat, wear bikinis all day long, just don't ever, ever look at us like you doubt how we feel about you."

Oh. Okay.

Wyatt looked shaken for a moment and then crossed his arms. "Yeah, well, I might love you, but I don't know about you bringing home a lowlife."

"I love you, Wyatt," Kallie said, watched his face go soft, and then she slapped him upside the head. "And I'll bring home who I want."

* * *

The moon had risen, three days past full, and lent additional light as they moved up the mountain. Their flashlights glimmered on dark tree trunks that seemed to press far too close to the trail. As every injury from yesterday ached, Kallie felt a twang of guilt that Jake had taken her pack to carry. Every time he shifted it, she remembered the club hitting his shoulder. Then again, her hip really, really hurt, and she'd probably have dumped the damn thing on the side of trail by now.

Seemed like he always showed up when she needed help, even when she didn't know she did. She carefully avoided thinking about anything other than having his friendship. They could be good friends. Really.

And she had something she needed to do. She stopped and turned to look at him. "Thank you for yesterday. Not just for saving my life"—she grinned at him—"although I really do appreciate that, but afterward too. To know why I was sent away…and that they loved me…it helps. I owe you."

"I think we're even. Seems like a little sub called me names and forced me to see things in a new light."

She winced. She'd called him a pussy, hadn't she? "You're not mad?"

His lips quirked. "We need to work on your confrontational skills a tad. But I needed to hear it. Thank you."

Relief lifted her spirits. He didn't hate her for her blunt words. *See? Friends.* Unfortunately, as they continued up the trail, her comfortable feeling fell prey to her memories of violence. Screaming. Death.

By the time the turnoff appeared, she'd started to cringe at the tiniest rustle in the brush. Although her brain recognized the sound of a mouse out for a night snack, the rest of her panicked. Soon the memory of the monster's roar overwhelmed the sound of Jake's limping footsteps behind her.

Her knees shook from more than exhaustion as she stopped at her rocks. They lay in an ugly mess, no longer spelling out her name. Maybe she should consider it a sign she didn't belong here. Shoulders slumping, she started to step over them. Jake made a noise, low in his throat, and she stopped.

As she stared down, moonlight colored the rocks with silver. She inhaled slowly. The murderer had scratched out her name, not her cousins. Not her *family*. She did belong here. Setting her jaw, she crouched and put the stones back into their places until her name shown clearly again. KALINDA.

My place.

Jake smiled, and the warmth from his understanding pushed a little of the chill away. His unspoken protest had made her stop and think. But he hadn't interfered after that. She'd made her own remedy, and he'd stood by in silent support. As he did now.

With that reassurance, she was able to turn and move down the tiny path toward the creek.

A little while later, she stood in the small clearing. Aside from trampled grass, no sign remained of the violence. And yet she kept seeing the murderer stalk out of the trees. When she turned, she saw Virgil helpless on the ground. She heard the thud of a club impacting flesh. A dog's yelp.

A warm hand closed on her shoulder, and she shuddered. Jake set the pack down and pulled her close. She laid her cheek on his broad chest and heard only the slow beat of his heart. The solid feel of him let her breathe again. Almost as if he shared from his own vast stores, courage flowed into her, strengthening her resolve. *I can do this.* No asshole monster would take this place from her.

She pulled back and stood on her own two feet. When Jake tilted his head, she nodded firmly. "I can do this."

"I have no doubt. You're one of the strongest people I've ever met."

The conviction in his voice stunned her. Strong? She bit her lip, captured her self-image again. *Damn right, I'm strong.* "I need to be alone."

Silence. His face tightened as he obviously warred with his need to shelter her. His protectiveness made her feel so safe and, oddly enough, helped her stand on her own feet. A contradiction, that—like how giving away love could increase it.

He caressed her cheek with gentle fingers, then walked back up the path, leaving her in the empty clearing, alone with her memories.

"My place," she whispered to the memory of the murderer. "I belong here. You don't."

When the murderer appeared again, she crossed her arms over her chest, then shrank his body to the size of a field mouse, gave him a tail and ears, and watched him scamper away. "Your balls were only mouse-sized too, you cowardly asshole," she muttered when he returned, cudgel held high. She turned him into a mouse over and over. Then she took the sounds of her screams, of yelps, of his roar and lowered the volume until the noise of violence disappeared under the happy tumbling of the creek.

She stepped back from the horrifying sight of Virgil,

helpless on the ground, and with jaw set, she substituted his laugh and groan when she'd told him that joke. Virgil's laugh could lighten any sadness, and a second later, she grinned. If he gave her any trouble before his ribs healed, she could start telling jokes.

Finally she came to the terror of Jake fighting the monster. She let fear drip like water from her fingers to the stubbly grass, and pulled Jake's protectiveness around her like a warm blanket.

She walked her clearing slowly, changing pain into pride. She'd done well. Her family was alive; Jake was alive. No more women would be killed.

Time passed. The moon rose until it floated high in the sky, outshining the stars. The creek's happy gurgling made her smile once again, and the pines blessed her with a motherly shushing sound. Distant barks came from coyotes running in the moonlight. And she knew the rustling in the underbrush meant a tiny shrew, not a monster.

She was shaking again…but whole. And her sanctuary belonged to her. She opened her arms, wishing for a way to embrace a place, to somehow return the comfort it had given her over the years. "Thank you," she whispered.

Turning, she realized she was still alone despite the passage of time. Had he gone back down the trail? Had he left her—as she'd asked? The sense of abandonment stabbed through her, and then she shook her head and laughed. Not Jake, Mr. Overprotective himself. The certainty stabilized the ground under her feet as if she'd moved from a rolling boat onto solid land. "Jake? Where are you?"

"Here." His voice came from up the slope. A minute or

two later, he appeared, walking down the tiny path. He must have gone back up the trail to leave her alone but stayed close enough to return if she needed him. Balancing her requests against his own needs.

"Thank you," she said as he walked up to her.

The moonlight showed how his gaze took her in, studying her face, her hands, her shoulders. He smiled slowly. "You look better."

"I am."

"As long as we're here, I want to talk to you without your cousins hovering over you."

She took a step back. Friends. Nothing more. She started to shake her head.

"Can't you trust me enough for that?"

A memory of the first time he'd asked for her trust stole into her mind: "*Can you trust me in here, surrounded by other people, to restrain you, spank you, and give you pleasure?*" Her cheeks heated, and from the way his eyebrow raised, he knew exactly what she'd thought. She straightened her shoulders. "Only to talk. I'm not going to start anything up again with you."

"Clear enough." He pulled a bottle of water from the side pocket of the backpack. "Drink, sprite."

The thought of never hearing his nickname for her again hurt. She took a couple of sips and handed the bottle back, watching him drink, the sight of his strong throat as he swallowed disconcertingly sexy. He unstrapped the sleeping bag from the bottom of the pack and flipped it open.

"Sit."

She dropped down and crossed her legs. Jake followed, and as she turned to look at him, she realized he'd positioned himself so the moonlight illuminated their faces. He not only wanted to talk but also see her reactions.

Why in the world had she agreed to stay? It would only hurt more. Already she felt her strength failing. *I can't do this again: needing him, wanting him, losing him. No no no.* "I changed my mind. I'm going to go back down now." She pushed up to her knees, then started to stand.

"No, you're not. Not unless you use your safe word." He grasped her wrist and gave her a level stare.

"Damn you, this isn't some game. I don't want to stay here." She tugged, and yet she couldn't…couldn't use her safe word and bring an end to everything.

He cupped her chin, keeping her from moving. "Look at me, Kallie."

Tears filled her eyes without warning, and his face softened. "Oh, sugar, don't do that. You'll break my heart." He stroked his thumb over the curve of her jaw.

"Why do you keep doing this?" She met his eyes. "I still…" She smothered the rest—*still love you*—and took a gulp of air. "I know you don't want anything serious. But I can't do this anymore."

"I'm damned sorry for the hurt I caused you, sprite. I was an idiot—and the coward you called me. When you said you loved me, it scared me spitless." His grim eyes trapped her gaze. "I just couldn't be responsible for another woman's happiness."

"I know," she whispered. It didn't help.

He brushed a wisp of hair from her face. "You see…I'd not only screwed up and had been so careless of Mimi that she had no hope, but somehow I hadn't realized she wanted to die. I'm a dom. To know I could miss that—I couldn't risk taking another submissive."

She curled her fingers around his strong hand. So strong, yet he'd been hurt so badly that her heart ached for him. His protectiveness was one of the things she loved about him—here was the reverse side. "You know you didn't miss anything, don't you? She didn't commit suicide. Andrew killed her."

"I know. Now." His face turned to stone, and rage flashed, turning his eyes to ice. "I shouldn't have killed him so quickly." He inhaled and exhaled in a long, controlled breath, and his gaze softened as he looked at her. "I'm sorry; I don't mean to scare you."

Maybe it shouldn't have, but his anger made her feel safe. He was a warrior like Virgil, and the world held too few of them. She raised her chin. "You don't frighten me, Hunt."

He snorted a laugh. "You think I'd know that by now." He rubbed his knuckles gently against her cheek and paused, his eyes on hers. "Kallie, even before I learned how Mimi died, I was already on my way to your house. For you."

The ground underneath her seemed to tilt. No. *I don't want this.* She'd needed his love so badly before, but not anymore. Too risky. Too much pain. "No."

"Oh yes. You were right; I ran…and I hurt you. I'm sorry, sprite." He looked so unhappy that he'd caused her pain; her heart broke for him. "Can you forgive me for being such a coward?"

He hadn't wanted to hurt her—she didn't want to hurt him now. "Of course I forgive you," she said before thinking it through.

Lifting her hand, he kissed her palm, his lips soft, his breath warm against her skin. "Thank you."

"Right. Well."

He didn't release her hand but used it to pull her closer. "Now the past is out of the way, we can move on..." After brushing his lips over hers, he deepened the kiss.

She could have kissed him all night, but eventually his words registered, and she slapped her palm on his wide chest and pushed him back. "Wait. Move on? To what?"

His lips quirked. "To the fact that I love you," he said, his rumbling voice only a murmur but very certain. When her mouth dropped open, he smiled and took her face between his hands, holding her gaze with his as he repeated, "I love you, Kalinda Masterson."

Hellfire, he never did anything halfway, did he? *Love*? The sweeping wonder died under the onslaught of fear. She couldn't risk this, couldn't stand to lose someone again. Her lip quivered, and he ran his thumb over it soothingly.

"No. I don't want you." She kept her hand on his chest to push him away, felt the contoured muscles, the warm skin, and wanted to stroke instead. The crisp hair scattered over his chest—she'd ruffled it once. A long, long time ago. Her breath hitched with the desire to touch, to be held.

The moonlight glimmered across his face, his hard cheekbones, shadowing the line between his brows, showing the way his eyes narrowed. "Little liar. Yes, you do."

Shoving his hands away, she shook her head no, yet wanted to bury her face against him and cry.

Jake watched Kallie, realizing more fully how much damage he'd done when he'd pushed her away. He'd reinforced her belief that no one cared for her. Her admission that she loved him had been a gift he didn't deserve. In fact, if she hadn't been half-asleep, he'd never have heard the words from her.

For now, he gave her time. Reaching out, he stroked her hair as she wrestled with her old fears of abandonment and believing no one wanted her. She had good reason for her anxiety. The world came with no guarantees. And he couldn't promise her they'd always be together. But if she risked her heart with him, every day of their life, he would show her exactly how very much he loved her.

And no matter how much she protested, she wanted to be loved so badly that it made his chest ache.

She was stuck, he realized, unable to move forward, unwilling to retreat back into her lonely space. If she'd been a different submissive—one with other problems—he might have mounted her on his cock and pressed for an answer…but she needed to come to him with both her mind and heart. "Kallie, do you love me?"

The straightforward question did it—because she couldn't deny what they both knew. Her eyes closed, and the answer came reluctantly. "Y-yes."

The laugh almost choked him, and her eyes popped open. "Sweetheart, you sound as if you're admitting to kicking puppies, not telling a man you love him."

She blinked, frowned, and then took a deep breath. "You're right." As he had done, she set a hand on each side of his face and stared into his eyes. "I love you, Jake Hunt."

And there it was. A future. Hope. Love. Joy fountained through him, lifting him from the depths where he'd lived for so long, to the heights to come. *Hell of a ride.*

She shivered, as if she'd opened a door, letting the air into her house, a clean, fresh, *scary* scent.

He pulled her into his lap and whispered, "Thank you, sprite."

As he held her and stroked her back, she realized she'd been trembling. With a sigh, she relaxed. For a while they simply sat, enjoying the closeness, the sounds of the forest and creek. Eventually he stirred. "The air has cooled—let's get into the bag."

She stilled. Spend the night? Before she could formulate a protest, he'd pushed her to her feet and stood up. He unzipped the bag. "Hop in."

After toeing off her boots, she bent to get in and squeaked when he gripped the neck of her shirt and pulled her upright. "I want you naked now."

She stared up at him, at his utter self-confidence and the power radiating from him, and she swallowed. "Yes, Jake."

He touched her face with his fingertip. "My sprite," and the sheer satisfaction in his voice stopped her breath.

Then he stepped back and crossed his arms over his chest. Excitement shot through her, and her fingers fumbled as she pulled off her clothes. The night air had chilled, and goose bumps rose on her skin; her nipples turned to tiny puckered buds. The air against her groin felt cool where she'd already grown wet. As she drew off the last sock, she stumbled. He caught her, setting her on her feet, then ran a hand over her breasts. As if he had the right.

She tried to take a step back, but he tangled his fingers in her hair, holding her in place, and deliberately palmed a breast. "My body, Kallie." Something had changed in his manner, the way he looked at her. No longer controlling, but possessive too, as if to say, *I am your dom.*

And she was his sub. The thought sent a thrill across her skin, and she answered without thinking, "Yes. Yes, Sir."

His lips curved in pleasure—pleasure she'd given him. He released her and patted her butt. "Get in the bag."

The inside of the bag felt like smooth ice against her skin. It would warm up quickly, but *brrr.*

By the time she'd squirmed her way in, he'd removed his clothing. The firelight flickered along his body to highlight the curves of his pectorals, dance over the ridges of his abdomen, and shadow his groin, and she wanted to touch him everywhere. He sheathed himself in a condom, then slid into the bag beside her. After bunching his shirt up to serve as a pillow, he rolled onto his side.

Shivering, she inched closer; his big body gave off heat like a roaring furnace.

"Little ice cube," he muttered and pulled her closer—a generous act if she'd ever seen one. As their legs tangled together, he ran his hands over her hips, pressing slightly, watching her face. "Any pain?"

She hissed when his fingers found the bruise from the club, and another spot on her shoulder.

"I remember the place on your back. Is that all the bad ones?"

She nodded.

"Good." He firmly pushed her legs apart, opening her, and an intense surge of desire made her moan. His smile was hard, satisfied as he stroked her folds, finding her wet, already slick for him.

Suddenly a surge of anxiety hit her, and she grabbed his wrist, wanting—needing—to stall. Yes, she'd admitted she loved him, but now to have him inside her, surrounding her… That seemed too intense, as if it would leave all her heart and emotions vulnerable to him. If he left her…

He didn't move. Didn't speak or try to reassure her. He just waited, his steady gaze on hers. A minute passed, and her fears seeped away. People loved her. No one had abandoned her. And Jake would never deliberately hurt her. He loved her, and she could trust him with…everything. She sighed and smiled at him. "Mini panic attack. You made me take off my big-girl panties."

He laughed and kissed her, so slow and sweet that it brought tears to her eyes. Lord help her, she'd turned into a damned faucet. "I love you, sprite," he whispered in his rumbling voice.

"I know," she whispered back and got another laugh. She released his wrist and grinned. "Where were we?"

Slowly, he slid his hand down over her mound and flattened it against her pussy. “I believe I was here.”

She shivered as her body sprang back to life. When he ran a finger up through her wetness, she sucked in a breath and then grinned at him. “No ropes. No cuffs. Are you sure you know how to do this without all that?”

He smiled slowly. “I thought I’d taught you that bondage can be more than just physical. Perhaps another lesson is indicated.”

And she remembered the rocks by the creek. Uh-oh.

He considered for a moment, then said, “Put your hands behind your head—lace your fingers.”

Her heart gave a jump. At the implacable look in his eyes, her body seemed to melt right down into the sleeping bag. The knowledge that he would insist she obey, would accept nothing less, somehow took her fears away. As if he stood between her and the world. She laced her fingers together.

He studied her. “Will having your arm in that position hurt your shoulder?”

Only a mild ache. “It’s okay.”

He gave a nod of approval. “Very good.” Smiling, he grasped her hair and tilted her face toward him, supporting himself on that elbow. He kissed her, deeply, thoroughly, as if asserting his possession, kissed her until her toes curled and her skin sizzled as if she’d been sunning all day.

After licking a finger, he ran it in a circle around one nipple, then the other. Desire surged through her, increasing with every repetition. She looked up at him and realized his gaze was focused on her face, not her breasts—watching her responses. From the way the corners of his eyes crinkled, from the way he claimed a kiss, she'd pleased him.

When he leaned back, cold air drifted in from the open sleeping bag, contracting her nipples to hard, jutting buds. His lips captured one, his mouth as hot as a furnace. He lifted his head, and air wafted across the wet nipple. He tongued the other. Hot. Cold. One, then the other. Her breasts swelled to aching tightness, and when he sucked strongly, her back arched as an electric current ran straight down to her pussy.

Her clit throbbed, slow and heavy. She needed more. His cock touched her thigh, the heat compelling. She raised her leg to press against it. "Stop teasing me and get—"

He pinched one nipple, and the edgy sting made her insides clench. "I will tease you"—he pinched the other breast—"anytime I want, little sub." His teeth closed on a nipple, holding it to the point of pain while his tongue flickered over the very peak. Her arms tensed; she wanted to touch, was afraid to move.

He slid a hand down her stomach, right to where she throbbed, and touched her with light strokes that only intensified her need. "Your clit is pushed out and swollen," he whispered in her ear. "Slick and aching for my hand."

She moaned and grabbed his shoulder, blinking up at him when he growled in disapproval. He removed his hand from her pussy and lifted his eyebrows at her.

Everything down there throbbed, and she whimpered,

"Please."

No answer.

She unclenched her fingers from his shoulder and forced herself to put her hands back under her head. Looking up at him, she managed not to beg.

His cheek creased, tempting her to touch. "Very good. Now open your legs wider."

She slid her thighs outward, and his hand flattened on her pussy, increasing the fire.

"There we go," he murmured. "Bound, whether by my will or my rope, open to me in all ways."

She shivered, unable to take her eyes from his face.

"This is how things will be between us, sprite," he said, his gaze level. "At least in the bedroom. Is this what you want?" His finger circled her clit until the pulsing encompassed her entire pussy.

"Yes. No." She shook her head, trembling with the need to move. Her own submission increased her arousal to fever pitch. *Think, Kallie.* His touch slowed… "Not all the time, right? You won't try to make me…"

He paused. "No, Kalinda. I don't want a slave—except in the bedroom." His smile flashed, and he teased the edge of her clit, the flicking touches igniting sparks everywhere. "In the bedroom, however, you will submit. Willingly. Respectfully. Giving me everything that is in you."

His eyes held hers as he released her hair, as he moved on top of her. His cock, thick and hard, slid into her wetness, stretching her. The feeling of being held in place as he pushed deep inside her—her face and feelings exposed, her most private areas available to whatever he wanted—shook her. Melted her.

"Yes," she whispered. "Yes, Jake."

"Good." He kissed her again, so tenderly she sighed. As he drew back, he smiled down at her, and his pleased expression wakened a spark of defiance. Had it all his own way, hadn't he?

He shouldn't have life so easy. With a sudden wrestling move Morgan had taught her years before, she reversed positions, rolling him onto his back, clamping her thighs around his hips, not letting him leave her.

"I think sometimes I should get to be on top," she announced and started up a forceful rhythm. His rough laugh made her heart melt. The way he looked when he laughed...

To her surprise, he let her work, setting her own pace, and everything inside her tightened as her climax approached at the speed of light. Every movement pushed her clit against his groin, and she increased the speed. Almost...almost...

He brushed his fingers up from her thighs, avoiding the bruise on her left hip. His gaze swept over her face.

And then those hard hands grasped her hips in an implacable hold and pushed her bottom upward until only the tip of his cock teased her opening. "On top," he murmured, letting her dip far enough for the thick head to enter her and leave. "But not in charge."

So close. How could he do this to her? "You bastard," she

hissed.

His rough laugh broke through the quiet. "Try again. Sir…or Jake. Master works too, especially when you really want something."

She really wanted his cock moving again. "Master. Please."

He grinned and slammed her hips down, driving into her, sending shock waves through her. Lifted her slowly, yanked her down again, and the waves of excitement built with each thrust, piling higher onto each other until her brain turned off completely and every sense focused on the next stretching impalement.

Her clit engorged, growing excruciatingly sensitive, yet the pressure expanded from the inside this time, pushing past any control. Suddenly the tsunami broke, exploding outward in wave after wave of pleasure, soaring higher as she tried to buck and he held her firmly in place. Unrelenting, he forced another orgasm out of her before taking his own release in forceful, pulsing thrusts.

Her head spun as he pulled her down to lie over him, limp except for little explosions that continued to spasm inside her. She laid her cheek on his damp skin and tried to figure out where all the air had gone. She could hear the strong, even beat of his heart.

Under her ear, his voice rumbled through his chest. "You brighten my life, Kalinda. I love you."

As if his words had echoed into the sky, the golden rays of the sun glimmered over the distant white-capped mountains. Sunrise. As it lightened his face, she lifted up enough to stare down at him, at the hard cheekbones, the strong jaw. Someone she could lean on, yet who valued what she had to offer. Someone she could fight with—and who she'd have to keep from stepping in front of her. Someone who loved her.

And God, she loved him. "I lo—" She choked on the words and then remembered she didn't have to hold them back. "I love you."

His eyes crinkled, and he caressed her cheek, holding her gaze with his. "I love you, Kallie Masterson," he murmured. "And I'll be telling you often so there're no misunderstandings."

Would there ever come a time when his words didn't send a surge of joy through her? She lifted her hand to trace his confident face, the mouth that curved under her fingers. "Are you really sure?"

"Completely." He rolled them over, putting her under him. His weight on her felt right, and she ran her hands up his biceps. He kissed her slowly. "And we'll be getting married before the year is out."

"Married?" She blinked and frowned, trying to ignore the thrill of happiness. "Aren't you supposed to ask me?"

"All right," he said with a deceptively agreeable smile. He ran a finger over her damp lower lip. "Do you want the wedding this month or next month?"

He sounded far too smug. She bit his finger—hard.

"Dammit," he swore, his complacent attitude disappearing like morning fog.

She giggled—and then he flipped her onto her stomach, and brought his hand down.

Major mistake. Ow, ow, ow!

First he spanked her.

Then he kept her on the edge of orgasm until her cries echoed through the mountain valleys.

Then he took her so hard she might never walk again.

An hour later, he smiled down at her and repeated the question. "So. Do you want the wedding this month or next month?"

When her head stopped spinning and she could breathe again, she managed to answer. "This month. Master. Sir. Oh captain of the universe." Oh honestly, just listen to her—what a wimp. She frowned at him. "You know, your new carving is going to have a really little penis."

His deep laugh rang through the clearing, and then his gaze focused on her, the heat almost perceptible. "So disrespectful," he murmured. "Looks like we'll have to do it all again until you get it right."

Hellfire. Her bottom still hurt. She glared at him, and then closed her eyes as various threats ran through her mind. *I'm going to glue brass balls onto your carving...and give it to you for Christmas...in public.*

Jake cupped her cheek and had to smile. Tough and soft and sweet. *My sub. My love...my problem.* He could almost hear Kallie's thoughts racing, and considering the expression on her face, whatever she was planning involved him—and not in a good way. He narrowed his eyes and studied her suspiciously.

A minute later, she looked up and saw his face. Her husky laugh rang out through the clearing, as open and happy as he'd never heard it before. "I love you, Jake Hunt, and you know what? You love me back."

Damn straight.

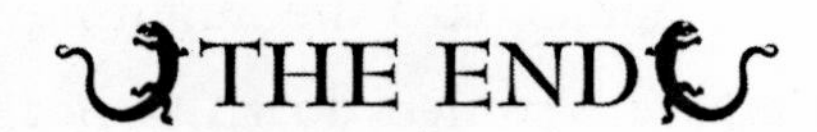

THE END

Cherise Sinclair

Now everyone thinks summer romances never go anywhere, right? Well…that's not always true.

I met my dearheart when vacationing in the Caribbean. Now I won't say it was love at first sight. Actually, since he was standing over me, enjoying the view down my swimsuit top, I might even have been a tad peeved—as well as attracted. But although our time together there was less than two days, and although we lived in opposite sides of the country, love can't be corralled by time or space.

We've now been married for many, many years. (And he still looks down my swimsuit tops.)

Nowadays, I live in the west with this obnoxious, beloved husband, two children, and various animals, including three cats who rule the household. I'm a gardener, and I love nurturing small plants until they're big and healthy and productive…and ripping defenseless weeds out by the roots when I'm angry. I enjoy thunderstorms, playing Scrabble and Risk, and being a soccer mom. My favorite way to spend an evening is curled up on a couch next to the master of my heart, watching the fire, reading, and…well…if you're reading this book, you obviously know what else happens in front of fires. :)

Cherise

Loose Id Titles by Cherise Sinclair

Master of the Abyss
Master of the Mountain
The Dom's Dungeon
The Starlight Rite

The MASTERS OF THE SHADOWLANDS Series
Club Shadowlands
Dark Citadel
Breaking Free
Lean on Me

"Simon Says: Mine"
Part of the anthology *Doms of Dark Haven*
With Sierra Cartwright and Belinda McBride

The above titles are available in e-book format at www.loose-id.com

Masters of the Shadowlands
(contains the titles *Club Shadowlands* and *Dark Citadel)*
Breaking Free
Lean on Me
Master of the Abyss
Master of the Mountain
The Dom's Dungeon

The above titles are available in print at your favorite bookstore

CPSIA information can be obtained at www.ICGtesting.com
Printed in the USA
LVOW080251210213
320930LV00001B/61/P